THE HOPEFUL HEARTS SERIES ◇ BOOK THREE

PERFECTLY MATCHED

LIANA GEORGE

Scrivenings
PRESS
Quench your thirst for story.
www.ScriveningsPress.com

Published by Scrivenings Press LLC
15 Lucky Lane
Morrilton, Arkansas 72110
https://ScriveningsPress.com

Printed in the United States of America

Paperback ISBN 978-1-64917-282-2

eBook ISBN 978-1-64917-283-9

Editors: Shannon Vannatter and K. Banks

Cover design by Linda Fulkerson - www.bookmarketinggraphics.com

To Sandra Byrd, my friend, my coach, my cheerleader. There's no doubt in my mind we were perfectly matched for this journey. I'm forever grateful to and for you.

ACKNOWLEDGMENTS

I've been blessed beyond measure to have the same crew supporting me over the *many* years it's taken me to write this series. To Teresa, Kathy, Angie, Lisa, Melanie, Brenda, Jon and Regina, your love and encouragement have helped me see this project to the end. I'm forever grateful for each of you.

A huge shout-out to the wonderful team at Scrivenings Press (Linda Fulkerson, Shannon Vannatter, and Kaci Banks) for all you've done to make this book the best it can be. I love being part of the Scrivenings family!

Deepest thanks to Kate Heister for being a fresh pair of eyes on the material and offering creative suggestions. I hope this is only the beginning of a wonderful, new relationship. Oh, did you like the ending?

This book wouldn't have been possible without the help of Brian Stuy. I appreciate all the time you generously provided to make sure I had my details straight. May you continue to do the good work you are doing to help adoptive families.

To my AWH Sisters (Danielle, Lisa, and Erika), working with you has been a true joy. Your patience as I juggled our work demands with my writing schedule means the world to me. I can't wait to see what God has in store for us in the future!

To my family, thank you for believing in me and giving me the time and space to follow my heart. Clint, I love you more; Kayley and Abbey, never stop reaching for your dreams.

Finally, to God, who has been with me since day one of this

adventure. You said not to be silent, but to go on speaking; to not fear because You would be with me (Acts 18:9-10). As always, You are faithful and true to Your Word.

1

When the map is unrolled, the dagger is revealed.
~ *Chinese Proverb*

Today's the day we're going to the chapel ...
    Today's the day we're gonna get ma-rr-ied ...
The modified 1960s lyrics play like a broken record in my head as our plane's wheels skid across the runway at Dallas-Fort Worth airport.

Did I really agree to marry Ben Carrington?

Technically, he accepted my proposal. But the details, usually important to a former professional organizer like me, are trivial now. All that matters is quickly and quietly tying the knot so we can catch the first flight back to China to officially begin the process of adopting Lei Ming and starting this unusual family of ours.

"Ready, Nicki?" Ben asks as the plane comes to a stop at the jetway, muting the music in my head.

I flinch as the simultaneous clicks of unbuckling seatbelts resonate through the cabin and weary travelers gather their belongings. Ready? For what? A marriage of convenience?

Parenthood? Or getting hitched at the Justice of the Peace in the middle of the week without our parents' knowledge?

Although everyone else is standing, I remain seated. A few days ago, our plan didn't sound all that crazy when we shared it with Director Wu and Julia. Now that we're home in the States and actually going to implement it—well, that's a different story.

"Nicki." Ben holds out his hand to me from the aisle. "It's time to go."

Gazing up at him, my pulse races. Despite the long flight and late hour, his face conveys a look of peace and joy. His green eyes sparkle, and his smile stretches from ear to ear, as if he can't wait to make me his bride.

That's Ben. Faithful to his commitments, firm in his faith, and fast to spring into action. A girl would be foolish to let a guy like that get away, and I am not a foolish girl. Lei Ming and I are lucky to have him.

I release the death grip on the metal seat divider and place my hand in his. An electric spark jolts through me when our fingers touch. Whatever fears and doubts had overtaken me when we first landed melt away. We're in this together, for better or for worse, till death do us part, regardless of how asinine our plan may be. "Let's go."

As we scuttle through the crowded airport, Texas seems nothing like what I thought it would be. I only spot a few Stetsons and Western boots at baggage claim, and as we make the two-hour drive toward his hometown of Kilgore, I notice there are more billboards than cows dotting the landscape.

"The Lone Star State isn't what I was expecting," I tell him as images from Westerns on TV and in movies flitter through my mind.

He cuts me a sideways glance and grins. "What were you thinking it would be? Cowboys and cattle around every corner?"

Thankful for the covering of night to hide my embarrassment, I gulp nervously. "No, of course not. I just thought—"

"You just thought there'd be lots of longhorns, ranch chaps, and spurs, didn't you?" He chuckles. "Don't worry. A lot of people think that at first, but Texas is like the rest of the States. We just have bigger belt buckles."

I throw my head back and laugh, grateful for the banter and momentary distraction. "So, did you reserve rooms for us at a hotel?" Although Ben and I don't know each other well, the fact that we're Christians means I can rest easy that he wouldn't have us staying in the same room before we're married.

At this point, I'm not even certain that will happen after we say *I do*, either.

"No." He removes his hand from the steering wheel and rubs his stubbled jawline. "I thought we'd stay at my parents' house."

A prick of fear jabs at my heart. "Why the sudden change? No one's supposed to know." It was a pact we made in China when we first agreed to this marital arrangement. While we knew our parents might not be happy with our hasty decision, we don't want them to talk us out of it—or worse, insist on a big celebration that we neither have the time nor desire for under the circumstances.

"Don't worry," Ben assures me. "They're not home."

His words flood me with relief, and my heartbeat returns to normal. "Where are they?"

"Visiting my brother and his family just outside of Houston. They emailed a few days ago and told me, so it works out perfectly." He places his hand back on the wheel at the two o'clock position. "By the time they return, we'll be Mr. and Mrs. and have sidestepped any drama surrounding our quick nuptials, keeping our efforts to get married without them safe." He furrows his eyebrows. "You didn't mention it to your mom, did you?"

"No, I didn't." Heavy-hearted, I peer out my window and study the moonlit terrain. Although it was hard to leave Lei Ming in her fragile condition and wrap my head around the fact that in order to give her a forever family, Ben and I would need to come home and get married. But that wasn't the most difficult part. It was the decision we made not to tell our parents, stabbing daggers into my heart.

For years, my mother has wanted me to find a knight in shining armor and supply her with a brood of grandchildren. If she knew I'd found Prince Charming and was starting a family sooner rather than later, she'd be over-the-moon excited. But she'd also insist on being present at the ceremony and involved with all the preparations. With Lei Ming's condition still hanging in the balance, we don't have the luxury or the time to plan a big wedding and include everyone.

That's why Ben and I agreed a private civil ceremony was the way to go. From afar, it sounded like a good idea. However, now that I'm back in the USA and hours away from exchanging vows with someone I've only known a few weeks, my stomach knots at the thought my mom won't be a part of my wedding. Even one at the local courthouse. I have no doubt she'd love to be there next to me.

"Hey, you okay?" Ben's voice pulls me out of my thoughts. "Not getting cold feet, are you?"

I look back at him. "What? No." I shake my head. "I was just thinking about my mom, that's all."

"I'm sorry. I know it wasn't easy for us to make the decision to leave our parents out of the loop, but it was the right one. We need to be on a plane back to China sooner than it would take for your mom to arrive here. Plus, my mother is a true-blooded Texan. She doesn't know how to do anything small, especially important events. I promise it would be a nightmare if we told them."

"You're right. It's just harder than I thought it'd be."

"Look, we'll do a nice reception, party, whatever you want with them once we come back with Lei Ming. In time they'll understand why we stayed silent and be happy for us." He pulls the car into a gated entrance.

"I hope you're right." I wrap my arms around my waist. I'm

not a hundred percent sure it will go over with everyone as smoothly as Ben thinks it will.

"Trust me. Everything will be fine." He rolls down the window and taps in the code to give us access to the estate.

After several minutes of driving down a windy path, the rental car's headlights finally flash on the front exterior of the Carrington mansion. As I take it all in, my mouth drops open. The sprawling residence looks like a photo straight out of *Architectural Digest*, only more Texas farmhouse than the usual New England Tudor I'm used to on the east coast. However, it's just as beautiful.

Ben wasn't kidding when he said his family had money. I squirm in the knowledge that one day I'll have to show my soon-to-be husband my mother's house, and it will lack sorely when compared to the Carrington's luxurious home. I can just imagine Ben staring at her place for the first time, his mouth hanging open too. But for totally different reasons.

I lean forward in my seat, anxious to see what the rest of the house looks like. But when Ben bypasses the circular driveway and keeps driving into the depths of the estate, I know I'll have to wait for another day to take it all in.

"Where are we going?" I glance back at the massive wood and iron front doors.

"I'm going to park over behind the guest house."

"Why?" I do my best to temper my fears. Is he embarrassed by me? I can't imagine that would be the issue. If no one is home, what would it matter? Or does his decision to avoid the main entrance mean he's uncomfortable flaunting his family's wealth?

"I don't want to tip Zelda off," he informs me, negating my worries. "If she sees a strange car at the front door, she'll call my parents right away."

"Who's Zelda?" I don't remember him mentioning a sister, but if she had a name like that, I probably would've.

"Our main housekeeper. She's been with our family for years

5

and knows every inch of this house. When my parents are away, she still comes to check on things. If she happened to stop by tomorrow before we can get to the courthouse ..."

"We'd be done for."

"Exactly. Zelda would make sure we didn't do anything until my parents returned." He brings the car to a stop. "And trust me when I say you don't want to mess with her."

I chuckle as we grab our bags from the trunk, imagining what the housekeeper looks like if Ben is afraid to stand up to her.

"You can sleep in the guesthouse, and I'll stay up in my room." Ben guides me down a lighted trail leading to a quaint cottage next to the pool, where the lingering smell of chlorine floats in the air. He opens the unlocked door, turns on the lights, and moves to the side.

"Wow." I scan the nautical-themed space that's double the size of my old apartment. "This is nice."

"I don't know why we call it a guesthouse. There are plenty of rooms in the main house. It's really my mother's she-shed." He puts air quotations around his last two words. "Her little sanctuary when she needs her alone time."

"I get that." I set my bag on the ceramic tile that looks like whitewashed wood planks. If I had the financial means, I'd have my own private retreat too.

"Do you want something to eat? We have a fully stocked kitchen with state-of-the-art appliances. I'd be happy to cook something for you. I make a mean quesadilla."

While it's sweet of him to offer, I don't think it's the best idea. I need to get some sleep before our big day tomorrow, and I'm not sure it's going to come easily. "Thanks, but I think I'll just send Director Wu a short email to check on Lei Ming and then go to bed. I need to be at my best for when I walk down the aisle as Nicki Mayfield one last time."

"I understand." Frowning, he steps back outside. "Get some rest then, Mrs. Carrington-to-be. I'll come get you in a few hours so we can head to the courthouse and seal the deal. Once that's done, we can tell our parents."

"Okay." I lean against the door and watch Ben slink away toward the main house. In China, he looks like a giant with his broad shoulders and towering frame. Here, however, he resembles a good ol' mama's boy—the kind who'd be a great catch for some lucky girl. And while I'm grateful to have hit the jackpot, I can't help but wonder if marrying Ben for convenience isn't robbing him and some debutante of true love.

"Ben, wait," I call out to him.

He quickly pivots in my direction. "Yeah?"

"Before I forget ... thank you."

He heads back toward me. "For what?"

Tears form in my eyes as I think about all Ben has done for me in the short amount of time we've known each other – supporting me at the hospital when Lei Ming was so sick, agreeing to tutor Tao so I could gain access to her in the ICU, visiting me in jail, then arranging this crazy marriage scheme. He's gone above and beyond the call of duty. "For doing this for me."

Ben inches closer toward me. "I'm doing this for you, Lei Ming, and me. We're a family now." He bends down and plants a kiss on my forehead. "Go to bed, Sleeping Beauty."

Heeding my Prince Charming's advice, I lock the door behind me, quickly shoot off my email and crawl straight into bed. But instead of sleeping, I lie there and repeat the words "I do" and attempt to pronounce my new name as casually as possible. "Hi, I'm Nicki May—Nicki Carrington."

After ten minutes, it still doesn't roll off my tongue easily.

Worried I'm creating problems where there aren't any, I take a deep breath and remind myself to relax. It will take time for me to grow accustomed to being Mrs. Benjamin Carrington or calling myself Nicki Carrington.

But just like love and intimacy in our relationship, it will have to develop naturally over time for both of us. I squirm underneath the covers imagining how that will all play out. Thankfully, jetlag finally takes over, and I drift off to sleep before a full picture forms in my mind.

I have no clue how long I've been dead to the world when the sound of the door handle rattling pulls me from my slumber. I bolt up in bed and wrap the covers around me.

As images of Western movie shootouts run through my head, I reach for my phone and call Ben.

"Hello?" His voice is groggy.

"Someone is trying to break into the guest house," I whisper, doing my best to mask my fear.

"What?"

I place my hand over the phone and raise my voice. "Someone is shaking the door handle violently and trying to get in."

"I'm on my way."

Afraid of what, or who, wants inside, I weigh my options. Hide in the closet or under the bed?

I'm leaning towards the former when the cavalry comes to my rescue.

"Mom." Ben's voice booms from the other side of the door.

His mother? I thought his parents were out of town.

I jump out of bed and peek out the front window blinds.

"Ben!" His mom releases her grip on the door handle and hugs her son. "What are you doing here?"

"I could ask you the same thing. I thought you were at Jacob's for a few more days." He wraps his arms around her, the look of disbelief on his face matching my thoughts.

"The kids weren't feeling well, so we left early this morning." She pulls back from his embrace. "Why didn't you tell us you were coming home?"

"I was going to surprise you." Ben leads her away from the cottage.

"Where are you going?"

"I thought we'd go inside and let Dad know I'm here."

She halts mid-step. "Sorry, but I need to get in my laps. Your brother doesn't have a pool, and I can't afford to miss any more days. You go inside and find your father, and when I'm done, you can fill me in on the reason for your unexpected visit." She marches back toward her she-shed and yanks on the handle again. "Why is this locked?"

"Maybe Zelda locked it since you were gone?"

"Zelda would never do that." His mom stops jiggling the hardware. "No, something else—"

I hold my breath waiting for her to finish her sentence, but she doesn't. Instead, she stoops down and picks up my black flats from under the bench next to the door. I slap my palm to my forehead. In China, we always take off our footwear before going inside, so it was a habit.

Now it was a downfall.

"Whose are these?" she asks.

"Aren't they yours?"

"No, they're way too small to be mine, and they aren't Zelda's either." She studies my scuffed-up shoes. "Benjamin Carrington, are you hiding something—or should I say someone—you don't want me to know about in the guest house?"

He guides her away from the cottage again. "My stomach's growling. Let's go inside and get something to eat. Then I'll help you figure out what's going on with the lock."

"No." She stops and tromps back toward her private retreat. "It's clear you don't want me going inside, which tells me there's someone in there you don't want me to know about." She returns to the door and bangs on it. "Whoever you are, open up."

I scramble away from the window. As I do, I catch a glimpse of myself in the mirror. Unsurprisingly, my hair's a mess, my eyes resemble that of a raccoon, my clothes are wrinkled worse than crumpled paper, and the stench wafting from my armpits makes it clear I haven't showered in days. Not the best way to make a good first impression.

Now what?

Technically, I wasn't supposed to meet his parents until after we said I do. However, like most things in my life lately, nothing is going according to plan. She knows I'm in here, so hiding won't do me any good. I might as well suck it up and get the introductions over with. Awkward as they may be.

Inhaling deeply, I reach for the lock and turn it to the right. The latch clicks open quietly.

My stomach coils tightly as I swing the door wide enough for them to see me. "Hi, Mrs. Carrington. It's so nice to meet you." I hold out my hand to her.

"Who—who are you?" She scans me from head to toe, then looks back at her son.

Blowing out a huge puff of air, Ben's eyes shift from me to his mother. "Mom, this is Nicki Mayfield." He pauses. "My fiancée."

THIRTY MINUTES LATER, cleaned up and dressed for my big day, I amble toward the main house. As the sun blares from its position straight overhead, sweat drips off me as if I'd just finished a spin class. I'm not sure if it's the sweltering East Texas heat in March or my nervousness about meeting Ben's parents causing me to need another shower, but I do my best to stay cool and calm. We need to advise them of our speedy marriage plans, alone and at the Justice of the Peace, without any drama.

"Nicki," Ben calls out to me from a Pergola-covered seating area next to the pool. "Over here."

I beeline it past the Olympic-sized, peapod-shaped pool and waterfall and straight for Ben.

"Mom, Dad." Ben's face beams. "This is Nicki Mayfield, your future daughter-in-law."

My heart pounds like a jackhammer, and my tongue sticks to the roof of my mouth. I want to say something rather than stand there like a statue, but my body refuses to cooperate. This is not how I envisioned meeting my in-laws for the first time.

"Nicki," Ben's mom squeals and sprints toward me. "Ben told us about your engagement." She draws me into her arms and squeezes tight. "I'm so excited."

I shoot Ben a sideways glance. How much did he tell them exactly?

Ben's lips stay firmly pressed together.

Uncertain of how to traverse this rocky terrain, I turn back to his mom and say, "That's great. Considering the circumstances in which we met earlier, I wasn't sure what to expect."

"I was just shocked before, that's all." She pulls back and holds me at arm's length. "It's not every day my son apparently falls in love so fast that he proposes before I even get a chance to hear about you."

"Yes, I can imagine how confusing this must all be, Mrs. Carrington, and I'm sorry for catching you off guard."

"Oh, please, don't call me Mrs. Carrington. That's my mother-in-law. You can call me Darlene." She beams. "Or Mom, if you'd like."

"Darlene is fine for now, Mom," Ben quickly admonishes her.

"Yes, darlin', I'm sure Nicki has a mother." Mr. Carrington steps out from behind his wife and holds out his hand to me. The sweet smell of pipe tobacco accompanies him. "I'm Hank, and you can call me whatever you like."

"Thank you, Mr.—I mean, Hank." I reluctantly place my sweaty hand in his.

"Why don't we all sit down?" Ben suggests.

Breaking huddle, we move to the dark chocolate wicker sofa and chairs covered in palm-tree fabric and coordinating throw pillows. A Texas-sized taco buffet is spread out on the square coffee table, including chips, salsa, fajitas, rice, and beans. Pitchers of lemonade and tea sit on a side table.

"Nicki, what can I get you?" Darlene asks as I plant myself under the ceiling fan.

"I'll just have some lemonade, thank you."

I cover my abdomen with my hand and push down on it,

hoping that might suppress any unwelcome hunger growls. Even though I haven't touched any food since the paltry meal on the plane, I can't bring myself to eat. Not only because I'm a sack of nerves, but with my luck, I'd spill salsa all over my *wedding dress*. Since it's the only one I have, I need to keep it spotless for a few more hours.

Ben's dad stops lathering his fajita meat in Tabasco sauce and glances at my stomach. His eyebrows raised high.

"Here ya go." Darlene passes a crystal flute to me. As she does, her enormous pear-shaped wedding ring flashes in my eyes, a subtle reminder that I don't have one. I'm not sure I will, either. It's not something Ben and I discussed.

"You have a lovely home," I tell her.

She brushes a strand of platinum blonde hair, which I'm sure she didn't acquire at the local drugstore, from her forehead. "Thank you, I'll show you around after we eat."

"Enough of the chitchat." Hank sets down the rich red bottle of liquid. "Nicki, Ben's told us all about you and the decision the two of you've made to get married, even though this is the first time we're hearing about you."

I sip my freshly squeezed drink, then do my best to set down what I can only imagine is very expensive stemware with both hands. "I know it must sound crazy, but I assure you that we've given this a lot of thought and prayer and feel strongly this is what we're supposed to do."

"Y'all are serious, then?" Hank's southern accent is even stronger than Ben's. "This isn't some joke?"

"No, we're definitely getting married." Ben props his elbows on his knees. "Today, in fact. At the Justice of the Peace."

"Today?" His mother chokes on her juice.

"A little fast, don't ya think, Son?"

"Is Nicki—" Darlene's eyes drift towards my stomach.

My eyes bulge at her comment as I recall I was rubbing it just moments ago. "Oh, that's not ..."

"Yes, we're expecting," Ben says.

I watch as the color drains from both his parents' faces. What is he doing?

"A little girl." Ben pulls out his phone. "She's eighteen months old, and her name is Lei Ming."

It takes a moment for them to process Ben's words, and once they have, their scrunched-up faces return to a normal state.

"So, Nicki's not pregnant?" Darlene's shoulders relax.

"No, but we've both fallen in love with this little girl in China, and we want to adopt her." He hands them his phone with what I can only assume is a picture of Lei Ming.

When they've finished fawning over her, I take over the conversation and explain the story from the very beginning until the moment we left her in the hospital a few days ago.

"Lei Ming's medical condition is day-to-day and may require more surgery." I wring my hands at the thought of her small body lying in the hospital the last time we saw her. Was she well? I'd checked my email before coming out here, but there was still no message from the director yet.

"If she does need more treatment," Ben picks up the conversation, "Nicki and I want to cover the cost and oversee her care, possibly even here in the States. To do that, though, we need to be her legal guardians – her parents. Even though we're doing this strictly as friends, the sooner we get married, the sooner we can get back and attend to her needs. Plus, we want to start the adoption process before she's matched with another family."

"I hear what you're saying and think it's noble that both of you want to do that for this little girl, but is this the best way to go about it?" His dad shakes his head. "I mean, you two barely know each other, and you want to start a family."

"I know all I need to about Nicki. If it's enough for me, then it can be enough for the both of you too."

My heart leaps at Ben defending me. Not that I need rescuing. I'm more than capable of standing up for myself, but still, it's nice. It's also somewhat alarming because, truth be told, Ben doesn't know all there is to know about me. Or my mom.

"Well, Nicki, since Ben seems to have such intimate knowledge about you, I'm curious as to what you can tell me about him." A hint of accusation peppers Hank's words.

My eyes dart between the two large men. Is this some kind of test? "Well, I've learned that he's fluent in Mandarin, good at sports, likes to dance, a devoted teacher, and an excellent preacher," I say, recalling the memory of listening to him on stage at church a few weeks ago, before turning back toward his father. "And I'm blessed God placed him in my life."

Unimpressed by my remarks, Ben's dad folds his arms over his chest and leans back against the chair cushion. "Let me get this straight, this arrangement you two have is simply a ploy to adopt a little girl, and y'all are just friends? Nothing ... more?"

"Yes." Ben takes a sip of his tea.

"Are y'all joining your finances, or will you have separate bank accounts?"

"Haven't given it much thought." Ben sets his glass down on the table. Hard.

"What about a prenup agreement?" Hank lurches forward.

"Don't need one. Nicki isn't marrying me for my money."

"That's true," I add, hoping to ease Mr. Carrington's worries.

"Okay, well, what are y'all planning to do about sleeping arrangements? If y'all are just friends, are you going to have your own rooms?"

My pulse skyrockets. Why does he need to know about that?

"None of your business, Dad."

"Hank, that's enough!" Darlene snaps. "It's clear Ben and Nicki have made up their minds, and being the adults they are, we need to support their decision."

"But what about love? Isn't that supposed to count for something in a marriage?"

"Don't be rude, dear. Not everybody is madly in love when they first get married. They can learn to love one another in time." She tilts her head at him and smirks. "Believe me when I say it's happened before."

"Thank you, Mom." Ben glares at his dad.

"Ignore your father, Son. He's just being his usual grumpy self." Darlene waves a hand at him. "I'm proud of what you're doing for Nicki and for this little girl, but you had to know we'd have questions and concerns. This is all so sudden, and I'm sure Nicki's mom feels the same as we do."

"She doesn't know." I bury the guilt festering inside of me.

"This is one of the reasons why we didn't want to say anything beforehand. We didn't want any drama." Ben crosses his arms over his chest. "Nicki and I are adults and have given this a lot of thought. Regardless of what you say or believe about our situation, we're getting married this afternoon. It would be great if you could be happy for us."

Darlene perches on the edge of the sofa. "Of course, we're happy, aren't we, Hank?"

The elder Carrington harrumphs.

"But I wish you'd wait," she continues. "Then we could have a small ceremony with a few close family and friends, which would quell any rumors, and would give me time to put on a wedding that's appropriate for a family of our stature." She shifts her gaze to me. "As well as enjoy your celebration. We could even arrange for Nicki's mom to come, too, 'cause it's all about family now, right?"

For some odd reason, her words strike a chord with me. Not just about my mom but about being family. Is this the best way to start ours? At odds with our parents?

"Nicki and I appreciate the offer, but we've made up our minds." Ben rises from his chair, obviously undeterred by his mother's words. "The most important thing is Lei Ming's well-being, and if we had the time for a traditional wedding, we'd have one. But we don't. We'll throw some type of party later, and we'll invite the whole city of Kilgore if you want, but for now, we're going to the JP."

He holds out his hand to me, an indication this conversation is over.

My eyes bounce between the three of them. I don't want to be the cause of a rift in their relationship. Hopefully, they'll be at peace with our decision someday soon. I place my hand in his and stand up next to him.

"Then you have our blessing." His mother cocks her eyebrow at her husband. "Right, Hank?"

Hank grunts something that sounds like a yes.

"Good," Ben says. "Now, if you'll excuse us, we're going to get married."

2

Better to bend in the wind than to break.
~ *Chinese Proverb*

Ben and I make a hasty exit before his parents, particularly his dad, can throw up any further objections or roadblocks to our impending ceremony. We arrive at the courthouse an hour before they close. Ready or not, I'm about to become Mrs. Benjamin Carrington.

"Can I help you?" The young girl behind the wooden counter asks when it's finally our turn.

"We're here to get married." Ben's voice is firm and doesn't carry the slightest trace of fear.

"I need to see your marriage license." She smacks her gums and holds out her hand.

"We don't have one yet," I inform her.

She rolls her eyes. "You'll need to go down the hall, show your IDs, and pay $75 to get one. Cash or credit card."

"Okay, then what?" I quickly glance in the direction of where we're supposed to obtain permission. "Do we come back here to you when we're done?"

"No," she cackles. "You have to wait 72 hours before you can officially tie the knot."

"What?" Ben and I blurt in unison.

"No one told us there was a waiting period," he says.

She taps a few buttons on her keyboard, then turns her computer screen toward us. "It's all right here on the county website. You've heard of the Internet, haven't you?"

"Of course," I reply. "We just didn't think—"

"If I had a dime for every time someone told me that, I wouldn't have to work behind this desk to pay for college." She cranes her neck past us. "Next in line."

Shell-shocked, Ben and I shuffle over to a nearby bench.

"So, do you have any other ideas of how we can become Mr. and Mrs.?" I plop onto the wooden slats.

He takes out his phone. "We could catch a flight to Las Vegas."

"Vegas?" I scrunch my nose. "I'm not big on celebratory fanfare, but I refuse to get married by an Elvis impersonator."

"It's the first thing that popped into my head." He rubs his hand over his face. "I can't believe I didn't think to check the requirements beforehand. I'm sorry."

I can see the frustration and regret in his eyes. "How were you to know? It's not like you get married every day." I grin, hoping to bring some lightness to the situation. "Or do you?"

"No, not every day." He winks at me. "But I try at least every few months. I was in a drought until you came along."

Once I've finished giggling like a schoolgirl, I ask, "Okay, so now what?"

Ben glances down the corridor. "Let me go see if I can find someone besides Miss Congeniality over there who might be able to help us. Maybe there's a loophole to all of this we can work around."

"That's a good idea. I'll wait here." I watch his large frame stomp through the corridors like a man on a mission. While it's hard to not try and take matters into my own hands, it's also nice having someone to lean on in difficult times. I might even grow accustomed to this.

After fifteen minutes of waiting, Ben still hasn't returned from his conquest. Rather than focus on the worries tumbling through my mind at the moment, I reach for a distraction. From the pit of my purse, I pull out my phone and check my email.

The bold font with Director Wu's name causes my pulse to race. I forsake all other messages and open hers.

Nicki,

So nice to hear from you! I pray your travels went smoothly. Lei Ming is doing well. The doctor informed me that she is recovering nicely and plans to release her to the Recovery Unit at New Hope soon. Please don't worry. She's in good hands. I'm keeping a close eye on her for you. Remember the red thread! Be in touch soon.

I stop holding my breath and release a huge sigh. Finally, some good news. If anyone needs some positivity right now, it's me. I type out a short response letting the director know that we are doing everything we can to get married and return to China as quickly as possible. At least knowing that Lei Ming is okay makes waiting three days bearable, if necessary.

Once the whooshing sound lets me know my reply is on its way, I dig in my purse once more and pull out the red thread the director gave me a few days ago. Maybe seeing it every day will remind me that if this little girl and I were meant to be together, then nothing can break our bond. Nothing.

I fashion the string around my right wrist like a bracelet just as Ben drops down on the bench next to me. "Okay, I talked to one of the registrars, and there's nothing we can do to get around the waiting period." He unfolds the paper he's holding in his hands. "But she did give me a list of other states where there's no time limitation, and guess what's on there?"

Oh, no. "Connecticut?" My stomach lurches at the thought that the one place I've been avoiding may be our only option to seal the deal.

"Exactly." Ben's face lights up. "I found a flight we can take later tonight. If we make it, we can be married in the morning and celebrate with your mom tomorrow evening."

"You want to go to Bridgeport ... tonight?" I can barely get the words out of my mouth.

"Yeah." His forehead wrinkles. "Is that a problem?"

To take Ben home? Yes, it's a problem. A big one. If we went back to Bridgeport, he'd expect us to go to my mother's house. I'm not sure we're at a point in our relationship yet for him to be confronted with the truth of her situation. There are some days when it's still hard for me to wrap my brain around.

No, I need a little more time to bare my soul, and my mother's illness, to my husband-to-be.

"Nicki?" he asks again.

"I ... I don't know."

"I don't understand. Are you changing your mind?"

"No. Of course not." I reach for his hands. "It's just that if we go to Connecticut, then it's only fair that we tell my mother about our wedding plans ahead of time since we told your family, and there's no guarantee how she'll react. She could be ecstatic or try to persuade us not to go through with it. I'm not sure I want any more parental discord."

"Okay, then." He holds up the paper from the registrar. "Certainly, we can find somewhere else on this list to get married."

"Thanks." I nestle my head against his shoulder and relax a bit.

But only for a moment.

As we study our options, our quiet searching is interrupted by Darlene's voice blaring through the empty corridor. "Ben, Nicki, wait!"

Ben and I watch in horror as his parents, dressed as if they were attending a black-tie event, barrel toward us.

"Mom, Dad." Ben leaps up from the bench. "What are you doing here?"

Darlene rests her hand on her chest, gasping for air. "You haven't gotten married yet, have you?"

"No." Ben grimaces. "We didn't realize there was a three-day waiting period."

"Well, maybe that's a sign, then." Hank lifts his cowboy hat before slapping Ben on the shoulder.

"Hank, stop it. We didn't come to fight." She straightens her sequin dress and primps her hair, ensuring that her up-do is still perfectly in place. "What are you going to do then?"

"We're looking for alternatives."

"What kind?" Hank scowls.

"Ones that will allow us to do what we came back to the States to do. Get married right away." Ben crosses his arms over his chest. "I don't understand. Why are you here?"

Darlene wipes the sweat from her forehead. "I understand why y'all are doing what you're doing and why you didn't want to tell us or Nicki's mom. But since we do know, I was hoping we could get here in time to see you get married." Her voice cracks. "It would mean so much to me."

Tears pool in the corner of her eyes, so I stand and give her a Kleenex from my purse.

"Thank you." She taps the tissue under her eyelashes so as not to smear her Tammy Faye mascara. "If I can't give you two a proper ceremony, the least you can do is let me watch."

Her gaze darts between Ben and me, pleading with us to let her be a part of this moment.

And that's when it hits me.

Looking into her eyes, all I see is a mother's love and the longing she has to be present when her child gets married. It's the look I imagine my mom would have if she were here. And it's the same one I'm sure I'll wear when Lei Ming walks down the aisle.

With that recognition, my chest tightens. Now I understand what Darlene must be going through. It's the same heartbreak my mother will experience when I break the news that I wed Ben without her. The loss of celebrating a life-changing event with your child.

How could I—we—possibly rob them of that joy?

I can't, and, if I'm being honest with myself, I don't want to. But I don't want to delay making Lei Ming our daughter one second longer than necessary either.

As my inner turmoil builds and threatens to tear my heart into pieces, I catch a glimpse of the red thread dangling from my wrist. If I truly believed God arranged for me to go to China and placed Lei Ming in my life, then I had to have faith that He could make a way for us to be matched, even if we had to wait a few extra days.

"Your mom's right," I say.

"About what?" Ben shifts his stare from his parents to me.

"If we're going through all these hoops to be a family, shouldn't we consider our families and include them as well?" I gulp. "I mean, since we have to wait three days anyway, why not go ahead and do a small ceremony where everyone can be present? It really would be great to have my mom here with me, and clearly, it's what your mom wants too. We can catch a flight back to China immediately after the ceremony."

"And what about Lei Ming?" Ben's cheeks burn red. "Are you forgetting the whole reason we're doing this in the first place?"

"Of course not," I say. "Lei Ming means the world to me."

"Well, what if she has another setback or some other family wants to adopt her?" Ben's lower lip quivers.

"We have to have faith, Ben, and trust that it's all going to be okay." I roll my fingers over the red thread. "I just received an email from Director Wu saying she's doing great and will be released from the hospital soon." I open my email and flash it in his direction.

He plucks the device from my hand and reads the message out loud. When he finishes, his shoulders relax. "So, she's really going to be okay?"

"Yes, and now that we know that Lei Ming is recovering nicely, it won't hurt anything to delay the wedding a few days—maybe a week—and have a small ceremony where all of our parents can be there with us." I cut a sideways glance at Darlene. "I think it would really make everyone happy. Including me." I smile.

"Are you sure about this?"

"I am."

"Okay, Mom." Ben turns toward his mom and holds his hands up in surrender. "You've got a week to plan something small."

She squeals in delight. "Oh, thank you." She wraps her son in a bear hug. When she pulls back from him, she's beaming. "Can I have ten days instead of seven?"

"Mom, don't push it."

"All right, all right." She grabs Hank's arm and drags him down the corridor. "We need to get home so I can start making plans."

Watching them go, lightness overtakes me. For better or worse, we did what was best for everyone.

Once they're out of sight, Ben looks back at me and shakes his head. "You have no idea the Pandora's Box you opened up, letting my mother plan what will no doubt be the social event of the spring."

"It won't be that bad," I narrow my eyes. "Will it?"

AFTER SEEING the joy on Darlene's face when we told her she could plan a small ceremony for us, I decide to leave for Connecticut the next day to visit my mom. I want to give her that same measure of happiness and tell her the news about my upcoming wedding in person, especially since she's been waiting for me to tie the knot for so long. But I'm going there on my own. Ben doesn't need to know about my mom's problems just yet.

"Why do you want to go alone?" Ben leans against the bedroom doorframe.

"It'll be easier that way." I throw my computer in my bag. "Heather was able to schedule a meeting with the O'Connor Foundation Board to review New Hope's grant submission early. That's scheduled for Monday afternoon. My mom and I will be back Tuesday morning. A quick trip, really."

"But I think it would be fun to see where you grew up."

"There's not much to it, and you'd just be bored hanging out in a strange place."

"I lived in China by myself, remember?" he chuckles. "I think I can handle Bridgeport for a few hours while you make your presentation."

"I appreciate the offer, but you should stay here and help your mom with the wedding. From the way she's talking, she's making a lot of plans, and I'm still not convinced your dad's on board and willing to help her." I scan the cottage for my computer charger. "Unless you're worried I won't come back."

"Very funny." He tilts his head. "I'm not concerned about that, but I do get the feeling you're hiding something from me."

I freeze. "What?"

"I think you don't want me to go with you because you've got a secret back home you're keeping from me."

"A secret?" I swallow the fear rising to my mouth.

"Yeah, some skeleton in your closet you're afraid I'll discover if I join you."

"That's ludicrous, Ben." I scurry around the room to avoid eye contact with him. It's not just a closet full of skeletons. It's an entire house.

"Is it?" He grabs my hand and pulls me toward him.

Standing so close to him, I can see that he hasn't shaved since we arrived back in the States. A scraggly beard has formed along his jawline, and I'm tempted to rub it. "What would I be keeping from you?"

"I don't know, a boyfriend?" He cracks a smile. "Some dude I'm going to have to fight for your hand?"

I belt out a hearty laugh. "I can assure you, there's no boyfriend. If you recall, I wasn't looking for a Prince Charming."

"No, you weren't, but he found you." His eyes bore into mine. "And he wants to be a part of whatever it is you're doing. Especially since we're planning to be a family."

My heart beats faster. While our arrangement, as Ben's dad so lovingly refers to it, is completely platonic, hearing Ben talk like that about our future family makes my insides quiver. In all the rush to get married, I didn't really stop to think about my feelings for him. Both now and in the future. Could we grow to love one another someday and truly be a family?

"I appreciate that. Really, I do." I take a step back from him, not only to protect my heart but to avoid seeing the disappointment in his eyes. "But you don't need to go. Like I said, you'd be bored."

"You're right. I don't need to go. I want to go." He gentles his voice. "I'd like to ask your mom for permission to marry you."

"You would?"

"Yes. One day when Lei Ming's boyfriend ..." He shakes his head. "I can't believe I'm actually saying those words, but when the time comes for our little girl to get married, I want her husband-to-be to do what's right by her as well and ask me for her hand in marriage."

A shiver runs down my spine, hearing him talk about Lei Ming that way. In just a short time, she's not only managed to capture my heart, but it seems she's done quite the number on him as well. It's also proof that the sacrifices we're making – and the craziness of it all—are worth it. If that's the case, then I need to be completely honest with him. No more secrets.

"Fine," I concede. "You can come to Connecticut with me—"

"Great, I'll go pack." He drops my hand and heads for the door.

"Ben, wait." I swallow. "I need to tell you something."

He stops and turns back toward me. "Ah, so there is a mysterious boyfriend."

"I wish it were as simple as that."

My legs go weak, and I drop into a low-back chair in the living room. Divulging the truth about my mom isn't going to be easy. Other than my organizing colleague who's been assisting Mom avoid eviction by getting things in order, I've never told anyone about her hoarding. But now I don't have a choice. If he's going to accompany me back home, he's going to see it all for himself, and it's best if I warn him ahead of time.

He plops into the matching chair across from me. "Okay, go ahead, tell me all about him. I can handle it."

When I don't reply to his joke, Ben scoots forward in the seat, deep concern etched on his face. "Nicki, what is it?"

"It's my mom." I take a deep breath and lower my gaze. "She's, well, she's a hoarder."

"You mean like the people on that TV show? The ones who don't get rid of anything?"

I nod.

"Oh."

A heavy silence falls over the room, leaving each of us lost in our own thoughts.

Finally, Ben speaks up. "I can see why you wouldn't want me to come, Nicki. It would be hard to hide that, but really I'm more confused than anything."

"What's there to be confused about? My mother loves to collect needless and worthless things to the point that her home is basically unlivable."

"I get that." He perches on the edge of his chair. "What I don't understand is how is it you're so organized, but your mom isn't? Has she been like this your whole life? And why did you not want me to know?"

"You're asking me to give you my whole life's story."

Tenderness flickers in his eyes. "Well, it's probably a good idea for me to know about it, don't you think? We are going to be husband and wife soon."

His words speak volumes. He's not mad. Even though I kept this from him, he still wants to marry me. What did I do to deserve someone like him?

"You mean you're not upset that I kept this from you and intended to keep it from you as long as I possibly could?"

"I told you my dark secret about Katie's death, and you didn't run. Why would I be upset that your mom has an illness?"

"I don't know, I just thought ..."

Ben springs from his seat and squats down beside me. "Nicki, we've made a huge commitment without really knowing each other that well. There will be things we learn about one another along the way that may be a jolt to our system. It's to be expected." He places his hand on mine. "But the only way this is going to work is if we're open and honest with one another. No secrets."

"Agreed, no more secrets." I tuck a strand of hair behind my ear. "So, you want me to tell you the whole story then?"

"I do." He stands. "But save it for the plane ride. I need to go pack so I can meet my future mother-in-law."

3

If one is in harmony with his family, he has found the secret of
success.
~ *Chinese Proverb*

I spend the majority of our three-hour flight filling in Ben on
the details of my mother's illness. How it began after my
father's death, the rift it caused in our relationship, and the
extreme measures it took for her to finally accept the help she
needed.

Of course, Ben was nothing but completely understanding
and compassionate as I poured out ten years of sorrow, pain, and
frustration on him. By the time our plane touched down in
Connecticut, I was certain my life and the events of the past two
days would qualify us for our own reality TV show. Or a full-
blown theatrical production. Especially once we bring my
mother up to speed on our upcoming nuptials. There's no telling
which side of the pendulum she'll swing to.

"Here we are." I slowly pull our rental car into my mom's
overly cluttered driveway.

Under a gray and cloudy sky, Ben surveys the scene in front

of him. He rakes his hand through his hair and lets out a slow whistle. "Wow, you weren't kidding, were you?"

"No," I say, unnerved not only by his reaction but also by the condition of my mom's yard. Not much has changed since I was here for Ms. O'Connor's funeral in February. There are still several dishwashers, garden gnomes, and tattered lawn chairs spread out across the patchy lawn, the welcoming committee to the chaos.

"She's supposed to be cleaning things up to satisfy the city and county orders, but from the looks of it, she hasn't made much progress out here."

"It probably looks better on the inside. Maybe it's been too cold to work outside right now. I'm sure March in Connecticut isn't as warm as Texas." He removes his seat belt. "Should we go in and find out?"

I hope he's right. They had to have made improvements inside. Otherwise, my mother will be homeless soon.

"Are you sure you're up to this?" I wince. "I wouldn't blame you if you didn't want to see everything. You could go to the hotel tonight, and we could meet you for breakfast in the morning."

Ben shifts his body and faces me. "Nicki, I've never been married, but I've been to enough weddings to know that whoever is officiating will say for better or for worse during the ceremony. When he does, I will say I do because I mean it. For better or worse, okay?" His eyes flick toward the mess. "And if we need to help her in any way, we will."

"Thanks, that means more than you realize." I gaze back at my mother's front yard and sigh. "If we're going to do this, there's no point in delaying it any longer, right?"

We exit the car and slither through the hodgepodge of items scattered between the driveway and the backdoor. I don't even have my hand on the doorknob when it suddenly swings open.

"Nicki!" My mother squeals in delight. "You're here!"

Before I can say a word, she hugs me tight. The smell of her watered-down rose perfume attacks my nostrils, and I inhale the familiar scent. I'm home.

"Mom." I gasp for air. "It's only been a few weeks."

She reluctantly releases me and holds me at arm's length. "It feels like ages ago."

Her eyes fall on Ben. "And you are?"

"I'm Ben." He holds out his hand to her. "It's so nice to—"

Instantly my mother wraps her arms around his chest.

"Meet you," Ben manages to finish, his face red as he reciprocates her gesture.

My mom releases Ben from her tight grip and beams. "Nicki said she was bringing someone home with her when she called, but I thought she was talking about her friend Julia or her boss Heather. I had no idea she was bringing a suitor to visit."

I step in between them and do my best to save Ben from her smothering. "A suitor, Mom, really? This is not the Victorian era. Ben is just a friend." Who also happens to be my fiancé. "Now, can we please go inside? Even though it's spring, it still feels like winter, and I'm freezing."

The three of us scoot inside the toasty house. Despite connecting my mom with a hoarding specialist, it doesn't look like much about the house has changed. Old newspapers and phone books line the main hallway, and piles of overflowing plastic bags from the local dollar store have yet to relinquish their duty as a barrier to the front entrance.

"Why is all this stuff still here?" I ask through gritted teeth.

My mom blinks rapidly. "What do you mean?"

"This." I wave my arms frantically around the space. "You were supposed to be clearing all of this out."

"Nicki," Ben's eyes convey a subtle warning. "Maybe now isn't the time."

I pivot back towards him. "She doesn't have time, Ben. The local officials are going to evict her soon, and this place looks the same as when I left." I look at my mom. "Is Ann still helping you?"

"She is, but when she brought her entire team in here, it was too much for me to handle. We decided to just work one-on-one instead and only a few hours twice a week." My mother rocks from side to side. "It's taken longer that way, but we've managed to make some progress in my bedroom, the bathroom, and part of the living room." She counts off each space on her fingers. "You don't need to worry about it. I've got everything under control."

"Not from where I'm standing."

The joy that had radiated from my mother's face when I first arrived evaporates, and she lowers her chin to her chest.

Immediately shame engulfs me. "I'm sorry, Mom," I whisper. "I'm just worried about you and what will happen if you don't meet the city or county's deadline."

"It's hard to let go, Nicki," my mother mutters.

"I know." I take her hands in mine. "We'll figure something out."

"We will," Ben says, stepping closer to me. "But for now, why don't we move on to other topics?"

My mother slowly lifts her head. "That sounds lovely. We can visit in the kitchen over some tea."

When we settle around the wobbly Formica table, my anger has simmered some. I'm not really upset with my mom. I'm mad at myself for not being here when she needed me most. Maybe if I'd stayed and had overseen the work she and Ann were doing, things would have improved at a faster rate. I would have made sure of it.

If I had, my mother would have a clean, livable house by now, and the threat of eviction wouldn't be an issue. However, had I done that, our bond would have been battered and bruised beyond repair once more, which is why I'd asked a third party to step in. Despite feeling as if I'd just been awarded the "World's Worst Daughter" title, I'm certain returning to China had been the right thing to do. For our relationship, for New Hope, and especially for Lei Ming.

I only worry what the future holds for my mother now.

"So, what brings the two of you back to the States? How long will you be staying?" She sets three chipped tea mugs, each filled with water and a seeping tea bag, and a bag of partially eaten, generic sugar cookies in the center of the table. "Nicki was rather vague on the phone."

"Actually, Mrs. Mayfield ..." Ben clears his throat.

"Stop right there." My mother wags her index finger before sitting down across from him. "There will be no formality here with me. Please, call me Ginny."

"O-kay, Ginny." Ben nods. "Well, Nicki and I ..."

"We're getting married!" I blurt.

My mother's eyes grow as wide as tea saucers. "M—married?" Her eyes dart back and forth between Ben and me as if trying to determine which one of us was going to yell out 'gotcha' first.

"We are." Ben gives me a side-eye. "We wanted to tell you in person."

"Really?" Mom clutches her chest, and for a moment, I worry she might have a heart attack. "The two of you are getting ... married?"

"Yes. In one week. In Texas."

"So soon? When did all this happen? And why so fast?" Her voice is a mix of joy and confusion. "I mean, I'm delighted by the news, but I don't understand."

I lean over and cover her hands with mine. "I'm sorry to drop this bombshell on you, but we have a good reason."

"I'm sure you do, dear." She shakes her head. "I'm just hoping one of you can start at the beginning and tell me how this all came about."

"Yes," Ben and I say together.

We spend the next hour tag team sharing all the details of the last few weeks – Assistant Director Chang's schemes to embezzle money from New Hope, Lei Ming's health issues, and the obstacles standing in my way to adopt her. When we finally reach the part about our decision to get married and the problems we encountered in Texas, we're both out of breath.

"I don't know what to say." My mother takes a long sip of her tea.

My mouth drops open. "Seriously? You've been dying for me to get married and supply you with grandchildren. Now that it's finally happening, you're speechless?" Fear shoots through me. "Unless you're not okay with our decision?"

"Oh, I am. I'm just shocked, that's all." She fans herself with her hand, and I'm not sure if she's trying to calm down or keep herself from crying. "But I am happy!"

I jump from my chair and squat down next to her. "I know it must sound like we've lost our minds." I flick my eyes at Ben. "Who knows, maybe we have, but as strange as it seems, it does feel right."

"It sounds pretty strange," my mom chuckles. "But it also sounds like love."

My breath hitches, and I almost topple over onto the floor. "Love?"

"Yes, dear. Love."

Obviously, we didn't explain the situation well enough to my mom. Ben and I are just friends. I mean, he's a great guy and has gone above and beyond, but that was all there was to it. Right? Otherwise, why were my mother's words throwing me so off balance?

"What the two of you are doing for that little girl," she continues, "is nothing short of love. God's love. And I couldn't be prouder." She cups my face in her hand. "It's not the way I always dreamed it would be, but who am I to stand in God's way? And if the two of you have prayed and feel strongly that this is what you're supposed to do, then I can't say no to that."

My legs tremble, and for a second, my spirits dip. The love she was referring to wasn't about Ben and me, after all. If all she sees in us is a strong friendship, maybe that's truly all there is.

"We have your blessing then?" Ben asks. "Even though Nicki

and I both agree that we need to do this, I still want to respect your wishes." He beams. "Mrs. Mayfield—I mean, Ginny—do I have your permission to marry your daughter?"

My mom looks down at me, her eyes glistening. "Your father would have been thrilled to have Ben ask him for your hand."

I gulp. "I know. I wish he could be here."

"Me too." She plants a soft kiss on my cheek before turning toward Ben. "Yes, you have my permission."

Springing to my feet, I give my mom a hug.

"Now I have so many questions I want to ask you about the wedding." She pulls back from me. "But first, I want to see the ring."

I freeze and stare at Ben with a "now what" expression.

"Oh, we're going ring shopping tomorrow," he says smoothly. "We wanted to wait and make sure it was okay with you before we put a ring on it."

My insides jiggle at his reference to one of Beyonce's most popular songs and that he was able to skirt around the fact it was a topic we hadn't really discussed.

"That makes sense," she says. "Then I guess all we need to do now is talk wedding details. I have a stack of bridal magazines around here somewhere, and I'm sure I can find my wedding gown for you. I set it aside many years ago in the hopes I could pass it on to my daughter. And that day has finally arrived!" She snaps her fingers. "It can count as both something old and something borrowed."

I rub my forehead. It's bad enough my mother even has a bridal magazine collection or that she held on to her dress all this time, but she's going to be disappointed when she learns that someone else is handling all the details of the big day.

"Um, Mom." I clear my throat. "Before you start making any plans, I need to talk to you about the wedding."

"Of course." She pushes back in her chair. "But a week isn't a long time to get a wedding coordinated. Can it wait?"

"Actually, there aren't many details you need to worry about."

I purse my lips. "Ben's family has generously offered to make all the arrangements for us in Texas."

"Every ... thing?" she cries. "You mean I don't have a part in my own daughter's wedding? But that's what the bride's family is supposed to do."

Seeing the anguish on her face, guilt ties my stomach in knots. She's wanted this for so long, and to see her in such pain, it's as if I just pulled the rug out from under her and robbed her of the entire experience. Not only that, but I don't have the heart to tell her that Darlene Carrington's idea for a high society event doesn't include clearance items from the local thrift shop or hors d'oeuvres from the freezer section of the big box stores.

"Well, it's just that weddings, even small ones, can be expensive, and you and I don't have the kind of resources they do. It only seemed logical to let them take care of it. Plus, not worrying about all the details will let us enjoy the moment more."

"I hadn't considered that." She drums her fingers on the table. "But isn't there anything I can do? I'm the mother of the bride!"

"I'm sure there is," Ben chimes in. "My mom is hiring an event planner to handle most of the details, but I have no doubt there'll be something special you can do."

"Yes," I grin, grateful for Ben's ability to think fast on his feet. "I have to present to the O'Connor Foundation in a few days. Then we'll all fly back to Dallas, and you can find a part of the ceremony to claim as your own. And if there isn't that much for you to do wedding-wise, I'd love it if you'd help me get things squared away for your granddaughter. I have no clue what a child requires, and you could go shopping with me and tell me what to buy."

My mother rises from her chair and paces the already worn-out laminate tiles. "I don't know," she mutters with each pass. "They aren't buying you a dress, though, are they?"

"No, now that I know I can borrow yours, that's one less thing anyone will have to worry about."

"You mean it, Nic? If I find it, you'll wear it?" My mother's eyes light up.

"I will." I have no clue if it will even fit, but for Mom's sake, I'll figure something out.

"Oh, that's wonderful." She claps her hands and scoots toward the kitchen door. "I'll go dig it up right now."

The cuckoo clock she's had for as long as I can remember belts out its hourly jangle. "It's getting late, Mom. Why don't we wait until tomorrow?"

"You're right." She waits for the antique timepiece to finish its tenth chime. "We have a few busy days ahead of us, and we're all going to need our rest. I'll set up the air mattress for Ben in the living room."

I walk over to her and break the bad news. "Ben and I thought it would be better if we didn't sleep here. We reserved two rooms at a hotel just off I-95."

"Don't be silly, Nicki." She swats her hand at me. "This is your home. You can't sleep at a hotel." Her eyes fill with determination. "You'll just sleep in your room, and we can put Ben on an air mattress in the living room."

"Mom—" I rub my temples. I could tolerate the house and all its chaos for a night or two, but it wasn't fair to make Ben endure such torture.

"An air mattress will be fine, Ginny," Ben says before I can debate the point.

Satisfied by her victory, my mother flashes a huge grin at him. "They're here somewhere. Just give me a minute to locate them." She retreats to the deep, dark recesses of her house in search of the bedding. I have no doubt she'll return with enough inflatable mattresses to supply an entire platoon of soldiers.

Once she's gone, I reach for my purse. "If you know what's good for you, you'll take the car key and get out now. I'll cover for you."

"It can't be that bad, Nicki."

"You have no idea." I pull the key fob from my bag and toss it to him. "She stores her freakishly scary collectible dolls in my bedroom, so there's no telling what may keep you company in the living room if you stay."

Catching the key as only a former baseball player could, Ben lets out a booming laugh. "Don't worry. If I can sleep on the rock-hard beds in China, I can handle an inflatable one for a night or two."

I inch closer to him and wrap his fingers around the black plastic. Better than anyone, I'm well aware of the creatures and critters that linger in dank spaces when expired food, trash, and unkempt spots go unchecked. Even if my mom has managed to make a dent in some of it, those who have been living rent-free in her house will retaliate. I'd really hate for Ben to be one of their victims.

Ben's shoulders bounce up and down as he drops the key on the table. "You may be easily spooked by a few dolls, but I'll be fine, I promise. You just worry about getting your rest for our big ring hunt tomorrow."

The mention of jewelry shopping leaves me breathless. "You were serious about that?"

"Of course." He takes the twisty tie off the cookie bag and begins shaping it into a circle. "We have to have something to slip on your finger unless you want one like this." He holds it up as if it were a priceless gem.

"I'm not big on fancy trinkets, but I think we can do better than that." A rush of adrenaline courses through me as I think about all the possibilities for my left hand.

"Agreed." Ben tucks his rustic creation into his jean pocket. "Now, if you'll excuse me, I need to get ready for bed." He swaggers out of the kitchen.

"Okay, but now you're the one who's opened Pandora's Box." I holler. "Don't say I didn't warn you."

4

Leaves emerge from where they should not.
~ *Chinese Proverb*

My mother's nonstop chattering awakens me the next morning. Listening to her rattle on about local artisans who could craft a unique, one-of-a-kind wedding ring set for us, I can only groan and imagine Ben patiently suffering at the kitchen table. The poor guy has no idea what's in store for him with a mother-in-law like Virginia Mayfield. Out of guilt and necessity, I rush to dress so I can be the one to rescue him this time. It's the least I can do.

Despite my mother's helpful suggestions, Ben and I manage to escape from the house with our own list of shops to check out. No matter how many stores we have to visit to find the perfect ring, we're up to the challenge. Buying a ring may be the one thing that will make this crazy situation of ours seem a little more normal.

Goosebumps pebble my arms as we drive to the ritzy part of Bridgeport. Not only am I excited about taking another step to cement our deal, but I'm also a little nervous too. This will be the first time Ben and I will have to work together toward a common goal. What if we don't see eye to eye on a ring? How will we reconcile our differences? And if we can't compromise, what does that mean for our relationship, both today and in the future?

I try not to dwell on the what-ifs too much and instead use small talk as a distraction. "Were you really okay in the living room last night?" I ask.

He shrugs. "I'm not complaining."

"That's because you're so nice. I hate that the house wasn't in better shape for you. I was certain she would've made more progress by this point."

"It was fine, Nicki." He clears his throat. "Plus, I didn't want to upset her anymore. I didn't have the heart to skip out on her hospitality after informing her there wouldn't be much for her to do for the wedding." He glances at me. "We'll make things right, though, and find a way to get her involved in the plans when we get back to Kilgore."

I flash a smile at him before turning my gaze out the window. Being the weekend, there are no morning rush hour commuters to contend with and none of the usual traffic wars of vehicles battling for space on the six-lane highway. Only a barren stretch of asphalt awaits us.

Honestly, I'm grateful for the reprieve. Thinking of my mother *helping* with the wedding causes my insides to wage a battle of their own. Even though the Carringtons were super friendly, I'm not sure they'll understand my mother's issues and how we come from a totally different world than theirs.

"Hey." Ben taps my knee with his fingers. "Earth to Nicki."

I whip my head in his direction. "What?"

"Are you still with me? You seem lost in thought over there."

"I'm good." I sit up straight.

"I don't think you are. Is everything okay?" His eyebrows knit together. "You're not still worried about your mom, are you?"

I fall silent and contemplate his question. Will I ever stop worrying about my mom? The way others perceive her and her illness? Her well-being and healing? What will happen to her if she doesn't meet the deadline for the house cleanup? I can't imagine there will ever be a day when I don't fret about her for one reason or another.

"Nicki?"

"What? Sorry, no, I was just thinking about what kind of ring we should get." I blink rapidly at my half-truth. Although it's important to have trust in a relationship, especially a marriage, I'm not ready to divulge all my worries to him just yet. And if I had to guess, he probably feels the same way about some aspects of his life too. It's a bridge we'll have to learn to cross together as time goes on.

"And what are you thinking?"

"Something simple's fine."

"I'm sure we can do better than that." He pulls the car off the highway and onto a side road. "Isn't there some kind of ring you've always dreamt about wearing?"

"No," I tell him. "Remember, I'm not big on jewelry."

He throws his head back. "I thought all women were."

"Clearly you don't know that much about women—or me." I cringe at my last word and quickly add, "Yet."

As the color drains from his face, my breakfast roils in my stomach.

"I'm sorry, Ben, I didn't mean that in a bad way."

"No, you're right. We don't know each other all that well." He pulls into a strip mall parking lot and pulls the car into a space near the entrance. "But I want to change that. I want to learn everything about you, Nicki Mayfield. I mean, the soon-to-be Nicki Carrington."

That's a scary proposition.

"Are you sure about that? What if you don't like what you find out?" My chest tightens. No one's perfect, but what if my headstrong and independent spirit are more than he can handle?

Will I pop his romantic bubble and possibly put our relationship —and Lei Ming's future—in danger?

"I'm not much of a gambler, but I'm willing to take that chance." He leans in close to me. "Plus, I have a few traits you probably won't be fond of either."

"Like what?" My breath hitches as I imagine him picking his teeth at the dinner table.

Opening the car door, he winks at me. "You'll just have to wait and see. Now let's go get you a ring."

An older man with oily black hair dressed in a three-piece suit greets us as soon as we enter, bringing our conversation to a close. "How can I help you two lovebirds today?"

"We'd like to look at wedding rings." Ben strides over to one of the display cases where large diamond rings sparkle under bright LED lights.

"Congratulations." The man claps his hands. "I could tell you two were madly in love the minute you walked in the door."

I stifle a laugh. I'm not sure what vibes Ben and I are giving off, but this guy is either clueless or really trying to butter us up. "Where are your wedding bands?" I glance around the superstore.

"Over there." The salesman points to a far corner of the building where the less-than-stellar jewelry has been banished. "But I think your fiancé already has his eye on something."

"He's not my—" I stop myself. At some point, I have to start referring to Ben for what he is—my fiancé. But before I can actually get the words out and clarify our unusual relationship, the jeweler jogs off in Ben's direction, eyes focused like an animal about to take down prey.

I sidle up next to my fiancé, whose face is so close to the glass counter his breath fogs up the display. "Why are you over here?"

"Where else would I be?" He tilts his head up at me.

"The plain wedding bands are over there." I cock my head toward the back of the store. "Simple, remember?"

Ben stiffens his back. "I do, but that doesn't mean it can't be nice too."

"A solid gold band is nice," I insist.

"Look, Nicki," he whispers. "I know this is a marriage of convenience, but I'd like to buy you something special." He bends his head down at the glittering rings lined up against a velvety purple backdrop.

My mouth falls open. Those aren't diamond rings—they're flawless boulders.

"I don't know, Ben. They look awfully expensive."

"Would you like to try one on, Miss?" The slick salesman quickly removes a keychain filled with tiny keys from his blazer pocket, which jingles as he unlocks the fortified case. His fingers dance over the dozen open boxes and land on the biggest jewel of the bunch. "This one looks like it's meant for you." He holds the ring up in the air like Mufasa, showcasing Simba in the Serengeti.

I take it from him and hold it between my fingers. I move the diamond back and forth, searching for a reason why I shouldn't even be admiring it, but at the moment, nothing comes to mind. The only thing I can think of is how absolutely breathtakingly stunning it is.

"That's a Princess cut Halo diamond engagement ring with luxe winding willow diamonds." He spouts off more details by memory. "It has a 1.5-carat diamond in the center with one carat worth of diamonds surrounding it. All mounted on a 14k rose-gold band. One of our finest."

"Here." Ben gently removes it from my fingers. "Let's see how it fits." He grips my left hand and places it on the appropriate finger. "What do you think?"

I brush my thumb over the smooth glass and watch as the lights glint off its surface, blinding me. "It's the most amazing ring I've ever seen ..." My hand falls to my side under its weight. "But I can't see myself wearing this."

Ben must hear the apprehension in my voice because he

quickly turns to the commission-hungry jeweler and says, "This one's a little over the top. Can you show us some other rings, a little less flashy?"

The elderly man pouts before offering, "This way."

A few cases down are rings that are just as beautiful yet not as flamboyant.

"What about that one?" Ben points to a ring as stunning as the Princess cut I had just tried on, only smaller in scale.

"It's nice, but again, I don't really need anything fancy."

Ben lifts his eyes from the display case. "I know, but my mother's ring is fancy, and if I bring you home with nothing to show—or show off—I'll be in trouble."

"Mama's boy, uh?" I nudge him.

"Sometimes, but when it comes to social status, my mother is a stickler. Not only that, but if we go back to Texas with nothing but a simple band, people might question our commitment. I don't want to be the brunt of my mother's wrath or her FBI inquiry, so help me out a little, please?" He cocks his head. "And I think it would look good on you."

"Fine," I concede. "I'll look and see if there's something that's more my style that might appease her, too."

I traipse up and down the display cases in search of something that will suit me and my mother-in-law-to-be. After two circles around the store, I find one that catches my eye. And my heart. The longer I stare at it, the faster my pulse races.

"This one." I tap on the glass where a pear-shaped topaz stone surrounded by a circle of tiny diamonds sits atop a white gold band. It's not your normal, run-of-the-mill wedding ring, but then again, our marriage arrangement is anything but normal. Maybe a unique, one-of-a-kind ring is better suited for our situation.

"Lovely choice," says the salesman dryly. His keys clank against the display case as he removes the ring from its tiny home.

Ben takes it from him and inspects it before slipping it on my left hand.

Once it's firmly in place, I fan out my fingers and tilt the ring up toward the light. While it's more than I had originally wanted, I'm mesmerized by its beauty. Not only is it gorgeous to look at, but it's a perfect fit, too. Just like Cinderella's glass slipper—as if it were made for a Princess who'd found her Prince Charming.

"I think we've found the one," Ben says.

I freeze at his declaration. "I like it, but we don't even know how much it costs."

"Trust me. It's worth every penny if it makes you smile like that." He grins. "Especially since you aren't that fond of jewelry."

"Aren't you the comedian?" I jab his ribs, my eyes still glued to the ring sitting atop my finger.

Our combined laughter almost drowns out the sound of my phone chiming from deep within my bag.

"Excuse me." I take the ring off and place it back on the glass counter. "It's probably my mother calling, anxious for an update. I should answer, or she'll keep bugging us. I'll go up front and let her know what we've found so far."

"No problem." Ben nods. "I'll wait for you here."

I rush over to an alcove near the entrance for privacy and retrieve my phone. But when I glance at the screen, my mother's name is not written across the top. The caller ID reads Julia.

"Hi, hello?" I drop into the closest chair.

"Nicki?" My sweet friend's groggy voice comes over the line.

Fear crashes down around me. "Julia? Is everything okay?"

"I'm not sure."

My mind whirrs at the possibilities of what could be so bad that it would prompt her to call me at this hour. With the twelve-hour time difference, it had to be late in China. Was it her sister? Director Wu? Or worse, Lei Ming?

"What's wrong?" A bitter taste forms in my mouth.

"I was on the Internet doing some ... research when an ad

popped up on my screen." She breathes heavily into the phone as if her life is being threatened.

"Okay, what about the ad that has you so spooked?"

"It's not just any ad, Nicki. It contained some disturbing information."

"It's the Internet, Julia." I manage a half smile. "You have to take most of it with a grain of salt."

"It's a missing child report." A thread of alarm fills her voice.

"Is someone trying to find you?" While I find it hard to believe after all these years, it's possible her birth parents might be trying to track her down.

"It's not me they're looking for."

And then she tells me. I'm not sure how much time passes before I put down my phone and digest the information Julia had just shared with me. All I know is the room is spinning, and I have to find a way to wrap my brain around her unexpected revelation.

"There you are." Ben sits down next to me. "I was beginning to think you got cold feet and changed your mind."

I stare into space and search for words, but they temporarily evade me.

"Nicki?" Ben bumps his leg against mine. "Are you ready to make a decision on that ring?"

"No," I mutter.

"That's fine. We can keep searching until we find something you like. And if nothing here suits your fancy, we can go to the next store on the list. We won't stop until we find the perfect ring."

Ben starts to stand, but I pull on his arm. "No, I mean, we may not need a ring after all."

"Why not?" He falls back into the seat.

"Because I just found out Lei Ming may not have been abandoned as we'd assumed." I swallow hard and push down the bile swirling in my mouth. "There's a chance she was taken from her family sometime last year and somehow ended up at New Hope."

"Taken? What are you talking about?"

"A little girl from Fujian province in Southern China was taken, and her family placed an ad on the Internet through some business website asking if anyone knows where she might be. Apparently, when kids are abducted, and parents want to find them, they sponsor ads on popular business websites, hoping that someone will recognize the child.

"Several ads popped up while Julia was doing research online. She said the photo of one of the missing children looked eerily similar to Lei Ming, so she thought I should know, just in case."

"Did she send you that picture?"

I open my phone and click on the image I'd asked Julia to forward me. With trembling hands, I pass it to him.

He studies the face on my screen. "It does look like Lei Ming, but it's hard to tell. I think we'd need more information to make any solid speculations. Do you have another picture of Lei Ming we can compare it to?"

"Of course." I retrieve my phone and scroll through my camera roll. As each image of her crosses the screen, daggers pierce my already tender heart. "Here." I stop at a close-up shot of her sweet face.

Ben clicks on the picture and enlarges it. "The eyes and hair coloring are the same, but the missing child's cheeks are puffier, and her skin tone is a shade darker than Lei Ming's. Then again, Lei Ming's had a lot of surgery and weight loss recently, so ..."

I take the phone from him and flip back and forth between the two photos. While I didn't want to believe the child in both pictures could be one and the same, there was just too much resemblance to count anything out. My chest constricts at the thought that Lei Ming had been stolen from her family. What an awful thing. For everyone.

"Do you know the history of how Lei Ming arrived at New Hope?" Ben asks. "Did someone drop her off? Was there a note left on her or anything like that?" His lips press together in a slight grimace.

I close my eyes and do my best to recall the details Julia had supplied to me that chilly morning in December when I first laid eyes on her. "According to the orphanage, Lei Ming had been brought there a few months before I visited. I assumed she was like most other young Chinese female babies and abandoned because she was a girl."

"That makes sense." He rubs his unshaven jawline. "But why would kidnappers drop her off at an orphanage in Beijing if they had taken her from somewhere in the south? There are local orphanages in every city in China, so why travel at least 1,000 miles to bring her to New Hope?"

"I don't know." I shrug. "Maybe whoever took her wanted to get her as far away as possible so it would be harder to track her down."

I shiver at the thought of my sweet baby being handled by rough criminals across the wide expanse between the northern and southern landscapes of China. "Or maybe they discovered she had a heart issue after they took her, heard about the work New Hope was doing for children with those medical conditions and left her there so they wouldn't have to deal with it."

Ben blows out a deep breath. "Possibly, but there's really no way of knowing. At least not from here."

"So, what do you suggest we do?" I whisper faintly.

"Well, that depends."

I cock my head. "On what?"

"Do you want the answer my heart is speaking or the one from my head?" Tears pool in the corners of his eyes.

Everything in me wants to hear from his heart, because I know that it beats for Lei Ming the same way mine does. That's why we're in this jewelry store in the first place. We've fallen head over heels in love with her and want to make her ours and give her a forever family. Neither of us can fathom anything else.

But I know the man Ben is, and I know he'll want to do the

right thing for her, even if it means breaking our plans, our hopes, and ultimately our hearts into tiny million pieces. It's the answer I'm afraid to hear, yet the one I need to.

I suck in my breath. "What's your head saying?"

"That we have to find out if this missing child is actually Lei Ming." The muscles in his jaw tighten. "It would be a terrible disservice to her and this family if we tried to adopt a child whose parents really did want her all this time. Wouldn't you agree?"

"I don't want to, but what other choice do we have?" I choke back a sob. "It would be wrong of us to be selfish and look away."

"And it would be way worse if we kept going with our plans only to have everything explode in our faces later. It's the only thing we can do, and it's the right decision." He wipes a tear from my cheek.

"You're right." I sniffle. "So now what?"

"Well, maybe Julia can reach out to the people who posted the ad and see if she can find out anything." Ben rubs the back of his neck. "Or we contact Director Wu and see if we can learn more about Lei Ming's arrival at the orphanage. Someone there could remember something that might clear up any discrepancies."

I retrieve a tissue from my purse and blow my nose. "And then what?" My ability to strategize has momentarily abandoned me, along with my hopes and dreams for the future. If we're going to solve this mystery, Ben will have to be the one leading the way.

"Once we hear back from them and you finish your presentation at the O'Connor Foundation on Monday, we can assess where we're at. If we don't get the information we need, we may have no choice but to return to China right away and discover the answer ourselves."

"And if we find out that Lei Ming does has a family that loves and wants her, then ..." A logjam forms in my throat.

"Then our plans are pointless, I guess." Ben's shoulders sag. "We wouldn't need to adopt her. Or get married, after all."

My stomach clenches. "But if she isn't the missing child, then we'd still go through with everything, right?"

"Of course." He juts out his chin. "Once we start digging, I'm sure this will end up being a case of mistaken identity. When it does, I plan on keeping my commitment. Won't you?"

"Yes, but I'm not sure what we're supposed to tell our families now. It's not fair to make them ride this roller coaster of doubt and uncertainty. Should we call everything off without any explanation, or do we inform them of what's happened and pray they'll understand and push pause on all the arrangements they've made?" I sigh. "Either way, we're sure to disappoint them, especially after giving them so much hope."

"Good point." Ben scratches his head and stays lost in thought for a moment. "Maybe we just tell them that after talking about it, we felt bad about spoiling their dreams of a big celebration, and we're willing to wait a bit to let them put something together. That way, we won't be party-poopers, and it will give us some time to straighten out this nightmare."

I scrunch my forehead. "Okay, but how long? If we don't give your mother a definitive time and we end up proceeding with our plans, this thing may explode to a size I'm not comfortable with."

"For someone who just met my mother, you certainly have her pegged." A smile breaks through his forlorn face. "What if we told her she has six weeks? That way, we'll still be within the 90-day limit on our marriage license, and that should give us ample time to run any tests we need to determine if Lei Ming is the missing child. We should be able to figure everything out by then."

I reach for Ben's hand and squeeze it. Hard. I'd never wanted a husband, kids, or a family of my own. Now that all of them are slipping through my unringed fingers like water in a sieve, I realize how much I really did want it. All of it. More than I'd ever wanted anything else.

"That sounds—"

"So, have you come to a decision yet?" The elderly salesman invades our privacy, bringing our conversation to an abrupt end. "Should I write up an invoice for the topaz ring you loved so much?"

Ben and I lock eyes.

"Not today, thanks." I stand and slowly pick up my purse, allowing my hair to fall and cover my face. I'm not ready to explain the shock and awe that must be evident on it right now.

"Can I show you something else?" he asks, desperation lacing his voice. "We have a wide selection to choose from, and I'm sure we can find a similar piece at a price you feel comfortable with."

Every fiber of my being is tempted to change my mind. To march over to the display case that holds the ring of my heart, slip the beautiful piece of jewelry back on my finger, and leave the store like a woman who's about to get married. It would be so much easier than dealing with the reality that Lei Ming may have been taken, and we might lose her.

But that wouldn't be the prudent thing to do. In fact, it might be even more damaging. It's probably best if we leave the store and postpone the ceremony until we find out the truth.

Ben must sense my dismay. He gently wraps his hand around mine and then addresses the jeweler. "Thank you for your help, but we're going to wait a bit. We'll be back, though." His gaze returns to me. "I promise."

5

Once the arrow is on the bowstring, it must be shot.
~ *Chinese Proverb*

In the two days since Julia's news turned my world upside down, I had yet to fully process my emotions. There hadn't been time. I'd been too busy juggling personal and professional problems to allow myself to feel anything beyond the numbness that the daughter I thought would be mine and the husband I thought would be mine might not be.

I did my best to contact Director Wu over the weekend for insights on Lei Ming's arrival at New Hope, but she had gone out of town, and no one could tell me when she'd be back. Julia had tracked down the business that promoted the ad, but every time she rang them, the line was busy. We weren't making any progress, and the suspense was killing me.

With each unanswered call, it became apparent that the only way to glean the information we needed was to track down the people who'd actually sponsored the ad—the missing child's family. Which, in a country of a billion people, wouldn't be easy.

Left in a state of limbo, I make every effort to bury my anxiety, pain, and anger. It's the only way I can survive the uncertainty of what's ahead. Otherwise, like a hard-boiled egg cracked too early, what comes out won't be pretty.

"You are number ten in the queue. Please wait," the automated phone message tells me. Again.

I bang on my computer keyboard at the announcement and move on to review my next PowerPoint slide. Thirty minutes earlier, I was number twelve. At this rate, I'd be finished with the board meeting before I could speak to a human being.

"Whatever's wrong dear, I don't think you should take it out on the laptop." My mother waltzes into the kitchen and kisses the crown of my head.

While I love my mother and her morning cheerfulness, she's clueless to the emotions swirling within me right now and the energy it's taking to not completely lose it. But she's right—I can't afford to damage my computer. I need it.

In fact, the only thing helping me hold it all together at the moment is my presentation prep for the O'Connor Foundation board meeting later this afternoon. Not only is it a good distraction, but it's also a worthwhile endeavor. I may not be able to control my life circumstances, but I can do everything in my power to ensure that the kids who depend on New Hope don't have their lives upended as well.

Which means convincing the Board that New Hope is still worth their financial investments and allowing the current management to stay in place for the time being. Although Director Wu's negligence played a part in its downfall, she's still the best person to oversee the orphanage until the embezzlement scandal dies down and it becomes a desirable employer once more.

"Morning, Mom." I look up from my computer screen and force out a smile for her sake. "I'm waiting to talk with a county official about extending your deadline."

"Don't waste your time. No one answers the phone there. You have to go to the office in person if you want to talk to someone."

"Maybe I can swing by there after my presentation." I push the end call button and rake my hand through my hair. Great. One more task to add to my ever-growing to-do list.

Before I can make another pass through my curly mane, my mother grabs my right hand and inspects the nubs at the end of my fingers. "You're going to present to the O'Connor Foundation with your nails looking like this?"

"They're fine." I study my fingers and the ravaged skin surrounding them. All nine and the one where a ring should be sitting. "I don't have time for a manicure. Too many other things need my attention right now." Hopefully, she takes the hint and leaves well enough alone because it won't take much for the emotions I've buried deep within me these past few days to seep out like an oil spill.

And I can't let that happen.

"That's not like you, Nic." My mother continues to hound me. "Why are they in such bad shape?"

I take a swig of overly sugared milk laced with a touch of coffee. "Mom, let it go." I slam down my mug on the table, allowing some of the light brown liquid to slosh onto the surface.

"What's going on with you? You're drinking coffee, which you never do. You're snapping at me—which you never do, either—and for someone who is about to stand up in front of some very important people and ask for money, you don't look your best."

"Gee, thanks."

"Do you want to talk about whatever has you in a tizzy? I haven't seen you this stressed since you shut down your organizing business six months ago. Is it because you haven't been able to find a ring you like?"

I glance up at her. Since Ben and I agreed not to say anything to our parents about the situation with Lei Ming or why we haven't pulled the trigger on a ring yet, I can't divulge the true reason for my frustration.

"I appreciate the offer, Mom, and I'm sorry for being testy

with you, but I have to get this presentation right, that's all. Director Wu and those kids are depending on me."

I pick up my phone and read aloud a text message the director had sent me a few days ago.

"Nicki, I wanted to let you know I've been praying for you and am certain you'll do everything you can to convince the Board to continue supporting New Hope. I'll be waiting to hear from you."

I let out a heavy sigh. "Yeah, no pressure there."

"Well, with your skills and God's help, I have no doubt you'll do great, and I, for one, can't wait to hear about it at dinner tonight." Mom smiles like she did when I was younger, and she believed I could do no wrong. I shiver and hope I'll have the chance to beam like that at Lei Ming one day too.

"Did someone mention dinner?" Ben strides into the kitchen wearing a blue Texas Rangers t-shirt and black sweatpants. "I'm just working on breakfast now but count me in for whatever you fix."

"Oh, you've given me a wonderful idea, Ben." My mom jumps up from her seat. "I'll make a special dinner to celebrate Nicki's success with the Board." She dashes over to a shelf stocked with cookbooks.

"Mom, don't go to any trouble ..."

"It's no trouble at all. In fact, I've got a recipe for beef stroganoff in my Better Homes and Garden cookbook. It was your favorite meal, and I would make it on special occasions like this one." She studies the spines of the various books looking for her favorite red and white checkered menu guide. "It may be in the living room. I'll go check."

Ben and I watch her race out of the room.

Once she's gone, he joins me at the table. "Now I see where you get all your spunk from." He pours himself a cup. Suddenly he stops filling his mug and looks at mine. "Are you drinking coffee?"

"If three tablespoons of sugar, a cup of milk, and a few drips of that stuff—" I nod at the carafe in his hand before continuing, "count as coffee, then, yes, I am."

"Wow. I never thought I'd see the day." He sets down the pot and takes a sip of his unadulterated brew. "Since our first meeting at the coffee shop, I've never seen you drink the stuff. Are you nervous about your presentation?"

"Yes. I mean, no." I pick at my unsightly cuticles.

"Wanna talk about it?"

I choke back the lump in my throat. "With all the chaos and uncertainty surrounding Lei Ming, the wedding, and my mother's eviction deadline, I haven't prepared as much as I'd like, and in a few hours, I have to convince a group of people I've never met to keep funding New Hope despite all the problems there, and—

"And failure isn't an option for you, am I right?"

I nod and fight back the tears before continuing, "I just worry that with all the distractions, any convincing arguments I plan to offer won't be up to my usual standards, which means failure is looming closer than I like."

"Look, you're probably more ready than you think, but even if you're not, you can't put so much pressure on yourself. You— we've got a lot going on." He places his hand on top of mine, his fingers brushing against the frayed red thread wrapped around my wrist. "What's that?" He points at my sad attempt at jewelry.

"Oh, remember the thread Director Wu gave me at her house when we were there last week? I decided to make it into a bracelet to serve as a visual reminder that if two people are meant to be together the thread between them can't be broken." I pull back my hand and slide it under the table. "Silly of me, huh?"

"Not at all. Probably a good idea under the circumstances." He takes another drink of coffee.

Watching him, I'm astounded by his ability not to crack under pressure. Was that part of his nature, or was there more there I wasn't aware of? A divine intervention I had yet to discover?

"How do you do it?" I'm curious to know his secret.

"Do what?" He sets his drink on the table.

"How do you manage to stay so calm?" I sigh. "I feel like a volcano about to erupt."

"Who said I was calm?"

"You've been nothing but cool and collected since we returned from the jewelers." I harrumph. "How is this not bothering you?"

"It is." His chin drops to his chest, and he fingers the rim of his mug. "I'm just choosing to stay busy, so I don't have to think about the fact we might lose Lei Ming. It's how I deal with hard stuff, Nicki."

My heart constricts. I've been so on edge with my emotions and keeping them from pouring out, I never stopped to consider how he might handle things. But then again, I've only known him for a few months, so how could I? But now that I do, I'll store it away for the future.

If we have one together.

"I'm sorry, Ben. I guess we just have different ways of handling stress." I brush my thumb against the side of his hand. "I know how much Lei Ming means to you too."

He raises his head. "I've been asking God for this to all be a huge misunderstanding. But if I'm being honest, praying hasn't come easily as it normally does. But it's all I can do right now as I try to make sense of it all."

"Ditto." My voice wavers. "I haven't been able to understand why all of this is happening, and I'm not really talking to God about it. I don't know if I'm angry or confused or both, but the words just won't come out."

Ben inches closer to me. "Would it help if we prayed together right now?" He holds out his palm to me.

Touched by his offer, I raise my hand to place it in his when my mother bursts back into the room.

"I can't find it." She makes a beeline for her bookshelf. "I know it's here somewhere."

"What are you talking about, Mom?" I try to hide my irritation at her abrupt intrusion on our sacred prayer time.

"My cookbook." Her face is flushed, and sweat lines her upper lip.

Honestly, in this house, there's no telling where it could be hiding, but I don't have the heart to remind her about that. She really has been working on cleaning things up around here, especially with Ben's help, these past few days. He's carried out at least twenty large trash bags to the curb since we arrived. That's nineteen more than has ever left the house in the past five years.

While it's not at the pace the county or I would prefer, she is making an effort.

"Would you like me to help you look?" Ben jumps up from his chair and flashes me an apologetic look.

My mother pivots. "That would be great. I'm sure together we could find it." She snaps her fingers. "The office. We should look there."

Once more, Ben and I watch her race out of the room.

"I better go help her." He pushes his chair in. "Otherwise, your celebratory feast will be PB & Js."

"I actually like that idea." I would be completely happy munching on sandwiches. Maybe a less elaborate meal would give us more time alone and allow us to finish what we almost started before my mother's frantic intrusion.

"I doubt she'll go for that. Spending time with your mom, I've learned where you get your determined spirit. And a kiddie meal won't be satisfactory for her." He winks at me before heading for the door.

"Ben, wait."

"Yeah?" He turns back in my direction.

I leap from my chair and kiss him on the cheek.

"What was that for?" He covers the spot of my affection with his hand and beams.

"For everything, but especially for all you've done with my mom. I have no clue how you managed to have her get rid of so much stuff, but you're a miracle worker."

"I am, aren't I?" He puffs out his chest like a superhero, then shrinks back to his normal posture. "Actually, she's the one doing most of the heavy lifting. I'm just holding the bags and hauling them outside. She's motivated."

"Of course, she is. If she doesn't get things cleaned up, she'll be homeless soon. The county officials will be here in a few days to see if she's done as they've asked."

"That's not it, Nicki."

My pulse races. What else could it be? Did she tell Ben something that I should know about? "What, what is it then?"

His eyes bore into mine. "It's you."

"Me?"

"Having you wear her wedding dress on your big day means the world to her. Unfortunately, she hasn't been able to locate it yet, so she's plowing through all her piles trying to find it, despite my reminders that she doesn't have to find it right away."

"She has?" I take a step back.

That my mom would be willing to work so hard to give me something special causes my insides to quiver. I always thought that she loved her discarded, broken, and expired items more than she did me, but this one act proves I was wrong. She really does love me. And just like what I want to do for Lei Ming in the future, my mother's doing the same for me now by going the extra mile.

If Lei Ming doesn't already have a mother, that is.

Before I can voice my doubts and fears about that possibility with Ben, the ever-reliable cuckoo clock indicates the top of the hour with a loud chime.

"I guess that's our signal to get moving." Ben grins. "We won't be eating well tonight if I don't help your mom find that cookbook, and if I'm not mistaken, you have an orphanage to save, right?" He gently kisses my cheek. "Knock their socks off, Nicki."

My skin is still tingling from his touch when I arrive at the O'Connor Foundation a little while later. I do my best not to linger on it, though. I need to have my head on straight for my pitch to the Board.

Thankfully a familiar face greets me outside the conference room. Heather Campbell, Ms. O'Connor's faithful assistant and my boss at the moment, is the boost I need to regain my focus.

I rush to embrace her. "What are you doing here?"

"I'm here to cheer you on." She holds me at arm's length.

As she does, I notice that her strawberry blonde hair reaches past her shoulders now, and she looks much happier than the last time I saw her. Wearing a dark navy business dress suit and heels, she's the consummate professional.

"You're an angel." I shift my eyes to the closed, double mahogany wood doors. "I'm not late, am I?"

"No, they're just finishing up their lunch." She smiles. "You okay?"

"I'm good." I wince at my half-truth. Although I may be a little off-kilter, thanks to all that's happened since I returned to the States, my head and heart are ready for battle. They have to be.

"It's okay if you're nervous," she says. "I would be too. That's why I came."

"I appreciate it more than you know, but I refuse to let my emotions get in the way of a solid presentation. So much is riding on this meeting and me doing well." I exhale deeply. "For lots of reasons, but especially for Katherine."

"She'd be proud of you." She points to a framed portrait of my former boss and her father posing together on the wall just to the left of the boardroom. "She always was, and no matter what happens today, she always will be."

I turn and gaze at the painting. My stomach flutters seeing

Ms. O'Connor up-close and personal again. In the picture, neither she nor her father are smiling. Was it because of their strained relationship? Or the fact that they were forced to spend time together? Either way, I'm sorry they never had a chance to reconcile and enjoy the father-daughter bond they both so desperately wanted.

Unfortunately, it was too late for them. But it didn't have to be for their legacy. If I could somehow pull myself together and make my case as to why the Board needed to continue funding the orphanage, maybe other children would have an opportunity to find forever homes and develop healthy relationships with their adoptive parents rather than suffer like the O' Connors had.

No pressure, Nicki!

Before I can share my thoughts with Heather, the handle to the boardroom clicks, and a middle-aged woman pulls on the doors, swinging them wide open. "Miss Mayfield, we're ready for you."

Heather and I exchange one final glance. Buoyed by her support and confidence, I square my shoulders, tug on the hem of my blazer the way Ms. O'Connor would when preparing for business, and march into the room.

The ample space is filled with an oblong table where six men and six women, all dressed in business attire, hold court. Sunshine bursts through a row of windows, which heats the room and makes it feel like a sauna. Or that could just be my body heat ramping up under twelve pairs of frosty eyes.

I'm offered a seat at the end of the table, where I quickly arrange my things and wait for permission to speak.

Finally, the middle-aged man with thinning hair and glasses sitting at the opposite end of the table addresses me. "Miss Mayfield, thank you for coming. I'm Mr. Caldwell, Chairman of the Board. We've been eager to speak with you."

Perching on the edge of my chair, I clasp my hands together. "Thank you for agreeing to see me on such short notice. I've been anxious to meet with you as well, and it's a pleasure to see all of you today."

He removes his glasses. "Normally, we'd wait for the submission period to be complete before listening to any presentations. However, since you're here in the States at the moment, and with New Hope's extenuating financial circumstances, we were willing to make an exception."

"I appreciate that." I open my computer. "I'm ready to start whenever you are."

"I'm sure you've put a lot of effort into your presentation Miss Mayfield, but after looking at the documents you submitted ..." He holds up a black folder bulging with the papers I asked Heather to provide them. "We have some questions we need answered first."

"Certainly." I promptly shut my laptop and push it aside.

An elderly woman, who, with her short gray hair and wire-rimmed glasses, reminds me of Mrs. Claus, clears her throat. "Miss Mayfield, while the documents and numbers you provided are a few of the topics we'd like to discuss with you today, we feel the first issue that needs to be tackled is the police report detailing the embezzlement charges against Assistant Director Chang."

My throat constricts. "What would you like to know?" While I really don't want to relive the nightmare of the past few weeks, I'm willing to do whatever's necessary to help them understand that New Hope's problems are the malicious act of one person and that the children shouldn't have to suffer because of her selfishness.

"Exactly how a serious scandal like this happened in the first place." Mrs. Claus narrows her eyes. "And given that, why we should entrust New Hope with more money."

Where do I even start? I ponder my options and decide that the very beginning is my best choice. I take a sip of the water in front of me and lick my lips. "I knew something was off the first day I arrived back in China."

LIANA GEORGE

I recap everything that occurred at the orphanage over the last few weeks as concisely as possible. It takes an hour and a half to detail the events between when I first met with AD Chang, and they carted her off in the police car after she confessed to stealing money so her son could attend college in Canada.

Occasionally one of the board members interrupts with a question or a request for clarification, but for the most part, I do all the talking. They simply nod or stare at me with steely gazes. When I finish with my detailed deposition, my throat is parched, and I guzzle down the rest of the water in my glass.

"That's quite a turn of events, and I appreciate you taking the time to recount it with such accuracy," Mr. Caldwell says. "However, you must be aware that the Board is not very happy with the situation. Scandals reflect poorly on everyone involved."

"Yes," I whisper.

"And it seems that AD Chang is not the only one who is at fault." Mr. Caldwell lowers his head and peers down at me from the top of his glasses. "It's quite evident that Director Wu's negligence played a part in this. She should have been the one to catch the financial discrepancies much earlier. As she didn't, she must be held accountable."

My spirit falls. I have nothing but the deepest respect and admiration for Director Wu and would never say anything derisive against her, but she did have some culpability. She even said so herself. I just worry that if I put a voice to my thoughts, my words might be misconstrued and cause even more damage. But what other choice did I have?

"Miss Mayfield?" Mrs. Claus taps her French-manicured fingernails on the table.

"Yes," I whisper. "Director Wu's lack of oversight did play a role."

All at once, everyone begins to murmur.

"But wait." I hold out my hand.

The board members' eyes fall back on me.

"Director Wu has given her life to New Hope and those children. She would never willingly let harm come to them. Never."

"Yet she did," Mrs. Claus snaps. "And this isn't the first time she's failed to lead responsibly. In recent years we've noticed a pattern of behavior—whether it be time away for personal reasons or her lack of organization—that has left the well-being of the orphanage and the children in jeopardy. That is not acceptable, and we need to hold her responsible."

I blanch. "How?"

"Miss Mayfield, we appreciate your time today, but you should know that we had discussed the situation before you arrived and had already made a decision," Mr. Caldwell says, interrupting our sparring. "We were just wanting to hear the details from you firsthand in order to confirm our suspicions."

I push back in my chair and brace myself for what is coming next.

"It is our feeling that although Director Wu has served New Hope well, we cannot continue to let her oversee the program. We expect her to step down as soon as a suitable replacement can be found, ideally in the next six to nine weeks before we make our final decision about next year's distributions."

My heart drops to my stomach. I'd failed in my efforts to save the director's job. Not that I was given much of a chance, really. Even if I'd laid out every conceivable reason why she should stay, I doubt the Board would have taken my suggestions. She was in trouble before I walked through the doors.

"And if she is still at the helm," he continues, "I can assure you that will influence our decision considerably, and not in a favorable manner."

I weigh their requests against their deadline. Six weeks isn't much time to fulfill their demands. Especially when I have my hands full with other insurmountable problems. But somehow, I would figure it out. There was no other alternative.

"If I find someone to take her place before your deadline, then you'll continue supporting the orphanage?" I ask, hopeful.

"Possibly." The chairman narrows his eyes. "We would need to see substantial and immediate improvements in both the operation and the finances of the orphanage before we could commit to any future funding, but ..."

There's a 'but'? A spark of optimism surges through me.

"We're not completely heartless, Miss Mayfield." Mr. Caldwell adjusts his glasses. "After much discussion, we've decided to give New Hope a temporary grant to assist them financially until the end of August, which should either give them time to meet our demands or secure help from another source."

I blink rapidly. "You have?" I scan the faces of all the board members, which don't seem as scary now. "Thank you so much."

"Don't thank us yet, Miss Mayfield. This is not a guarantee. However, we do want things to improve at New Hope, so there's good reason for us to continue funding it." Mr. Caldwell arches both his eyebrows. "In the meantime, we expect you to deliver the news and our expectations moving forward to the director and anyone else at New Hope who needs to know." He bangs a gavel on the stand next to him. "Meeting adjourned."

As the board members collect their belongings and rush out the door, I stay glued to my seat. The shock of the Board's decision reverberates through my body, and I mentally begin formulating a plan to find someone to replace the director and manage the orphanage.

Unfortunately, almost every option that comes to mind will take months to complete. To properly interview and train someone for such an important position won't happen overnight. Whomever it is will need to be familiar with the ins and outs of running an orphanage and be able to start right away. Where would I possibly find someone with those qualifications at a moment's notice?

And more importantly, how can I finish it all by their deadline while juggling my own issues?

I rest my head on the luxurious table and ponder how I became trapped in a house of horrors with no escape route.

"You alive in here?" Heather's voice booms through the empty room.

"Barely." I lift my head. "It was brutal."

"I heard." She walks toward me. "Mr. Caldwell informed me of their decision to replace the director. I'm sorry, Nicki."

"Me too, but I think she's expecting it. The last time we spoke, she hinted that it might be the end for her." I place my computer in my bag and then sling it over my shoulder. "Still won't be easy telling her, though."

"I imagine it won't." Heather grimaces. "Are you throwing your name into the ring as her replacement?"

"Hardly," I huff. "I'm happy to return to China and assist her with the recruiting process, but I think I've done all I can for New Hope." And hopefully, not all of it bad.

We leave the conference room and amble over to the elevators, where the strong smell of lemon cleaner lingers in the air.

Heather pushes the down button. "Do you think you'll be able to find someone quickly?"

"I'm not sure." I shrug my shoulders. "The Chinese are very superstitious, and I can't imagine they'll be lining up to take a job that's been marred in scandal. Not only that, but I'm not sure how long I'll be able to stay in China."

"You'll be returning to the States, then?"

The elevator dings, and the large metal doors invite us in.

"That's the plan." I step inside and hold the door open for my boss. "But I'm learning that plans don't always work the way you expect them to, so who knows." Particularly when the child you want to adopt may have been kidnapped.

"Well, when you do come back, I have a spot for you at the O'Connor Foundation if you're interested."

"You want me to work with you?" Blood rushes in my ears. I'd been so busy worrying about all the other problems staring me in the face, I hadn't had time to consider my employment options when I returned. Now it seemed I didn't have to.

"I do. But more importantly, Katherine wanted you to as well." Heather tilts her head. "She hoped you'd continue her legacy and you'd be in a powerful position to help the less fortunate."

"I ... I don't know what to say."

The elevator comes to a stop, and we move into the lobby.

"Yes would be good, but don't feel like you need to give me an answer right away. Just think about it. I'd hate for you to make a hasty decision you'll regret later."

Oh, Heather, if you only knew. Rash decisions are becoming my specialty these days.

"Once you've broken the news to the director and helped her find someone else to take her position, we can talk." A grin springs across her face. "Hopefully, that won't take too long, and we can start working together to bring Katherine's dreams to pass."

A cold sweat runs down my spine. That Ms. O'Connor would want me to be part of her legacy was an honor I didn't feel worthy of. "I will, thanks."

Heather checks her watch. "I've got to run, but I'll be waiting to hear from you." She darts out the main entrance door.

Did she mean about Wu? Or my position with the O'Connor Foundation? I'm not sure.

Contemplating both dilemmas there in the lobby, I arrive at a solution that might solve the first one. It's an unlikely answer but could definitely work. I just have to present a compelling enough argument.

I rummage through my purse and pull up the director's contact info. My thumb hovers over the call button, but I don't push it. For one, I don't have the guts to tell her about my meeting with the Board or my idea just yet. And two, with the time difference, she's still sleeping.

I slip the phone back into my purse. I'll have to wait a little longer to inform her of today's events. But that's okay. That just gives me some time to enlist the one person I think would be the perfect candidate for the job.

All I need her to do is say yes.

6

A carp in a dry rut.
~ *Chinese Proverb*

I sit in my car in front of my mom's house, replaying the meeting in my head. With each loop of the recording, my anxiety rises another level. If my idea for Wu's replacement doesn't pan out, then what? The Board's timeframe doesn't give us much time to thoroughly vet and interview a new director. And we can't afford to let just anyone run the place.

Which means returning to Beijing is no longer a priority. It's an urgency.

Not only for New Hope but for Lei Ming as well. Since we haven't been able to get the answers we need, I'm left with no choice but to find them myself. I only hope my decision to leave sooner than later doesn't cause an uproar with anyone.

Firm in my plans to leave in the next twenty-four hours, I slide out of the car and head inside. As the last pops of color in the sky fade into the dark of night, I drag my body through the messy yard, grateful my mom chose to cook for me after all. That way, I can eat and go straight to bed. Maybe a good night's rest and a clear head will make the circumstances I'm facing more manageable.

But when I open the back door, no spicy smells or sounds of searing beef greet me—only silence.

"Mom? Ben?" I drop my bag onto the dining table and inspect the immaculate kitchen. Well, immaculate in the culinary sense. Not the organized one.

"Nicki, you're home." My mom bounces into the kitchen. "We've been waiting for you."

"What happened to dinner? Did you not find your cookbook?"

"Oh, I did. In the office of all places. But there was a problem with the oven."

I glance at the rusty stove top. "I'm surprised it's lasted as long as it did. I think you've had that since I was in middle school. I'm not surprised it finally quit working."

"I'm sure it can be fixed. Or at least that's what Ben said when he looked at it earlier. Something about a funny odor and loose cords. He's going to call a repairman tomorrow."

My knight in shining armor—the one I thought I didn't want but found out I might need—comes to the rescue again.

"Where is Ben anyway?" I crane my neck toward the hallway.

"Getting ready for dinner."

"What do you mean getting ready?" I grimace. "Like going out to eat ready?"

"Yes. Since we can't eat here, we decided to go to Luigi's instead. We have a lot to celebrate."

My shoulders sag. "Mom, I'm not really up for going out. It's been a long day. I'll just make a PB&J and call it a night." I head for the fridge.

"Nicki, a sandwich is no way to mark your success."

That's my mother for you. Ever the optimist. She's certain my meeting with the Board was a victory. And it was in some ways, but not completely. At least not in the way she thinks, and it will be sad to burst her bubble later. However, I could use a bit of her positivity right now.

"It's fine. We can eat out another time." I open the fridge door and stick my head inside. "Do you have any grape jelly?"

"No."

"Okay, what about strawberry then?"

Her footsteps pound against the floor as she marches over to me. "No, we are not going to eat out another time." She yanks on the door handle. "We're going to Luigi's. Tonight."

Startled by her tone and insistence, I straighten back up. "Mom, I know what you're trying to do, and I appreciate it, but today wasn't a total success, and I'd rather stay in. I promise when I get some things resolved, we can have a big party then, okay?" Like when I get back from China.

"I'm sorry you had a rough day, and I want to know what happened at the meeting—good or bad—but you aren't the only one with something to celebrate."

My pulse races. "Did something happen?"

"Yes." She closes the refrigerator door.

"What?"

A slow smile breaks out across her face. "I don't want to tell you just yet. It's a surprise, and I'll tell you all about it at dinner."

I blow out a puff of air and rub my face, tired of the cat-and-mouse game she's playing with me. "Can you please just tell me? I'm too tired from the events of the last few hours—no, the past weeks—to guess what your big news might be."

"Nicki, I don't want to tell you—"

"What's going on in here?" Ben's voice interrupts our back and forth.

I spin in his direction. Ben stands in the doorway, dressed in a plaid, long-sleeve button-down and slacks. He definitely knows how to look good for an evening out. Too bad we aren't going anywhere.

"I could hear the two of you bickering from the bathroom. Everything okay?" he asks.

"It's fine," I tell him. "I was just explaining to my mother why I don't want to go out tonight."

"You don't want to eat at Luigi's?" He frowns. "Why not? Your mom's had me craving pasta all afternoon the way she's raved about that place."

My stomach flips. Now I have to convince him too? With two against one, the odds aren't in my favor here.

"I tried to explain we have a surprise for her, but she refuses to go." My mother's voice cracks.

"I'm worn out, that's all." I drop into one of the kitchen chairs. "Is it really that important to the two of you?"

"Yes," they say in unison.

While I don't think their big announcement has anything to do with the problems weighing heavy on my heart, I have to admit their united front and secrecy have the hairs on the back of my neck standing up. "Fine." I wave my hands in the air in surrender. "Give me ten minutes to freshen up."

When we step inside the doors of my favorite restaurant thirty minutes later, the familiar mix of onions, garlic, and Italian seasoning lingers in the air. Inhaling deeply, my earlier resistance to dining out dissipates, and a new burst of energy flows through me. I hate to admit it, but coming here was the right choice.

"Nicki!" Luigi, the elderly owner of the establishment, shouts from across the room. He races over to me and kisses both my cheeks.

"It's so good to see you!" I reciprocate his welcoming gesture. "You're still your charming self."

"Of course, *bella*." He winks. "After the food, I'm what keeps people coming back."

I laugh. "Well, just between the two of us, you have a slight edge over the food in my heart." I pat my chest. "But don't tell that to your chef."

"It's in the vault." He zips his fingers over his lips before peering over my shoulder. "And who is this young man with your mother? An *amore, bella*?"

"He's not my *amore*, Luigi." At least, I don't think so. My heart beats harder against my chest. Is it trying to tell me a different story? Before I can explain the situation and properly introduce Ben, the tiny Italian races across the entryway to meet my mom and fiancé.

"Pick any table you want, and I will get things ready for you in the kitchen." He claps his hands. "*La mia famiglia preferita* is back in the house."

Fortunately, our favorite booth is available, and the three of us quickly settle in.

"Things didn't go well with the Board, Nicki?" Ben asks after a waiter deposits water, fresh garlic bread, and olive oil on our table.

"Yes and no." I dredge a breadstick through the sauce.

"Which one is it?" My mother's forehead wrinkles.

"It's a long story." I swallow. "Buckle up."

As we munch on the delicious bread, I rehash the afternoon showdown with the O'Connor Foundation board. When I finish telling them of my orders to inform the director of her forced retirement, Luigi arrives at our booth with steaming plates of pasta.

"But we haven't even told you what we wanted." I push the breadbasket to the far end of the table to make way for the spaghetti and meatball platter Luigi passes to me.

"You didn't need to, *bella*." He hands a bowl of fettuccine to my mom and sets down a plate of cheesy lasagna for Ben. "Luigi knows what his favorite customers like." He holds up a pepper mill and carefully twists it over our food, allowing small black flakes to float down onto our entrees. When he's finished, he steps back and admires his work. "*Buon appetito!*"

Ben offers up a sweet blessing for our meal then we all dig in, abandoning our earlier conversation to savor our food.

When he's finished, Ben pushes his spotless plate toward the center of the table. "Do you think Director Wu will be okay with the Board's decision, Nicki?"

I wipe a stray noodle off my chin. "She told me she was going to retire soon, so I'm hoping that will be the case. I don't think she expects it to happen this quickly, though, and to have it forced on her. Under no circumstances do I want her to lose face."

"I guess I don't understand the problem." My mother carefully spins her pasta onto her fork and joins in on the conversation. "Shouldn't it be easy to find someone else to take over? Who wouldn't want to run such a worthy cause?"

"The Chinese are very leery of taking on anything that represents bad luck. Between the stealing scandal and the demands of the Board, it's going to take some time to find a replacement, and time isn't on our side. They want Director Wu gone in six weeks, or else the orphanage's funding is in serious jeopardy. I can't let that happen. Ms. O'Connor wanted me to continue her legacy there. If I can't get the financial support, I'll be disappointing her even though she's gone."

"So, what did you have in mind?" Ben places his elbows on the table and leans toward me.

"We need to get back to Beijing right away. For both New Hope and Lei Ming." My eyes bore into Ben's, and I pray he picks up the subtle message in my words so I don't have to explain that nightmare to my mother before I'm ready.

"How soon?" Mom sets down her fettuccine-wrapped utensil. "We haven't had time to discuss all the wedding details. There's still so much to go over."

While I know my mother would never play the guilt card on me, I can't help but feel bad for abandoning her at such an important time. But the wedding and all its details are at the bottom of my priority list. I only hope I can convince her of that without having to offer up too many explanations or excuses.

"I'm sure we can handle it by phone or video call, Mom," I assure her. "You and Darlene can talk and do whatever you like. I don't have to be involved in every decision. Even though we're waiting another month or so, it's still going to be a small wedding."

"I guess, but it would be more fun if you were here to help," she says.

I reach for her hand. "I'll be back before you know it." And if all goes according to plan, with the adoption process in full motion. If Lei Ming isn't the missing child, perhaps the decision-making board will fast-track our application, and she could come home with us for the wedding. She'd make the cutest flower girl. "Plus, you can keep searching for your wedding gown while I'm gone. I can't get married naked, you know."

My mom and Ben exchange sly glances.

"What?" My eyes dart between the two of them.

"Well, that's why I was so anxious to come here and celebrate. I have something exciting to tell you." Her eyes light up.

"O-kay, what is it?"

"Ben and I found my wedding gown today."

"You did?"

"Yes, isn't that wonderful?"

"Actually, you found it, Ginny," Ben chimes in. "All I did was pull the trunk out of the office closet for you."

"It doesn't matter who discovered it." I squeeze my mother's hand. "I'm just glad you were able to locate it." Seeing her so happy makes my heart full.

"Me too." Tears pool at the corner of her eyes. "I can't wait to show it to you."

"What are we waiting for? Let's go and see it." I scoot out of the booth. "After the day I've had, I need something good to focus on."

After paying the bill and promising Luigi we'll come again soon, we head back home. My mother talks the entire drive. It's been a long time since I've seen her this excited. Who knew my getting married would have such a positive impact? First her house, then her happiness. I pray I don't have to shatter her joy anytime soon with the news that there's no wedding because Lei Ming is the kidnapped child.

"Nicki, stop!" Mom screams.

I slam on the brakes. "Don't scare me like that." I catch my breath. "What's wrong?"

"Why are there fire trucks in front of my house?" She points out the front windshield.

I follow her shaking fingers. Red and blue flashing lights cut through the darkness and illuminate the area in front of her house, putting her clutter front and center. A cold sweat chills my spine.

"The dress!" Mom jumps out of the car and races in the direction of the chaos.

I put the car in park so I can chase after her. The minute I open the door, a strong burning smell hits me, and my fear is confirmed. Her house is on fire. And with it, my plans to return to China.

"Nicki!" Ben calls out from the back seat. "What are you doing?"

"I have to stop her." I jump out of the car.

He opens his door and joins me. "I'll move the car to a safer spot and meet you there."

Relieved he didn't try to stand in my way, I sprint down the street. Heavy smoke sears my lungs and my eyes. The heat bears down on me the closer I draw to the house. When I finally arrive at the driveway, I halt and stare at the flames slowly eating away at my mother's possessions.

Where is she? Certainly she didn't try to go back in to save her wedding gown for me. *Please, Lord, don't let her have done something so foolish.*

I scan the frantic bodies moving across the lawn, but I don't see her anywhere. As I make my way toward the house, a hand takes hold of my arm, keeping me from going any farther.

"You can't go in there."

I swirl to confront the commanding voice only to be meet with a familiar face. "Ben?"

"Where do you think you're going?" He pulls me closer to him. "And where is your mom?"

"I think she went inside to save her wedding dress." I cough. "We have to find her."

"We will." His voice cracks, betraying the confident front he's displaying. "Follow me." He takes my hand and leads me to one of the firefighters positioned near the mailbox, who's overseeing the rescue efforts.

"Excuse us, but we're looking for an older woman, curly strawberry blonde hair, about this high." Ben holds his hand up to the middle of his chest.

The fireman pulls his eyes off the inferno and toward us. "Yeah, she ran back in the house."

My legs buckle. "That was my mother! Why didn't you stop her?"

"We tried Miss, but she evaded my men."

Stepping back, I bump into Ben's chest. I turn and bury my head in it. "Why would she try to save it? We could get another one."

Ben pulls me tight for reassurance. "I'm sure they caught her before she actually made it in."

"I sent my men after her, but they haven't responded yet." The fire chief reaches for his walkie-talkie. "I'll see if I can get an update. Stay here."

Even in Ben's strong arms, my body shakes uncontrollably. "What if she doesn't make it out?" I clench his jacket in my fingers.

"They'll get her out, Nicki." He raises my head. "How about I pray for that right now?"

Unable to speak, I nod.

"Lord, we ask for a covering over Ginny right now." Ben's words are gentle yet powerful. "As You did with Shadrach,

Meshach, and Abednego, don't let the fire touch her. May Your Mighty Hand lead her back to safety and to us. We ask this in Jesus' name. Amen."

"Amen," I mutter, grateful for the heartfelt plea and for the man who spoke it.

Although my mother and I haven't had the best relationship these past few years, things were finally taking a turn for the better, and we were growing closer. I couldn't lose that now. Not like this.

I pull back from Ben's comforting embrace and watch as the flames eat away the dilapidated wood. The old house creaks and moans under the heat's intensity. With all the junk stored inside, it won't take long for it to burn to the ground, leaving my mother's treasures as ashes to be blown away by the wind. I shudder thinking about what all this might mean for her. If she makes it out alive.

It seems like ages before the fire chief reports back to us. "They've got her and are tending to her in the backyard. They'll bring her out in a minute."

"Thank you." I breathe out a huge sigh of relief, followed by a silent song of praise to God.

"When will you know what caused the fire in the first place?" Ben asks.

"Not for a few hours. We caught it before it could do too much damage or get too out of control, so we should have it contained soon. Once it is, we can investigate and have a definitive answer, but in houses like these, it's usually related to some faulty electrical cords." The burly man looks back at the house. "Between all the fire damage and its poor condition, the city will likely condemn it anyway. Sorry, folks." He walks back to the smoldering house.

"Better?" Ben asks once the fireman's outline has melted into the darkness.

"That helps, but ..."

"But what?"

I dig my foot into the gravel. How do I explain my concern without sounding like I'm complaining? "Well, what do we do now?"

"I imagine we'll go to a hotel for the night." Ben shrugs his shoulders.

"Not that." I shake my head. "We need to head back to China right away, but how can I possibly leave my mother under the circumstances?"

"I don't know. It's something we'll have to discuss and make a decision about once things calm down."

"That's the problem." My chest tightens. "Time isn't on our side right now. We need to figure out what's going on with Lei Ming, and New Hope needs a new director, but I can't leave my mother after this. She's basically homeless now." My chest aches. "How am I supposed to know what to do?"

"I'm sorry, Nicki." Ben hangs his head.

"For what?"

"For putting you in this position in the first place."

I rake my fingers through my hair. He's the last person who needs to be apologizing to me. "What are you talking about?"

Ben turns his head and presses his lips together. "If what the fireman said was true, then I'm to blame for all this." He points back toward the house. "When I messed around with those cords and connections from the stove, I probably set things in motion."

"You can't blame yourself. We're not even sure that was the cause. You have to remember, with all the tinder she had stockpiled in there, my mother's house was a fire waiting to happen."

"But still ..."

"What started the fire isn't important right now." I grab his hand. "All that matters is where we go from here. Okay?"

When he looks back at me, steely determination fills his eyes. "Then maybe we should take your mom back to Texas."

I snap my head back. "To Kilgore?"

"Yeah, she can stay with my parents while we're gone. That will give her some time to deal with the fallout from this fire while we go back to China and figure things out there."

"You're joking, right? My mother doesn't even know your parents and vice versa. How could we ask them to do that?" I study his face, waiting for his lips to curve upward, but they don't. "Ben?"

"Nicki, your mother needs help getting settled, and from the sound of it, you and I have to catch the next plane out of here. Do you have any better ideas?"

Unfortunately, I don't. Asking my mother to move to the Lone Star State does sound like the best option available to her. Who knows, if things really are better there as the locals claim, it might be exactly what she needs.

Although I can't imagine my mother willing to leave this place. Other than me, it was the last connection to my dad she had left. Could she just pick up and walk away that easily?

"What if she says no?" I ask, not certain she'll agree to the idea.

"Then we'll have to convince her otherwise." His eyes move past me. "Sooner rather than later because here she comes."

I spin around to see my mother, flanked by two firemen, walking toward us. "Mom!" I sprint to meet her.

Before she can say anything or before I can reprimand her for taking such a dangerous risk, I wrap my arms around her. She smells like she's been smoking all day in an unventilated room, but I don't care. She's safe, and that's all that matters.

"I'm fine." She wiggles out of my arms.

"What were you thinking going in a burning house? You could have been killed."

"I had to get this." She holds up a thick wad of yellowed lace, its edges frayed and singed. "This dress is the only thing I have for your wedding. I didn't have any other choice."

A lump forms in my throat. How can I be upset with her for

doing something that, while completely foolish, was also so very special?

My heart swells with love. "Mom, you shouldn't have."

"It's what mothers do." She rubs her face, smearing black marks all over it and making her look like an NFL linebacker. "You'll understand soon enough once you've adopted Lei Ming."

Oh, how I pray she's right.

"I'm glad you're okay, Ginny." Ben joins us.

"Thank you." She coughs. "I wish I could say the same about my house."

The three of us pivot and watch as streams of water extinguish the last of the flames and dark smoke clouds snake their way into the night sky.

"I'm sorry, Mom, but they won't be able to save any of it." I put my arm over her shoulder.

"I know." Tears streak down her charcoal-stained face. "It hurts to see it all disappear so quickly, but maybe it's for the best."

I gasp. Although I see her lips moving, the words coming out don't match up with the junk-hungry woman my mom is. "We need to let the paramedics look you over again," I tell her. "I think you're in shock."

"I am, but not like that." She clears her throat. "It's going to take some time for me to deal with losing all of this, but perhaps it's God's way of offering me an opportunity for a fresh start." She pats my hand. "Decluttering and letting go of all that stuff this week as I searched for my wedding dress made me realize what I'd been doing all these years since your dad died. I'm not sure I want to go back to that way of life. It won't be easy, but I'm willing to try."

"Really?" I blink in numb astonishment.

"Yes, I think I'm ready for something different ... something simpler."

"Like what?" Ben asks.

"I don't know." She peels her eyes off the smoldering mess

strewn across her front yard and onto us. "But I'm open to any suggestions you might have. Heaven knows I'm clueless on how exactly to do that."

"Actually, Mom," I shoot a sideways glance at Ben and smile, "Ben and I have an idea we'd like you to consider."

7

No sooner has one pushed a gourd under water than another
pops up.
~ *Chinese Proverb*

Fatigue settles over me like a warm blanket as our rental car
speeds toward the Carrington Ranch on what should have
been my wedding day. *If* everything had gone according to
schedule. But I'm learning that making perfectly arranged plans
is no longer one of my organizing superpowers. Now, it seems to
be my Kryptonite.

That's why I let Ben book our tickets back to China
tomorrow. With how things have been going for me lately, I
didn't want to take any chances and jinx our trip. For so many
reasons, we had to return to Beijing without any delays or
disruptions.

The loud buzzing of the ranch's entry gates brings me back
to reality and lets me know we're almost home.

"This place is amazing, Ben," my mother says as we drive by a
pasture filled with a mix of black, brown, and white cattle. "It's
just like you see on TV or in a magazine. Do you have horses
too?"

"We do." Ben navigates the sedan around a large onyx-colored cow situated in the middle of the road. "I'm sure my mother would love to take you out for a ride if you're up for it."

"Would I need boots?" Worry laces her voice.

"You don't." He glances in her direction. "My mother has plenty of options for you to try on." His gaze returns to the road ahead. "Speaking of Mother, there she is."

I scoot towards the edge of my seat in the back and peer out the front windshield, where I spot Darlene waiting for us by the front doors. My heart pounds against my chest like a jackhammer as I watch the Texas socialite's tiny frame grow larger in my line of vision. Ready or not, it's go time.

"Welcome to Texas, y'all!" Darlene waves her arms over her perfectly coiffed hair.

Once the car stops in the circular driveway, my mother jumps out of the vehicle to meet her.

"Mom, wait." I want to pull her back into the car, but she's already out of reach.

"Don't worry, Nicki, she'll be fine." Ben turns off the engine and looks back at me. "They've been talking on the phone with each other for a few days, and it seems like they're hitting it off. Look at them." Ben points at the two women huddled together, chatting and laughing. "Does it look like they're not getting along?"

I follow his finger and see the smiles radiating from our mothers' faces. "No, they seem to be enjoying each other's company." I look back at him. "You have to understand that since my dad died, I've been the one to watch over her. I'm worried that once the reality of what happened to her house sinks in, she might go back to her hoarding ways." I lower my head. "Like here. At your house. What would your parents think of us Mayfields, then?"

"I know you're concerned, Nicki, but I'm sure my mother has so many activities planned there won't be time for your mom to start stockpiling anything."

Ben doesn't really know my mom all that well, and with an illness like hers, you can never be too sure. "I hope so."

"You have to have faith that everything's going to be fine until we get back. Otherwise, you won't be able to focus on Lei Ming and New Hope like you need to."

I thumb the red thread roped around my wrist. My faith is wavering right now. I'm trying to wrap my brain around how I could have so misunderstood God. I'd been certain He placed me in China to adopt Lei Ming. Why build up my hope for a family only to have it all crash down around me now?

"I don't have as much faith as you do, Ben." I take a deep breath and look into his calm, yet ever-so-handsome face. "When I pray but don't receive an immediate answer, I don't think all I should do is have faith. I want to take action."

"Nicki, God isn't a Pez dispenser waiting to dole out your requests like candy." He shifts in his seat. "Sometimes believing Him requires trust and faith that things will happen when they're supposed to. And as we've learned these past few days, that doesn't always happen on our timetable."

"Yes, but why all the struggle in the first place? If being a family is what He has called us to be, why are we facing so many obstacles?"

He shakes his head. "I don't have all the answers. All I know is that there are times when faith requires us to be okay with unanswered questions in life."

"I'm not sure I can do that, have that kind of belief."

"Then I guess I'll have to believe for the both of us." He opens the car door and saunters to the trunk to retrieve our bags.

I jump out of the backseat and meet him on the driveway. "So, you're not worried then?"

"About what?"

"Everything?" Frustration spreads across my chest. "Discovering that Lei Ming may not truly be up for adoption? My mother staying here? Not getting married after all?"

"No, because you have to trust me when I tell you that your mom is in good hands here." He removes our luggage and then slams the trunk closed. "And as for our daughter and our wedding plans, there's nothing we can do until we get back to China. So rather than fret, I'm going to focus on what I can do, which is check on our flight arrangements for tomorrow." He marches toward the house, looking like a bellboy.

I chase after him through the open front door. "Why? Is there a problem with our flight? Is it delayed? Or worse, canceled?"

"No, I just got an email from the airline when we landed at DFW asking me to call, that's all." He drops the bags on the foyer's marble floor, causing a booming thud to echo throughout the large house. "It happens all the time. Probably just a change of seats or meal choice follow-up."

I let out a sigh of relief. "If you— "

Loud shrieks erupt from the kitchen, putting a halt to our conversation. We exchange curious glances before heading in that direction. When we arrive at the threshold, we find our mothers hunched together at the large island, laughing at something on a screen.

"What's going on?" Ben asks.

Both moms glance up from an iPad, their four raised eyebrows looking like a mountain range.

"Oh," my mom says, "we were watching a social media post of these kids falling asleep at the dinner table. It's hilarious."

"Yes, ever since y'all connected us, we've been sharing stories and videos of kids so we can get ready for Lei Ming's arrival." Darlene wipes tears from her eyes. "We can't wait to be grandmothers!"

My knees buckle. I'm glad they're bonding and finding common ground, but what if we discover Lei Ming really was taken, and we can't be a family? It kills me to think we might have to pop their grandparent bubble.

I lean against the doorframe. "I didn't know you were on social media, Mom."

"When I told Darlene I'd bought a new tablet since my Dell was destroyed in the fire, she suggested I get on. And I'm so glad she did." My mother beams. "I had no idea all the funny things people put on YouTube. Did you?"

Seeing her so happy, I choke up. "Yes, and maybe we can watch some together later."

"Look at this, honey." She taps the device's home screen, where an app with a long list pops up. "I've been making notes of all the details Darlene and I have come up with for the wedding."

"The two of you have already made plans?" I stand up straight.

"Of course." Darlene reaches for a large three-ring binder sitting next to a freshly baked pecan pie, whose sweet aroma fills the room. "We haven't just been exchanging funny memes these past few days. We've come up with a master plan, and I have it all printed and categorized in here."

"You have a wedding ... binder?" My eyes widen at the bulging notebook full of paper beautifully lined up with index tabs. Did she print the entire internet?

"I assumed you'd appreciate having all the information perfectly arranged." Darlene chuckles then passes it to me.

My arms drop under its weight. What were they possibly planning? A ceremony fit for a king? "Um, I thought we agreed on a simple wedding." I glance at Ben for backup, but seeing him stifle a laugh lets me know I'm on my own here.

"We did," Darlene says. "But even one of that nature requires a lot of details."

"And since you only get married once, Nic, we want to make sure it's special," my mother adds.

Ben clears his throat. "I'll let you ladies have fun with that." He points back in the direction of the foyer. "I'm going to check on our flight."

Before I can protest and offer reasons why he should stay, he darts out of the room.

With no other choice, I study the tome in my hands and push down the anxiety creeping its way into my bones. What if they've done all this work, and we don't need to get married after all? *Lord, please don't let that be the case.*

"Let's get started then, shall we?" Darlene settles onto one of the bar stools and pats the one next to her. "Ginny, join me." Then she points at the stool directly across from them. "Nicki, you can sit there, so it's easier for you to see."

I slide onto the chair, quickly noting the power seating arrangement in play here. I'm doomed. Oh well, I'll let them enjoy the moment for now. Who knows what the future holds?

"All right." I flash a smile at them. "Show me what you've got."

After Darlene cuts into the pie and passes us plates with a Texas-sized serving, both mothers take turns explaining their individual and combined ideas for every aspect of the wedding. Themes. Invitations. Table settings. Flowers. Photography. Food. For a wedding that's still a few weeks away, every detail has been addressed, including a list of guests. Of which there are many. Scanning the names, I don't recognize ninety percent of the people invited.

"Wow." I lick the last of the pecan filling from my fork. "You two thought of everything, haven't you?" A rush of excitement creeps into my heart. If we do get to have this ceremony, it will be an unforgettable day.

"Darlene already had most of it lined up. I just suggested a few things here and there." Mom's eyes sparkle with delight.

"I'm glad you were able to offer some input, Mom."

"Oh, she had some really good ideas, too." My future mother-in-law chimes in. "I never thought about giving guests disposable cameras to capture the day's events. So creative! I can't wait to see what they come up with."

My mother's cheeks turn a light shade of pink. "It's the least I can do for all you and Hank are doing."

Darlene wraps her hands around my mother's. "We're family now, and that's what families do."

Watching the tender exchange between the two of them, I swallow the lump lodged in my throat. I'd heard stories from some of my married friends about the nightmare mothers-in-law could be. But that didn't seem to be the case with us. We're blessed with Darlene Carrington.

"Nicki." Ben's voice interrupts my warm, fuzzy moment. "Can I see you for a minute? It's urgent."

I jump down from my perch. "I'll be right back."

"Take your time, sweetheart," Darlene says. "Ginny and I can discuss what type of fascinators we should wear with our dresses while you're gone."

I shake my head at her comment, then dash out to join Ben. "What's a fascinator?" I ask when I'm far enough away not to be overheard by the wedding planners.

"An English hat." He scrunches his eyebrows together. "Why?"

"Your mom mentioned wearing one at the wedding."

"There's a problem."

I blow out a puff of air. "Tell me about it. I think I'm going to have to say no to that."

Ben rubs his temples. "That's not the problem."

"Are you sure? Because it definitely sounds like one to me. I don't want fancy English hats at my simple—"

"I can't go to China," he blurts.

"What do you mean?" I study his face to discern what he could even be talking about. "Are you saying you can't go or don't want to?" I shudder at the implications of the latter.

"Can't."

"Why not?" Although I'm relieved by his answer, worry still gnaws at me.

He takes me by the hand and leads me into a study just off

the entryway. "My work visa was revoked, so I have no way to get into the country." He shuts the door behind us.

"How, how is that possible?"

He shrugs. "I guess the school misunderstood what I meant when I said I was leaving and going back home. It seems they were under the belief that I was quitting before my contract actually expired in July."

"But you didn't, did you?"

"Of course not. I knew we'd be returning right after the wedding, so I just told them I was going home. As I said, they misunderstood."

"Okay." I scratch my head. "Can you call them and see if they can fix it?"

"It's the weekend." He wrinkles his nose. "Plus, they won't be back in the office until Wednesday because of the Qing Ming festival observances on April third and fourth."

"Wait, is today April 1?" I poke his ribs with my fingers. "Is this some kind of April Fool's joke?" A lightness overtakes me. "You had me there for a minute."

He flattens my hand against his chest. "I wish it were, Nicki, but it's not."

My breath hitches. "So, you're not kidding? You really can't go back with me tomorrow?"

"No." He falls onto the leather sofa and buries his head in his hands. "I can't believe I could let something like this happen. I should have explained more clearly."

"It's not your fault." I kneel next to him. "It was a misunderstanding, that's all."

"There's no time for misunderstandings." He pops his head up. "We have to get back to China and figure out if Lei Ming and the missing child are one and the same. And you need to take care of things at New Hope. We can't afford anything getting in the way of all that."

"Look, we just need to make a few phone calls. I'm certain we can straighten everything out before we have to fly out."

"It doesn't work like that, Nicki. You just don't prance into China unannounced. You have to have the proper paperwork, and that takes time." His Adam's apple bobs. "Time we don't have."

His words take me back four months. Hadn't I said the same thing to Ms. O'Connor when she first asked me to go to China with her? I had, and if I recall, she refused to accept that as an excuse.

Now, neither would I.

"I don't know what it's going to take, but we will find a way to leave here as planned. Ms. O'Connor managed to make it happen, and if she can do it, so can I." I leap up off the floor and head for the door.

"Where are you going?"

"To get my phone and call the travel service company that assisted Ms. O'Connor the first time we went to Asia. They worked their magic getting us into China quickly then, and I'm going to need them to do it for us now."

After three hours of intense back-and-forth conversations with Lisa, the visa specialist, we finally find a solution. Just not the one I was expecting.

"So, what did they say?" Ben stops pacing when I enter the study.

"Do you want the good news or the bad news?" I settle onto the couch.

The hopeful glimmer in his eyes fades. "Good?"

I try to stay calm. "The good news is we can get you a visa, and we can leave for China as planned."

"That's great!" He pumps his fist.

"Wait." I hold up my hand. "I haven't told you the bad news."

"It doesn't matter. We can be on the plane tomorrow. That's all I care about. Whatever bad news we have to deal with, I'm sure we can figure out a way to overcome it." His lips curve upward. "I mean, how bad can it be anyways?"

"The visa is only good for 144 hours, and you can't leave the Beijing region at all."

His head jerks back. From the lines etched in his forehead, I can tell he's doing the math. "That's only ..."

"Six days."

He resumes his pacing. "Can I get an extension once I'm there?"

"I asked." I watch him move across the room. "Normally, you could apply for an extension, but because your visa was revoked under unusual circumstances, they won't consider it. They have very strict rules and regulations. We won't know until we get there if there are other options for you to stay."

"But we can't possibly get the answers we need in six days." Anger tinges his words.

"I know, but what else are we going to do? We can't sit around here for three more days and hope to get approved for an emergency visa once the embassy opens. If we don't take the 144-hour visa, it could be weeks before you're allowed in." I wince. "I don't want to take that chance, do you?"

"No, but we both know that isn't enough time."

"We'll just have to do what we can and pray for a miracle."

"Unless ..." He halts.

My chest squeezes with fear. "What?"

"Well, what if you went by yourself tomorrow and got things underway with Lei Ming and New Hope?"

"And what about you?"

"I'll stay here and join you once I have a proper tourist visa. If I can get it expedited, then I'd be a week behind you at most, but at least we wouldn't always be watching the clock."

I roll around his suggestion over in my mind a few times. While traveling to China alone doesn't scare me, the thought of handling the situation with Lei Ming on my own does. From the moment we agreed to this crazy scheme, we formed an alliance. One that could deal with the good and the bad as long as we were together making joint decisions for our family.

However, now is not the time to divide and conquer. No—now, more than ever, we need to stay a unit. Even if it has a limited lifespan.

"I say we take our chances and see what we can do in six days. Things may come up that need both of us to decide on the spot." I stiffen my spine. "I don't want to make any decision about our future by myself. As they say, it takes teamwork to make the dream work, and that's what we've become. A team."

His shoulders relax for the first time since we started this discussion. "I do like the sound of that." He ambles over to the couch and drops down next to me. "I'm willing to give it a try, but only if you're sure."

With everything coming at us the way it has, I'm not a hundred percent certain of anything these days. But I do believe we are better together.

I hold out my hand to him, a symbolic gesture to seal the deal. "For better or worse, right?"

8

A storm tests the strength of a blade of grass.
~ *Chinese Proverb*

"Welcome back, Mr. and Mrs. Carrington." Director Wu greets us from the front door of her house the day after we arrive back in China.

"Director Wu." I race from the car toward her without even stopping to smell the blooming roses in her garden or correct her mistake in our titles. Ben's timer started ticking as soon as we landed in Beijing, and we can't afford to waste a single minute. "Thank you for meeting with us this morning."

"It's my pleasure, dear. I'm sorry I was unavailable when you rang last week. I went to visit family for the holidays, and phone reception was spotty. But now that you're here, we can visit, and you can fill me in on everything."

"We have a lot to tell you." Ben rushes up behind me.

"Don't keep me in suspense then." She waves us inside. "Come in."

We follow her back to the small sitting room, where only two weeks ago we announced our decision to get married, albeit out of convenience rather than love. Funny how quickly life can change.

"Have a seat. Can I offer you something to eat or drink?" She points to a simple spread laid out on a card table, filled with an assortment of Chinese goodies. Both familiar and unfamiliar. "I brought them back with me. Leftovers from the Qing Ming festival this past weekend."

As tempting as her offer is, and despite how yummy the food looks, my stomach can't handle anything right now. "Maybe we could eat after we visit?"

"Of course, Nicki." The director leads me to the small sofa. "Is everything okay? You look a little pale."

"No, actually, it's not." I choke back the tears.

"Well, sit down and let me get you some water." She reaches for a small kettle.

I grab her arm. "That's okay. I'd rather just talk." With only 144 hours together to resolve this, we need to determine as quickly as possible if the missing child is Lei Ming. It's the only way we'll be able to move forward with our lives. One way or the other.

"What's wrong, dear?" She slowly lowers herself onto the couch next to me.

My tongue sticks to the roof of my mouth. Getting the words out of my mouth is harder than I imagined.

Ben must sense my trouble. "Director, Nicki and I didn't get married. At least not yet."

"Why not?" Her joyful demeanor fades. "Did something happen?"

"Yes." Ben pulls out his cell phone and taps on the screen before passing it to Director Wu. "This."

The director takes his phone in her hands and studies it. Her lips move along as she reads what I can only assume is the missing child ad. "Oh, this is disturbing." She places Ben's phone in her lap and then turns her gaze on me. "And you think the child is Lei Ming?"

"We're not sure," I whisper. "That's why we didn't go through with our plan."

"We want ... no, we need, to make sure this is not our little girl first," Ben adds. "We felt it was in our, I mean, everyone's best interest if we straightened this out before making such a huge commitment, even if we were willing to do it. It's the right thing to do for everyone involved."

"I see." The director passes the phone back to Ben. "Well, I have to admit I wasn't expecting this. I assumed you were coming here to get the adoption paperwork started." Her eyes flick toward a thick folder on the coffee table.

A chill runs down my spine as I shift my eyes toward the small table. And onto the crisp red folder with a New Hope seal engraved on the front. Seeing what should have been unleashes the waterworks I've held at bay since Julia first notified us about the report.

Tears spill down my cheeks. "Do you think Lei Ming could be the missing child?"

"The picture does resemble her, and I have to admit the facial features are quite similar." The director sighs. "Not only that, but my secretary notified me that someone had called last week while I was away specifically asking about the children who had been admitted within the last six months, which, if I recall correctly, Lei Ming was."

"What did she tell them?" I pull a tissue out of my purse to plug my dripping nose.

"Nothing. We don't discuss matters like that over the phone, and she assured me she didn't divulge any information."

I turn toward Ben to gauge his response to the news. He's as white as the director's walls.

"Do you think they're related?" There's an edge to his voice.

"I can't say for certain," she admits. "How did the two of you find this ad?"

"Julia. She called while we were ring ... ring shopping. She saw it on a website while she was doing some research and thought we would want to know."

"And did you?" she asks, her voice gentle.

"Not at first. When we started comparing the picture Julia sent to our pictures of Lei Ming, we saw some differences and thought it might just be a mistake."

"Yeah." Ben opens his phone and flashes a photo he took of Lei Ming and her stuffed bear in the hospital at us. "Look closer, and you'll see that Lei Ming's face is thinner, and her frame is larger compared to the missing child's."

The director squints at the screen, her expression void of any signs she's leaning one way or another. "I can see why you might think that, but from the sound of it, I take it you aren't completely convinced."

"We aren't, and we both agreed we can't turn our back on this for our own happiness." I sniffle. "It wouldn't be right. We need to make sure Lei Ming hasn't been taken from her family, one that really does want her."

"That's very noble of you both."

"Honestly, we don't want to be noble, Director." Ben sits on the armrest next to me and places his hands on my shoulders. "More than anything, we want this child not to be Lei Ming so we can be a family, unconventional as it may be."

"I'm sure it was difficult to make a decision like that, and it must be taking its toll on you both."

I wipe my nose. "I'm basically a mess on the inside and doing the best I can to put up a good front on the outside. What makes it even worse is that I don't understand how something like this happens in the first place." Anger scalds my lungs. "Why Lei Ming? Why us?"

"Are you looking for the practical answer?" She levels her gaze on me. "Or the spiritual one?"

The hair on the back of my neck stands up. While I probably need both at the moment, my heart can only handle one.

"Practical," I say without elaborating on my lackluster faith as of late.

"Okay." She sits ramrod straight. "I wish I could tell you this is an unusual situation, but unfortunately, it's not."

Ben squeezes my left shoulder. I reach back and cover his hand with mine as a sign of solidarity. For better or worse. And this definitely sounds like it belongs in the worse category.

"When international adoptions opened up," the director continues, "many children were kidnapped and sold to orphanages because of the high demand for babies."

I balk. "Not New Hope, though, right?"

"No, of course not. But it was a highly lucrative business in the country for a while. Once the adoption laws and the one-child policy changed, things like this weren't as common." Her fingers roll over her pearl necklace. "Sadly, babies are still taken, though."

"But why would someone take Lei Ming from her home in the South and bring her to an orphanage in the North, miles away from where she lived? It doesn't make sense." Ben asks, his words putting voice to my thoughts. "There are orphanages in every major and mid-size city in this country. Why New Hope?"

"That's the million-dollar question, isn't it?" The director sighs. "I'd like to think that someone realized how serious her medical condition was and brought her here because they heard of the work we were doing. But it could have just been a series of unrelated events that led them to drop her off, or it could have been divine intervention. We may never know. We must be grateful that for whatever reasons, she did end up here with us—and you."

Her words, while comforting, don't offer us any insights into how this situation came to pass. Or provide any proof that Lei Ming is the missing child.

"So, what should we do next?" I ask. "I mean, we need solid evidence that Lei Ming is or isn't the child in this ad."

"I agree." She purses her lips. "We would need to run a DNA

test on Lei Ming and then submit the results to the police in the village where the missing child was taken to see if she's a match to the parents. We would know in a few days, a week at most."

My heart pounds so hard against my chest I'm afraid it might burst open. Hearing the director confirm our next steps brings my fears to fruition. But that isn't all that scares me. Not only does that eat up all the time Ben has here in China, but if we contact the police, I worry what it will do for New Hope in the process. The orphanage can't suffer through another scandal. Housing a kidnapped child and allowing her to be adopted when her family truly wanted her is more than just a scandal. It's a nightmare.

"That won't work," I blurt.

The director blinks her eyes. "It's really the most concrete testing to determine if Lei Ming is a match or not, Nicki. What else would you suggest we do?"

"I'm sorry, that's not what I meant." I stand and rock from side to side, trying to determine which part of my reasoning I want to explain. I choose the most pressing matter. "Of course, we should do a DNA test, but is there any way we could expedite it?"

"I can see if that would be possible, but why the rush?" She narrows her eyes. Ben and I exchange glances before unloading the rest of our problems on her—the marriage fiasco at the courthouse, my mother's house fire, and Ben's visa woes. I purposely stop short of divulging my meeting with the O'Connor Foundation. For now.

After running New Hope for over thirty years, she deserves to have that conversation separately, not mixed up with all our drama. I'll fill her in on the Board's demands in the next day or two. My brain has compartmentalized all the emergencies vying for my attention, and I can only unlock one section at a time.

"Sounds like it's been a few rough weeks for the two of you. I'm sorry you're having so much trouble. Especially when all you're trying to do is the right thing for this little girl." She rises from the couch. "I can ask the police if we can expedite it, but I can't make any promises."

"About that." I stand to match her stance. "Is there any way we can keep the police out of this until we have the results?"

"That's an odd request." She stares at me, confusion clouding her eyes. "Why are you asking?"

I look down at the ground, searching for the words to say what I need to without hurting this dear woman's heart, or worse, causing her to lose face. "Well, it's just that ..." I lift my head. "New Hope can't afford another scandal at the moment, and involving the police might create one."

Her lips twitch, but she holds her head up high. "I can understand your concern. We're still dealing with the aftereffects of Chang's deception, and admitting we may or may not have an abducted child might cause even more problems."

"Ones that wouldn't fare well for us." I stammer.

"Or for the O'Connor Foundation. I assume you spoke with them while you were home, yes?" She raises an eyebrow as if aware I didn't divulge everything earlier.

"I did, and I promise I'll share all the details of my meeting soon, but right now, I just want to focus on solving this mystery with Lei Ming as quickly as possible. We really need to know."

"I appreciate your honesty, Nicki." She brings her hands together. "However, I'm not sure we can do much without getting the police involved at some point. I can call the lab to see if we can run the test privately, but you have to remember, things don't work here like they do in the US. There may be no way of avoiding the police, especially in a possible kidnapping case. We may have no choice but to notify them of the situation."

"I keep forgetting things may not work here as they would back home." I clench my fist. "You're right. I seriously doubt there's any way of getting around the police."

"Let's go ahead and run the test." Ben rises and takes over for me, for which I'm grateful. "We'll just have to pray for the best."

"I agree." The director stands, her face conveying nothing but compassion. "Let me go change and then we can head over to New Hope and get things moving."

When we arrive a little while later, the orphanage is bursting with activity. Children play outside in the bright sunshine, cries and laughter echo through the hallways, and the front desk workers busy themselves with a group of visitors.

"Potential adopters," the director informs us as we gawk at their presence. "A company brings them in occasionally to tour the facilities."

"That's good, right?" I ask. Even though I know none of them will be matched with Lei Ming under the circumstances, I can't help but wonder if there are other children here by mistake. What if one of these families adopts a child only to find out their family wanted them all along? Then what?

"It's always good when we can find forever homes for our children." She leads us toward her office. "That's why we do what we do."

"*Dǎoxiàng qì,*" one of the receptionists calls out in our direction.

Director Wu turns her head.

"Wait here." The elderly woman shuffles back toward the information desk.

"What are they saying?" I ask Ben as I watch the two women converse.

He twists his mouth. "I'm not sure, but I think I heard the receptionist mention Lei Ming's name."

My pulse races. Had something happened to her at the hospital? Or had someone already figured out Lei Ming was the missing child? I hold my breath as the director makes her way back to us.

"I have some news you may be interested in," she says.

Ben and I draw closer to one another for support. Whatever it is, we're ready for it. Together.

"Yes?" I manage to eek the simple word out of my mouth.

"The receptionist let me know ..." Her lips slowly curve upward. "Lei Ming was released from the hospital and brought back here to the Recovery Unit earlier this morning."

"Really?" My knees wobble, and I hold onto Ben's arm to keep from falling. "Can we see her?"

"I told her to let them know you're coming." She hands us two lanyards. "You two go ahead. While you visit with Lei Ming, I'll see what I can find out from the village police about getting the testing done."

Without hesitating, Ben and I snatch our permission passes from her and drape them around our necks. I pay no mind to the havoc it's wreaking on my hair.

"Here, let me help you." Ben gently loosens a strand of curls tangled in the rope. "You can't see our daughter looking like Medusa, can you?'

I quiver at his touch. And his words. Our daughter. Despite our fears that she and the confiscated child could be one and the same, he still holds out hope that we'll be a family. It not only melts my heart but also infuses new faith in my weakened spirit that we will be too. "Thanks."

He wraps his hand around mine. "Lead the way."

With our fingers intertwined, I can't help but feel as if we're walking into our future—one of happiness. And maybe even love. If that's what the warm, fuzzy emotions swirling in my heart are trying to tell me.

Floating on a cloud, I take us through the maze of hallways that lead to the Recovery Unit. I use the time to fill Ben in on New Hope's history with the O'Connor family, the reasons why they started offering medical resources to the orphanage, and how their donations are saving the lives of so many children.

"Wow," Ben says as we arrive at the entrance of the off-limits area. "That's amazing."

"It is, and Ms. O'Connor is counting on me to make sure that it continues for years to come." I tap on the intercom, letting the staff know we've arrived.

"How are you going to do that?" he asks as a loud buzz sounds and the double doors leading to the Recovery Unit slowly swing open.

"I don't know yet. I can only handle one thing at a time." I shrug my shoulders. "And right now, I have to focus on Lei Ming."

The hospital-like room is dark and chilly when we enter. Monitors beep in a rhythmic pattern among the different beds in the unit. A mix of baby powder and disinfectant floats through the tiny space, making it hard to breathe.

Or maybe that's just me, anxious to see the little girl with silky black hair and big chocolate eyes who stole my heart. I survey the room in search of her. It doesn't take me long to spot her snuggled up with her bear. "There she is." My trembling finger points in her direction.

We race over to the side of her bed, where her small body is hooked up to a bunch of colorful wires, and an IV tube drips fluid into her arm.

Seeing her so weak and fragile, I fall back against Ben's strong frame. "She looks so helpless."

"But she's alive." He places his hands on my shoulders. "That's all that matters."

My head bobs up and down as tears pool in the corner of my eyes. Instinctively, I reach out to touch her arm, which is as cold as ice. I tuck the blanket around her tighter.

Just as I'm about to pull my hand out from under the fluffy covering, her body twitches, and her eyes spring open.

"Hey, sweetheart." I brush my fingers over one of her cheeks. "It's so good to see you."

"Yeah." Ben leans over my shoulder and into her crib. "Remember us?"

Her eyes bounce between the two of us before a huge wail erupts from her blue-tinted lips.

"I guess not." I reach down to pick her up, but the octopus-like cords keep me from doing it gracefully or quickly.

Every effort to hold or comfort her causes her cries to rise to another level.

"Let me help." Ben tries to maneuver the wires out of the way, but they only become more entangled.

"Shh." I pat her chest. "It's okay; we'll figure it out. Hold on." Lei Ming pushes my hand away.

"What are we going to do?" Desperation laces my voice.

"I don't know, but you have to stay calm, or else you'll make things worse."

I step back and let him take over. Maybe he can work his magic with her.

But when large tears stream down Lei Ming's face at his attempts, it's clear neither of us can get through to her.

A nurse rushes to her bed, speaking rapid and very stern Mandarin.

Ben switches to his second language, and the two exchange words. After a few minutes, the nurse turns her back to us and comforts Lei Ming.

"She wants us to leave," he says, forlornly stepping away from her crib.

"Leave?" I watch the nurse rewrap the blanket around Lei Ming and speak to her gently in her native tongue. "But we just got here."

He pulls me aside. "The nurse says Lei Ming needs to rest and that waking her was a mistake. And she doesn't want the other patients to get upset."

My stomach sinks. Once again, my motherly ways are a failure. "But I didn't mean to. I just wanted to make sure she was warm." I glance over my shoulder as we walk toward the hallway.

"I know, Nicki, and it's not your fault. It's bad timing, that's all." He pushes the entrance doors open and stands to the side so I can walk through.

When we're back in the light, I lean against the wall and close my eyes. Why did I ever think I could be a mother? I am the last thing this child needs.

I stay lost in my thoughts until the clacking of shoes against the hallway tiles brings me back to the present.

Opening my eyes, I spring away from the wall when I see Director Wu marching our way. "Director, what are you doing here?" My heart beats faster, worried that the harsh-speaking nurse ratted us out, effectively ending our chances of returning to see Lei Ming anytime soon.

"We need to talk." She stops directly in front of me. "I spoke with the village police."

Ben sidles up next to me, our faces almost pressed together. "And? Are they willing to expedite the DNA test?"

"I'm afraid not," she says apologetically.

I stiffen my back. "Did they say why they wouldn't?"

"Because according to their records, they don't know about any missing child from their village."

"What?" Ben and I say at the same time, our heads almost bumping into each other.

"I don't understand." I rub my forehead. "Are you sure you called the right police station?"

"I did," she confirms.

"So does that mean that this was all a mistake and we can follow through with the adoption as we'd planned?" Hope swells within me.

The director sighs. "I'm sorry, Nicki, but I can't say just yet."

"Why not?" Ben asks.

"After I spoke to the police, I called the Family Planning Bureau in the area, and they, too, denied any knowledge of a missing or confiscated child."

"So how are we going to get the testing done then and know for sure?" I wring my hands.

"I think the only way to know for certain is to go to the village and speak with the family directly to request the tests. The local officials aren't always reliable sources. They either don't want to get involved to save face or to keep their reputation with the higher-ups in good standing."

"That's not possible." I press my lips together. "We don't have the time, and Ben's visa doesn't allow him to leave the region."

The director's eyes bulge, and she looks directly at Ben. "You can't?"

"Unfortunately, no."

She taps her chin. "Then I guess it's up to the two of you how you want to proceed."

Ben and I lock eyes.

"What do you think, Nicki?" His tone is soft and gentle. Just like he is. "Do we believe the police and go ahead with our original plans? Or ..."

"Do we see this through like we said we would?" I lower my head and internally debate the questions. My stomach knots as I quickly race through our options once more.

Indecision washes over me, and I long to hear Ben's opinion. But when I raise my eyes and study his face, I see a mixture of sorrow and clarity written across it. Instantly I know what he's thinking. We have to do the right thing for Lei Ming, even if it costs us everything.

I clear my throat. "Director, let's see if we can speak with the family and, if they're willing, get the testing done to find out for certain if Lei Ming is their child or not." I pause. "And since Ben can't go, I will."

Ben's eyebrows knit together in puzzlement. "How will you speak with them?"

"I'll go with her," the director offers.

My mouth falls open. Is she serious?

"What?" Her head juts back. "I may be old, but I'm not incapable of traveling. I just visited my family, remember?"

Relieved I won't have to go alone, I hug her. "Thank you, that would be great."

"Ben can stay here and work on extending his visa, and you and I can sort out this mess together." She pulls out of my embrace. "I'm proud of you for making the right decision."

I nod at her compliment.

"I'll go check on travel arrangements then." She retreats to her office.

Watching her figure disappear from my sight, the tears start to flow again as the reality of the moment hits me like a wrecking ball.

"One way or the other, it'll be okay," Ben whispers in my ear before kissing my temple.

I look back at the Recovery Unit where Lei Ming sleeps. I hope he's right because I have a sinking suspicion we may have just lost our daughter for good.

9

Send charcoal in a snowstorm.
~ *Chinese Proverb*

While we wait for Director Wu to finalize the plans for the trip to the village, Ben and I return to the city to see what can be done about extending his visa.

He stops at the entrance of the coffee shop where we first met. "I can meet with Longchen alone to discuss my visa issues if you'd rather go back to the hotel to nap or prepare for your trip tomorrow."

"I'm anxious to hear Longchen's thoughts or suggestions on the situation." I open the door and inhale the strong coffee aromas while I wait for him to come inside. "Plus, how could I possibly pass up the opportunity to revisit the spot where we first met?" Memories flit through my mind, and I smile.

"Yeah, little did we know then that five months later, we'd be planning a wedding and starting a family together." He chuckles as we merge with others to form a line. "God definitely works in mysterious ways."

"You can say that again."

He opens his mouth, likely to repeat his last sentence, but

quickly closes it when someone behind me catches his attention. "Longchen!" Ben waves him over.

I turn around to see my old friend, who has been a huge help to me since the first day I arrived in China, standing at the entrance.

"It's so good to see you," I say when Longchen joins us.

He takes my hand in his. "You look as lovely as ever, Nicki." His eyes flick toward Ben. "If he's smart, he'll snatch you up."

Ben inches closer to me. "I'm trying." He holds out his hand to Longchen. "Good to see you, friend. Thanks for meeting us."

"You said it was urgent."

"It is," Ben and I say together.

Longchen arches his eyebrow. "Then we should find a table and talk."

"The line is really long." I point to the slow-moving, snake-like line behind me. "Why don't the two of you find us a table, and I'll order our drinks. We may be here awhile."

"You sure?" Ben asks.

"Yes, I'll take care of this, and you can tell Longchen all about our adventures since we last saw him." I push them toward the crowded seating area. While I'd love to tell the grandfather-I-never-had everything that's happened, the two men have known each other longer and are closer. It's only fitting that Ben be the one to update him.

I watch them maneuver through the packed and noisy restaurant before claiming my spot at the tail end of the line. After people-watching for a few minutes, I pull out my phone and begin to scroll through my email to see if there's any update from my mom or Darlene. I need some type of distraction to take my mind off all our problems and the fact that I might possibly be meeting Lei Ming's birth parents soon.

But there's only spam and a few emails from friends. I close my inbox and pull up the director's info. Maybe I can call and see if she's finalized our itinerary yet. My thumb hovers over the call button. Should I give her more time? Or will I just be bothering her while she's trying to arrange all the details?

As I debate my options, my phone vibrates in my hand. I answer the call, surprised by the uncanny timing of the director's daughter's call. "Hello, Victoria?"

"Nicki, I need to speak with you. Do you have a moment to talk?"

I glance up at the gaping distance between me and the counter. "I do. How are you?"

"I'm fine," she says in a curt and unfriendly manner.

I gulp at the sharp tone of her words. Where was the sweet woman who'd arranged for a lawyer to get me out of jail and who took extra measures to make sure my visa wasn't revoked? She's usually not this angry. "Is everything okay?"

"Not really. I'm at New Hope."

"Oh, I just left. It would have been great to see you again."

"I wish I could say the same."

"Did I do something wrong?" I rack my brain for how I might have upset her, but nothing comes to mind.

"Yes. As soon as I arrived here, Mother informed me of your upcoming trip to Fujian Province and that she was planning on going with you. I waited until she left her office for a moment to call you." Her icy tone turns fiery. "How could you think this was a good idea? She's in no condition to travel halfway across the country."

"Since she'd just visited family, I assumed she was up for the journey," I respond.

"Both her doctor and I advised her from going on that trip, but she went anyway."

I wince. "She didn't mention that to me."

"I doubt she would have." Victoria's voice softens. "Nicki, you must understand that although my mother is a humble woman, she can still be proud and hard-headed at times. And for whatever reason, she refuses to believe that her health is fragile.

The more she continues to push herself, the more her well-being is at risk."

"I ... I didn't realize how serious her situation really was or consider it from that perspective." My face heats with shame.

"No, you didn't."

"I'm sorry, Victoria. I was so caught up in the moment that when your mother offered to accompany me, I didn't consider the toll it might take on her and her health. I always see her as the strong, independent woman she is." Like Ms. O'Connor was, I want to say, but I shake my head and quickly bury the pain of losing my former boss. "I do need her to help me figure out this situation with Lei Ming, though. People there won't respond to me as they will with her."

"Mother told me about that," she says, her voice even gentler now. "I can't imagine how hard this must be for you ... and I'm sorry ... but my mother can't join you. She may look and act like she's doing well, but she can't take any chances. Most days, she's not fully up to the task of running the orphanage anymore."

My breath hitches. Was the director aware of the Board's decision before I had a chance to discuss things with her?

"In fact," Victoria continues. "I'm taking a short leave of absence from the law firm to keep an eye on her and lighten her load a bit. Maybe in doing so, she'll realize that being in charge is no longer an option for her and that she needs to let someone else take over for her at New Hope."

New Hope. Another problem I had yet to solve. But with my current dilemma taking up most of my time and attention, I had no idea when I could do what the Board had asked of me. The clock was ticking but finding this family and uncovering the truth about Lei Ming's identity took priority.

I drop my gaze to the floor, where coffee splatters ink on the white tiles like tattoos, and bring my focus to the matter at hand. If the director doesn't go with me to the village, how will I get anyone there to talk to me? Not speaking the language and being a Westerner won't get me very far there.

Nor will it allow me to obtain the information I so desperately need.

I must find another way.

"Victoria, I totally understand where you're coming from, and I respect your decision." I move out of the line and back toward the table where Longchen and Ben are huddled together. "Please have her send me the travel details she's already arranged, and I'll take care of things from here."

"Thank you, Nicki." Victoria blows out a sigh of relief. "When she learns of what I've done and stops being angry at me for interfering, I'll have her forward the information to you."

Heavy-hearted, I hang up the phone and drop it in my purse. I have to come up with a Plan B and fast.

Ben and Longchen are so deep in conversation that they don't even notice when I sidle up next to the table. I clear my throat. "Hey."

Both their heads pop up.

"Where's the coffee and tea?" Ben studies my empty hands.

I pull out the chair next to him and drop into it. "I got a call and had to step out of the line."

"Everything okay?" Ben's face goes pale. He's probably just as weary of the problems as I am.

"Not really." My voice cracks. "Director Wu can't go with me to the village after all."

"Is there a problem?" Ben asks.

"Her daughter doesn't think it's a good idea for her to travel such a long distance. She doesn't think she's physically up for it. The director wasn't supposed to visit her family last week. But she did."

"Oh." Ben's eyes grow wide.

"Yeah, I was so excited that we actually had a lead I didn't stop to think about how it might jeopardize her health. I didn't realize how frail she still is. Sadly, it doesn't look like that's going to improve any time soon either."

"I'm sure her daughter knows you would never do anything

that would cause the director harm." Longchen tilts his head at me and smiles. "However, it does seem like you'll need to come up with another plan, though. For the trip ... and maybe for the orphanage too."

"I would if I could, but ideas aren't stocked in a vending machine where I can easily just get another one. They're in short supply in here." I tap my head and then glance over at Ben. "Did you tell him about the craziness that is our life these days?"

Ben nods.

"He did," Longchen chimes in. "Before we discuss that situation, however, I should say congratulations on your engagement." He leans over and kisses me on the cheek. "When I saw the two of you together at my house at Chinese New Year, I hoped you might hit it off."

"Thank you." I blush. "But you know why we're doing what we're doing, right?"

Longchen pushes back in his seat. "I do. I think it's noble of you both, and I'm happy to do what I can to help the two of you succeed."

"I appreciate that more than you know." I purse my lips. "If you have any ideas on how we can get Ben's visa extended so he can come with me to the village, that would be most helpful."

Both men groan.

"Longchen and I were just talking about that when you showed up. He's familiar with the rules regarding visas because of his close work with the tourism industry." Ben's shoulders droop. "It doesn't look good."

I turn toward Longchen. "Why not?"

"Because of the miscommunication between Ben and the school and their subsequent revocation of Ben's visa so quickly, the government isn't likely to extend his temporary visa into a tourist one."

"Then what can he do?"

"The only option I have is to state a new purpose for a visa," Ben whispers.

"New purpose? Like what?" I ask.

"Like a different job altogether." Longchen pushes back against his chair. "He can't go back to his position at the school. They would require him to have a job in another field to meet the work visa criteria."

"Then what's he supposed to do?" My voice rises a notch. "He's a teacher."

Ben covers my hand with his. "I can ask around and see if any of my friends here might have openings at their companies. I'm willing to do anything—sort mail, sweep floors, whatever—if it means I can stay in the country longer so we can figure everything out."

"But if you get a new job, they aren't going to let you off right away to look for Lei Ming's family. They'll expect you to stay there and work. You have more flexibility as a teacher." I shake my head. "We have to come up with an alternate solution."

"There aren't any. They're in short supply in here." He taps his head, mimicking my earlier actions.

"Well ..." An idea pops into my head before I even have time to consider the ramifications. "What if you just went with me to the village without anyone knowing? It's not like you have a monitor strapped around your ankle. How would they find out? We could go and be back in five days."

"It's China, Nicki. Somehow, they'll find out." Ben's jaw clenches. "And we both know what it would mean for me if I broke the law."

Images of the dark, dank jail cell where I spent three long days and nights float through my mind. It was a terrible experience I wouldn't wish on anyone. I shudder thinking about Ben having to suffer through such a nightmare.

"Not only that," he continues, "but any mark on my record would disqualify us from adopting." Sorrow clouds his eyes. "If Lei Ming ends up not being the missing child, I don't really want to take that risk, do you?"

I guess I'd truly emptied the vending machine of its last

remaining options. "No, of course not, but how else are we going to get the truth?"

"Why do you need to go to Fujian Province in person?" Longchen asks. "Couldn't you send Lei Ming's DNA results to the police there once you have them and ask them to confirm one way or another?"

Ben and I exchange glances. "The village police claim they know nothing about a missing child." I quickly recount the director's earlier phone conversation.

"I see." Longchen's face conveys the same look of skepticism that Director Wu expressed when she dropped that bomb on us.

Despite the loud music blaring through the speakers and the rising and falling of Mandarin being spoken all around us, silence descends on our table.

Finally, Longchen's grandfatherly voice pops the quiet bubble enveloping us. "I don't know if this will help, but my wife's cousin works at the main headquarters of the Family Planning Offices here in Beijing. I could ask if she might be able to supply us with any information that might help you."

"Family Planning?" Ben props his elbows on the table. "How could that offer us any insights?"

Longchen lowers his voice. "Their office keeps the official records of all the children born in China. It's possible my wife's cousin has access to the birth permit for this missing child, which might have pertinent details that could assist you in your search."

"Do you think you could ask her to meet us here so we could talk?" My voice lilts higher.

"Don't forget where you are, Nicki." Longchen smirks. "There are eyes and ears everywhere. Considering the sensitive nature of this matter, it would be better if we arranged to visit with her at my home." He removes his phone from his shirt pocket and types out a message.

After several minutes of back-and-forth texting between our friend and his relative, Longchen places his phone on the table.

"She said she'd meet us at my apartment when she gets off work in an hour."

"Wonderful!" Ben pats Longchen on the back.

"It is," I whisper, but my face must convey my despair.

Longchen frowns. "You don't sound very convincing."

"No, I'm sorry, it's just that talking with her might solve one issue for us, but it still doesn't erase our other problems."

"I don't understand." The elderly man shakes his head.

"Well, Ben still doesn't have a job or visa that will allow him to stay in the country longer. If we do need to travel to Fujian province, there's no one who can go with me." I arch my eyebrow at Longchen. "Unless you might be available?"

"I'd love to, but I'm booked with tours all this week and next." He scratches his chin. "Have you thought about asking Julia to accompany you?"

Ben sits up straight as a board. "Of course. Why didn't we think of that, Nicki? She'd be the best person to go with you, and she's always been willing to help you if she can."

The muscles in my shoulders tighten at their suggestions. I had considered that but let the idea flitter away like dandelion seeds in the wind. Even though Julia is one of my closest friends, I can't keep asking her to bail me out of situations.

"I don't want her to think I only see her as my Chinese fixer. Since the beginning, our relationship has been one-sided, with me seeming to *take* all the time without giving much back in return. That's not how friendships are supposed to work."

I take a breath before continuing, "And I'm not sure she'd be able to, or even want to, leave her sister," I say unconvincingly. "Not only that, but she's so young I'm not sure people would take her seriously and give us the answer we're wanting." I pause. "Then there's always the concern about how this might play on her emotions. I'd hate for this to upset her in any way or cause her to question how she and Mingyu arrived at Mother's Love all those years ago."

Longchen narrows his eyes. "Isn't that a decision Julia should make, not you?"

"Probably. I just hate that I always need her assistance." I wring my hands together. "And like I said, what have I given her in return for all she's done for me? A bunch of *People* magazines? I should be finding ways to help her rather than asking her to bail me out again."

"I'm sure that's not how she'll see it," Longchen says. "But you have to give her a chance to decide on her own. If she does, and you do end up traveling there, you'll have what you need."

"Longchen's right," Ben adds. "You should ask her."

I squirm in my seat under their stares. I guess it couldn't hurt to ask.

"Okay, I'll call her." If traveling to the village is the only way to uncover the truth, she may be my only hope. I pull my phone back out of my purse, bring up her contact info, and press to connect. I just have to find something meaningful to offer her in return.

Instantly that sweet, familiar voice comes across the line. "Nicki, I've been waiting to hear from you. What took you so long?"

10

Studying the past helps to understand the present.
~ *Chinese Proverb*

I t doesn't take much to convince Julia to go with me to Fujian province. From her immediate response to my request, she must have known I'd venture down this trail at some point. And that I couldn't go alone. While I hate being so predictable, I'm grateful she's willing to accompany me and for her generous spirit to bail me out time and time again.

We agree to meet at Longchen's apartment a short time later to arrange the trip details before meeting with his cousin, knocking out two birds with one stone. Every organizer's productivity dream. Especially when the clock is working against us.

When I step into the hallway of Longchen's apartment building thirty minutes later, the highrise is unrecognizable.

It's no longer the festive environment that welcomed me before. Gone are the gold and red Chinese New Year decorations that wallpapered every flat surface and swung from the ceiling rafters. With plain white walls and quiet hallways, it's rather sterile.

Then again, it's not like we're here for a party or a social visit. My only goal at the moment is to gather any information on the missing child we can from Longchen's cousin. If she can provide that and it helps us verify Lei Ming's true identity, *then* we might have a reason to celebrate. No decorations required.

"*Yéyé!*" A child's voice greets us when we cross the threshold of Longchen's home.

Surprised by the sound, I peer around my host's frame and spot a little girl with braided black hair and chubby cheeks wobbling in our direction.

Longchen swoops down and hoists the child into his arms. He promptly swings back toward us. "Nicki, Ben, I'd like you to meet my youngest granddaughter, Jiā Lì."

"*Nǐ hǎo.*" I smile and wiggle my fingers at the sweet face that resembles Lei Ming's. "*Nǐ hǎo ma?*"

Jiā Li buries her head in her grandfather's shoulder.

"She's shy," Longchen says, rubbing her back. "But she'll warm up to you in a few minutes."

"Completely understandable." I remove my shoes and set down my purse. Every fiber of my being wants to hold out my arms and invite her into my embrace, but after my earlier experience with Lei Ming in the Recovery Unit, my parental confidence is shaken. And I'm not sure anything will be able to restore it.

Longchen glances around the apartment. "Her *nǎinai* is likely in the kitchen cooking. I told her we were coming, so she's probably in there making a feast."

Ben's face lights up. "I'm always happy to taste test if she needs someone to sample a plate ... or two."

"Don't I know it." Longchen bursts into a laugh, causing Jiā Li's body to jiggle. "I'll go see if I can be of any use to my wife. You and Nicki can make yourselves comfortable in the living room while you wait for Julia to arrive."

"Did someone say my name?" A familiar voice asks.

The three of us pivot towards the open door where Julia is standing.

"Julia!" I rush to give her a hug.

"Nicki," she gasps. "We've only been apart for a few weeks."

"I know, but I'm just so happy to see you." I squeeze her tighter. If it hadn't been for her, I wouldn't have survived in China. And now, my family and my future are dependent on her once more.

"Nicki, her lips are turning blue," Ben says from behind me.

I jump back and scan my friend's face. It's as beautiful as always, with her creamy porcelain skin and rich brown eyes hidden behind Harry Potter glasses. "They are not." I swat his arm.

"Hi, Julia." Ben inches forward and gives her a friendly embrace. "I apologize for my fiancée's over-the-top affection. Thanks for coming and helping us."

Julia pushes up her glasses. "My pleasure. Anything for friends."

"*Nǐ hǎo*, Julia." Longchen nods in her direction. "I'll let the three of you catch up while I check on my wife. Excuse me." He and Jiā Li retreat toward the kitchen.

"Shall we, ladies?" Ben extends out his arm and directs us to the living room.

Once we're settled into the tiny space, Ben and I take turns sharing all that had occurred since Julia first called me and told me about the missing child, as well as the latest development with the village police. Julia's head swivels back and forth as she listens to us detail the highs and lows of the past few weeks that I didn't have time to discuss on the phone.

"I had no idea," my friend says once Ben and I bring our story to a close. "No wonder it took you so long to reach out."

"Yes, and I'm sorry for not calling sooner, but as you can see, things have become complicated, and we have to be careful in how we handle everything."

"Of course. Is there anything else I can do?"

Ben leans forward. "Were you ever able to get more information from the business that ran the missing child ad you saw?"

"I tried contacting them several times, but the line was always busy. I could never get through." Julia blows out her lips. "It's been so frustrating, and I can only imagine how other parents must feel."

"No, that's okay." Ben's eyes are filled with compassion. "Nicki and I appreciate everything you've done for us so far."

Before I can affirm his statement, Jiā Li comes barreling into the room, her grandfather fast on her heels, bringing our conversation to a halt.

Ben springs from his seat and picks up Jiā Li in his arms. The young toddler giggles at her capture.

"She escaped while I was helping my wife," Longchen says, out of breath.

"No problem." Ben tickles her tummy. "Want us to watch her for you?"

Goosebumps pebble my skin. Considering what happened to us when we tried to take care of Lei Ming earlier, is that really a good idea?

"If you wouldn't mind, that would be great. My wife must think it's Chinese New Year again. She's fixing at least ten different dishes."

"It's cool, right Nicki?"

I gulp. "Sure."

"Thanks, I won't be too long." Longchen returns to the kitchen.

"Well, I'll leave you two to babysit, and I'll go see what I can do to get us a flight tomorrow." Julia rises from the couch and follows suit after our host.

"I guess it's just the three of us, then." Ben sits down next to me in the spot Julia had just vacated.

I watch as he smoothly situates himself into the seat with Jiā Li. He makes it look so easy. So natural.

"Want to hold her?" Ben offers.

My breath hitches. More than anything, I want to hold her, but fear paralyzes me. What if she reacts like Lei Ming had when I tried to comfort her? Then what?

"Nicki." Ben's voice holds a thread of assurance. "You'll be fine, I promise." He hands Jiā Li to me.

"O-kay." I quickly open my arms and take her from him. She falls right in, allowing my heart to slow back to its normal rate. "Well, that went surprisingly well."

"Here, this should help." Ben reaches for a ball lying on the coffee table. "And don't worry ... you're a natural."

"Thanks." I pluck the ball from his hands and pass it to Jiā Li.

For the next few minutes, the three of us play a game of catch. Jiā Li's happy shrills echo through the room, and I imagine this is what it might be like one day in our own home, with Lei Ming. The thought warms my insides and fills my heart with hope that not only could we be a family, but I might just make it as a mom after all.

"Sorry to interrupt all the fun." Longchen strides back into the living room, followed by Julia. "But my cousin has arrived."

A petite woman with the same salt and pepper hair as his steps out from behind them. "Hello, it's nice to meet you. I'm Nian Zhen."

Ben stands, and I follow his lead with Jiā Li cradled on my hip.

"It's nice to meet you," I say before quickly reverting to her native tongue. "*Xièxiè nǐ de dàolái.*"

"You're welcome, although after what Longchen has told me, I'm not sure how much assistance I can be."

"Cousin," Longchen takes her by the elbow. "Please sit."

I drop back down on the couch and place Jiā Li on my lap. She leans back against my chest and sucks her thumb. Julia, who must have completed our trip arrangements, joins us in the living room as well.

"I'm assuming Longchen has explained our situation to you," Ben says to Nian Zhen, not wasting any time on formalities.

"Yes." Nian Zhen nods. "I wish I could say it was uncommon, but unfortunately, it's not."

"Can you give us any insight as to how something like this happened?" Ben asks.

"I have heard rumors ..." Longchen's relative squirms in her seat. "But I am not proud of what I know and how it reflects on my beloved country. I am not certain I should share."

"I understand." I brush my hand over Jiā Li's braids. "All countries have things they've done that, in hindsight, probably weren't the best approach, but I promise we aren't here to pass judgment on China. We're just looking for answers to better know how to proceed with our situation, and we're running out of resources."

Nian Zhen turns to Longchen.

"It's okay, Cousin. I trust these people. You can too."

She nods and looks back at us. "Then I guess I should start at the beginning and explain how this might have come about." She perches on the edge of her seat and clears her throat. "In every city, town, and village, there are Family Planning Offices run by volunteer community members. Their job is to ensure that people in their community are adhering to the government's strict family policies."

"How do they do that?" I ask.

"There are various ways." She purses her lips. "One is to authorize birthing permits, which gives a family permission to have a child. Without one, a child will not be legal in the eyes of the country. They have also been known to record women's cycles so they would know if they had become pregnant and to watch for women who were displaying any signs of morning sickness."

"And if they missed a cycle or were sick, then what?" I squeak out the question, slightly embarrassed to be discussing such delicate issues in front of Ben and Longchen. However, it must be standard jargon for Nian Zhen as her face doesn't show any signs of discomfort.

"Then it would depend on if they had already exceeded the child limit. There were exemptions in certain situations, like if the firstborn child was a girl, then they were allowed to try for a boy. However, if they already had a boy and became pregnant once more, then other measures were taken ... measures in which they did not have a choice." She lowers her head to her chest, her leg shaking. "They would be required to terminate the fetus or find other means to deal with the children."

A heavy silence hangs over the room, each of us lost in our thoughts at Nian Zhen's admission.

"But I'm guessing not all families followed the rules, right?" Ben finally shatters the quiet and keeps the discussion moving forward.

She slowly lifts her head, her upper lip quivering. "No, many did not. And that is when things get complicated."

"Complicated? In what ways?" My heart thumps like a punching bag imagining how bad things could get.

"For their efforts to control the population, Family Planning Officials were awarded if they met their quotas and received distinct recognition from the government. However, when people refused to cooperate, then that put the officials' good standing in jeopardy, which was a problem."

I watch Jiā Li's chest rise and fall in a steady rhythm, certain that her still body has fallen asleep. Startled by Nian Zhen's answer, I avert my eyes from the napping child. "So, what would they do?"

"The officials began to punish those who had more children or refused to get sterilized. It was not uncommon to hear of officials going into a house and taking all of a family's possessions or destroying their roofs to make it impossible for them to live there. Or they would fine them heavily—usually some exorbitant amount—that they knew was practically impossible for the families to pay."

Listening to Nian Zhen recount these stories, my heart squeezes so tight I can barely breathe. And while I wanted to cover my ears and not listen anymore, I can't turn away. I need to know the rest of the story. It might very well be Lei Ming's.

"If the families endured all that hardship and still wouldn't abide by the rules, then many officials resorted to taking a child – usually the one that created the issue—and demanded a fee for his or her return. When the families would raise that amount, the officials would require a new, higher amount and play that game until finally, the family had no choice but to give up." Her voice wavers, and tears pool in the corners of her eyes.

"And what, what would happen to the confiscated child?" Julia joins the conversation.

Nian Zhen wipes her nose and stiffens her back. "They would be handed over to orphanages and eventually adopted out. At the time, to foreign families, but more recently to local Chinese."

"So not all children who are in orphanages were abandoned or unwanted ... as we've always been led to believe?" Julia's face ripples with anguish. "Some were there even though their families truly wanted them?"

Nian Zhen looks at Longchen. "Could I have some water, please?"

"Of course." He springs from his chair and races to the kitchen.

"Sadly, yes." Nian Zhen locks eyes with Julia. "And it seems that if this family from Fujian province is looking for their child, that could be the case, although I can't say for certain."

"Here, Cousin." Longchen hands Nian Zhen a bottle of water.

"*Xièxie.*" She takes a drink and sets it down on the floor next to her. "I'm sorry to have to share such gruesome details with you. As I said, it is a black mark on my country's history and not one I am proud of. Thankfully, the policies are changing, and, hopefully, things like this will cease to happen."

"Let's pray that's the case." Ben reaches for my hand. "However, if this did happen to the little girl Nicki and I are wanting to adopt, we need to know so we can try and make things right. Unfortunately, it hasn't been that easy."

Nian Zhen's eyebrows knit together. "And you believe I can help you?"

"Yes," we both blurt.

She takes another drink of water. "What exactly do you need from me?"

Longchen steps in. "Cousin, I told them you might be able to look up their missing child's information in your database and see if there was anything that might provide some insight into her true identity so Nicki and Ben could know for certain."

"You do know what you're asking of me, correct?" Her eyes narrow. "I could face severe repercussions if anyone were to find out that I was providing you with private information."

"I do." Longchen nods. "And I would not ask you unless it was extremely important. As Ben mentioned, they cannot get the answers they are looking for. I thought perhaps you might be able to give them a lead that might be of some assistance."

The uniformed woman rises from her seat and walks back toward the door.

A tremor of mingled fear and dread shoot through me. Is she leaving?

Worried she's gone without giving us anything more to go on, I'm tempted to question Longchen about her unusual exit when I see her small frame heading in our direction.

"Do you have the ad for the missing child by chance?" She returns to her seat, a computer bag in her hand.

"I do." Julia reaches for her pocket and pulls out her phone. After a few quick taps, she hands the phone to Longchen's cousin. "Here it is. It only lists the gender, date of birth, and the village name and province."

Nian Zhen removes a pair of reading glasses from her bag and props them on the edge of her pointed nose before reading what's on Julia's screen. "Okay, let me see what, if anything, I can find." She sets the phone down next to her and opens her laptop.

Watching her type information into her computer, I pray we learn something. Anything that might give us some clue as to who these people are so we can connect with them as soon as possible.

"Hmmm." Nian Zhen removes her glasses. "There is no *hukou* for a child born in that village on the day listed here."

"*Hukou*? What is that?" I scan the room, desperate for an answer.

"A *hukou* is the government's record of a child's birth." Longchen's usually chipper voice drops to a somber note. "Without it, a child is not legally registered and will not be able to acquire most of his or her rights, including healthcare and education. Most likely, the little girl who is missing doesn't have one because hers was not a permitted birth." He pauses. "If that's the case, then unfortunately she wouldn't be able to live a full life here in China. She'd be a ghost."

"And so that ... that's why they took her?" My stomach knots as I recall Nian Zhen's earlier remarks about those situations. "Because she wasn't permitted, and they wanted to punish the parents?" What a terrible atrocity for that entire family.

"It is possible, Nicki." The corners of Longchen's mouth dip. "There's only one way left for you to find out."

Although I know what he's referring to—visiting the village and speaking with the family—he's wrong. It's not my only option.

If Lei Ming is the missing child and her birth was not legally sanctioned, then the reality is returning her to her family might be the worst thing we could do for her. She will face a rough and challenging life in China without any government documents. If I want to do what is truly right in this situation, then perhaps the best thing would be to move forward with our plans and give her a life without so many hardships.

Yet when I close my eyes, all I can see is a sobbing mother

yearning for her child, longing for her empty arms to be filled once more.

If I could possibly replace what she had lost, why wouldn't I? But in doing so, what would I be losing?

"Nicki?" Ben pats my leg. "What are you thinking?"

I open my eyes and turn to him, swallowing hard to bring my heart down from my throat. "I'm going to the village to locate that family."

EARLY THE NEXT MORNING, Julia and I travel to Sanji village in the Fujian province, which requires a plane ride, a short rail trip, and a taxi drive through the patchwork of rice fields and tea plantations tucked within the Wuyi mountains. When we finally arrive at our destination later that afternoon, we're deposited at the doorsteps of the local police office.

If you could call it that.

The station is a ten-by-twelve, gray-brick, shed-like structure with orange window frames and a scuffed red door. A blue banner hangs across the width of the building with what I assume are the Chinese characters for police. The red, blue, and gold national emblem looms large next to the symbols. Not exactly the bustling command center for safety like I've seen on TV or in the movies.

Once we step inside, Julia points at a wooden chair propped against the wall. "Have a seat over there. I'll go see if I can find someone who can help us locate the family or at least give us a name."

I do as I'm told and plop down in the chair. Stale cigarette smoke lingers in the air like dense fog, and a creaking ceiling fan resonates through the tiny space, providing very little air or relief from the warm temperatures. I peel my damp shirt from my chest and shake it, hoping the effort might offer me a reprieve from the stifling heat. If Julia doesn't return soon, I may melt in a few minutes.

Thankfully, she drops down in the seat next to me before that can happen.

"So, what did the officer say?" I cock my head in the direction of a lone male agent seated at one of two desks.

"The Commander's out at a meeting, and he's the one we need to speak with."

"When will he be back?"

"He wouldn't tell me." She leans her head back against the wall and closes her eyes. "I guess we'll just have to wait."

"Patience is not my best virtue," I remind her. "Especially when I have to sit in a sauna."

She cocks one eye open. "Do you want to leave and come back later?"

"No." I pull my hair into a ponytail. "We need to speak with someone today, and I don't want to miss him."

"Okay, then, we wait." She crosses her arms and resumes her sleeping position.

I do my best to copy her efforts, but the hard wooden chair and rising heat make it impossible for me to rest. Plus, my brain refuses to turn off anyway. Now that I'm actually sitting still for a few moments, it's running at warp speed, thinking of all the tasks I still need to attend to.

Like New Hope.

What if more than one child there had been brought under the same circumstances as Lei Ming? Who would ever know or fight to find out the truth for them? Worse yet, what will happen if I am not able to meet the Board's deadline? Then all the children there might suffer. Not just those who might be collateral damage of tragic circumstances.

A cold shiver runs down my spine pondering New Hope's possibilities. The clock is ticking, and if I want to ensure its future is secure, I need to make my move now. Thankfully, I'm with the one person who might be able to keep the orphanage from falling apart.

I tap Julia on the shoulder. "Hey," I whisper in her ear. "Are you asleep?"

"I was," she mumbles.

"I'm sorry to bother you, but I really need to talk to you about something."

"Can it wait?"

"Not really."

She sits up straight, stretches her arms over her head, and focuses her attention on me. "Okay, I'm awake. What is it?"

The chair squeaks as I shift my weight and turn my body fully in her direction. "New Hope."

"What about it?"

Beads of sweat prickle my hairline. "Would you consider taking over the orphanage and replacing Director Wu ... like immediately?"

A flicker of shock causes Julia's eyes to double in size. "You're kidding, right?"

"No." I take a deep breath and quickly relay the Board's decision and demands to continue funding.

"So, they want her to step down, and you think I'm the best person to replace her?"

"I know it may sound crazy—"

"May?" Julia throws her head back. "How about it does?"

I hold my hands up. "I understand why you think that, but you, better than anyone, know that no one is going to take that position because of the difficulties it's faced recently. Almost every Chinese person will see it as a bad omen, even though we both know that's not the case."

"True, but why me? Why not you?"

"Because for the foreseeable future, my focus needs to be on my family, or the one I'm trying to make. If we find out that Lei Ming isn't the missing child, then she and Ben need to be my priority."

"That's admirable of you, and I applaud you for putting family first, but Nicki, I'm not sure I'm the best person for the job."

"Why not?" I scrunch my nose. "You've practically been doing it these last few years at Mother's Love. You know the ins and outs of running an orphanage, so training wouldn't take long, and sorry, but being one means you understand what these kids need more than anything."

"You're right, I do have a heart for orphans, and hearing Nian Zhen talk about those kids being taken from their families and put up for adoption tore me up inside. As an orphan, you live believing you aren't wanted, but in their cases, that's simply not true."

"See, you have what the position needs—a deep passion for those kids. And I have no doubt you would do an incredible job." I bump her shoulder. "Of course, I'll do what I can from the States to assist you, and I know the director would be happy to guide you as well."

She twists her mouth. "Can I think about it? I would need to pray first and see if it's what God would have me to do. And I have to admit Nian Zhen's insights have been weighing heavily on my heart and mind."

"Absolutely, but remember, time is not on our side here. The Board gave me a deadline of six weeks to get someone in place, and there isn't much time left."

"As soon as I feel confident in what I should do, I will let you —"

The door to the station flies open, and an older gentleman dressed in a forest-green uniform saunters across the threshold. After speaking with his inferior, he stomps toward us.

"Nĭ hăo." He stands ramrod straight, his hands behind his back.

Julia and I peel ourselves up off the chairs. "Nĭ hăo."

His charcoal eyes study us intently before he addresses Julia in Chinese.

The two converse for several minutes before Julia turns back to me. "He says he can't help us because they don't get involved in these types of cases."

"That doesn't make any sense." My stomach clenches. "Why aren't the police investigating a possible child abduction?"

Julia spins back around and rattles off more Mandarin at the Commander.

His face grows a deep shade of red, and he spits out a few more words before storming off to his desk.

"What did you say?" I watch him as he flings his hat onto his desktop.

"I told him that I knew for a fact there was a missing child from this village, and we would find out one way or another, so he might as well tell us what he knows before we bring in other authorities."

"Did you really?" I knew Julia was courageous, but I didn't think she'd be so bold. Especially with a police officer. Good for her. After having my own run-in with the law, I don't think I could do that.

"I did, and he told me I was pushing my limits." She crosses her arms over her chest. "Then he said it was pointless for us to come because the parents who claim their child was taken don't live here anymore."

"Don't live here? Why would they leave?" I rub my forehead. "Where did they go?"

"Sorry, but he didn't divulge that information."

"Did he at least give you a name? Something we can go on to track them down?"

"No, he wouldn't ..." She retrieves her purse from the chair and loops it over her shoulder. "But in China, it's not uncommon for parents in small villages like this one to go work in a larger city so they can support the family. When they do, they usually leave the children at home with the grandparents."

"So, you think we should locate the grandparents then?"

"Yes, because if we can get their DNA, then that should be

enough to let us know if Lei Ming is a match or not." She heads for the exit and pushes the door open.

"But how are we going to find them? We don't even know who we're looking for." I grab my purse and chase after her.

She waits for me on the sidewalk. "We're just going to ask around. It's a small village, and I'm sure everyone knows each other."

Not certain that it could be that easy, I arch my eyebrow. "But what if they don't want to talk to us because I'm, you know, a Westerner? Or what if they're afraid to talk because of what might happen if they do?" Nian Zhen's words from yesterday sear my mind.

"It's a chance we'll have to take." She places her hands on her hips. "But it's ultimately up to you."

I look up and down the main road and contemplate my options. But there's only one. "Okay, where do we start?"

11

One step decides the outcome.

~ *Chinese Proverb*

I t took most of the night to gather information from different villagers about the Zhongs, the family whose child had been taken, and their address, but we finally obtained the information we needed. Now, all that was left for me to do was secure their DNA this morning and discover what my future holds.

"What's in there?" Julia asks as we quickly scarf down our breakfast in the hotel restaurant.

My eyes follow her chopsticks, which are pointing at my overly stuffed bag in the chair next to me.

"Oh," I draw my backpack onto my lap. "A blanket."

Julia arches her eyebrow. "Why are you carrying a blanket around with you?"

I slowly unzip the upper pocket and remove the soft pink quilt Director Wu had given me before I left on this trip. "The director said this was with Lei Ming when she arrived on New Hope's doorstep a few months ago." My finger traces the tiny white hearts embedded in the fabric.

"She said they hold onto these types of items and give them to the adoptive families once the kids are officially adopted out. I brought it with me so if we did find the family, I could show it to them and that it might—or might not—offer further proof about Lei Ming's connection to them."

"Oh." Julia reaches across the table and brushes her fingers along one of the corners.

"Was anything left when you and Mingyu were dropped off?" I ask.

"No." She pulls her hands back and lowers her chin, which trembles slightly. "There was no note, blanket, or keepsake—just five yuan tucked inside the flap of each of our pants.

"When we got past the age of adopting out, the only thing they had to pass on to us were our finding ads, which are basically clippings from the local newspaper with our gender, the place we were found, and our personal statistics. I have mine and Mingyu's somewhere in my room at Mother's Love, but I don't bother to look at them. They are just terrible reminders that our future was sealed."

I set my fork down. "What do you mean ... sealed?"

Her head pops up. "Finding ads are what orphanages post in a sad attempt to give parents the opportunity to change their minds. Families have sixty days to claim their child. If they don't, then the child becomes a ward of the state. So, when our sixty days were up, that was it for us, whether we were wanted or not."

"I'm sorry." My stomach sinks, listening to her replay her heartbreaking history. "I shouldn't have asked."

"Don't feel bad. It's part of God's plan, and I've learned to accept it."

Every fiber of my being wants to take her at her word, but part of me can't help wondering if being here and learning about her country's past with children may be too much for her. And if it is, how can I possibly expect her to go with me? "If you want, I could find a translator here in town to accompany me to the Zhong house," I suggest.

"What?" Her long, slick ponytail swings from side to side. "Why would you do that?"

"Because I don't want to upset you or conjure up any emotions about your parents or the situation you may have worked so hard to put behind you."

"I appreciate your concern, but God has healed me of that anger and pain, so you don't need to worry. I will be fine." She smiles at me then continues, "But thinking about this situation and what this family must be going through is sad. I can't help but wonder how many other children have been taken from their families, families who truly did want them, only to have them adopted out by people who were clueless to the situation."

"Yeah, I wonder what they would do if they knew the truth," I say. "But I guess they never will."

"Probably not." Julia shrugs her shoulder. "But maybe one day there'll be a way to reunite those kids with their biological parents. It seems like the right thing to do for them, too, don't you think?"

"I do." I tuck the blanket back into my bag. "And that's why Ben and I are going to all this trouble to make sure we aren't adding to the problem. We want to avoid all the heartache a situation like this creates."

"And I think it's great that you are. But if Lei Ming isn't a match to this family, that means their child is still out there somewhere." She places her napkin over her empty plate.

"I guess it's time we find out." I push my chair away from the table, the legs screeching against the floor. "I just hope the odds are in our favor once we know the truth."

Since the village is small, we walk to the Zhongs' house. I enjoy being outdoors in the spring air as trekking through the town gives me a glimpse of rural Chinese life, as well as insight into the place where Lei Ming might have been born. To be honest, I'm not sure how I feel about that just yet. While it would be great to be able to share some of that history and knowledge with her when she's older, if this is truly her birthplace, then I will never get that chance.

I brush aside my momentary fears and force myself to focus on what's in front of me instead.

Unlike most cities in China, where highways are lined with vehicles of every kind, there are only two main roads in Sanji, with very few cars or bikes occupying them. Several local shops are open and offering their wares to people, but as I peek in the window, I see that there isn't much to choose from. As we continue to traverse the village center, I notice large red symbols painted on the sides of the buildings.

"What do those symbols say?" I stop and point to one long stretch of lettering.

Julia halts and studies the writing on the wall. "It says, 'Better to shed a river of blood than birth another child.'"

A cold shiver runs down my spine as the reality of the country's policy over the past forty years hits me in the face. "Is that still a common belief?"

She slowly turns her face toward me. "No, as Nian Zhen said, things are changing, but in remote villages like this, it doesn't happen right away."

Or it seems, even in the past few months, if indeed, that's when Lei Ming was taken.

"Come on." Julia tugs on my shirt sleeve. "Let's keep walking."

We traverse down a few alleyways, where loose chickens and donkeys roam free and provide momentary entertainment.

"Where are we going?" I ask Julia as we pass deteriorating shacks whose lawn décor includes lines of laundry drying out front.

"To the Zhongs', where else?"

"But here?" I study the impoverished surroundings again, my chest aching for the harsh conditions the inhabitants must reside in.

"Remote villages like this don't have stylish houses or

apartments, Nicki." She slows down her pace and squints at the symbols on the concrete walls. "They are either shacks, huts, or cutouts in large buildings. This is normal for a village like this."

I can only nod, my throat logjammed by my Western arrogance and ignorance. Why do I always expect life to be just as it is *back home*? Even if Lei Ming isn't a match for this family, there's a possibility she came from something similar. Rather than be judgmental, I need to be taking it all in so that one day I can give her a proper picture of her heritage.

"This should be the house we're looking for." Julia stops in front of a gray circular opening.

My breakfast churns in my stomach as the reality of the moment dawns on me. The minute we step into the courtyard and announce ourselves and our reasons for being here, I'm putting into motion a chain of events that might change the trajectory of my well-arranged life. For good.

Lord, give me strength and wisdom for what I'm about to do.

Although my emotions swirl within me, I look at my friend and guide and say with as much courage as I can muster, "Let's go in, then."

Julia reaches for my hand and squeezes it before leading us into the courtyard. There are no signs of life except for a skinny, orange tabby cat lounging in the sun and a cast iron pot bubbling over a stack of sticks, saturating the space with the aroma of chicken.

"*Nǐ hǎo,*" Julia calls out.

Within seconds, an elderly woman emerges from the dark recesses of a walled room adjacent to the courtyard. Her tanned, leathery skin wrinkles around her eyes and the corners of her mouth when she smiles and greets us from the doorway. "*Nǐ hǎo.*"

Julia wastes no time and begins to chat with the woman as if they were old friends.

While they exchange pleasantries, I take in the tiny space. In addition to the makeshift stove, there's a small wooden table with four stools next to a laundry line filled with tattered kids' and adult clothing. Several pairs of shoes line up against the wall near the door in adult and children's sizes.

The sight of it causes my heart to race and fill with fear all at the same time. If children live here, then there's a possibility Lei Ming could have been taken from them for violating the country's strict family planning policies, just as Nian Zhen mentioned.

"Nicki, did you hear me?" Julia asks.

I push down my worries and pull my eyes away from the family's personal items and onto my friend. "I'm sorry, what did you say?"

"This is the Zhong residence." She pushes up her glasses. "According to the grandmother, they still haven't found their granddaughter, although many people have claimed to know where she is or said they have her."

"Would she be willing to answer some questions for us about her grandchild's disappearance?"

Julia quickly rattles off more words in Mandarin before answering. "Yes. She'll go get her husband so we can all talk out here."

My eyes shift from my friend toward our hostess. I nod and smile at her willingness to visit with us. She reciprocates before rushing back inside the house.

Once she's out of my range of vision, I turn back to Julia to ask her if the woman mentioned anything else that might be useful about her possible connection to Lei Ming. But before the words escape my lips, a loud commotion erupts inside the house.

Julia and I crane our necks inside the doorway for a better look. Less than a minute later, the grandmother returns, her face red and sweaty. Squatting like she's in a game of tug and war, she pulls the grandfather into the doorway and out into the courtyard.

"Nǐ hǎo," I say, hoping that might help calm the situation.

The old man mumbles something under his breath. I'm not

sure what he said, but it's clear from his tone he's not happy to be included in the conversation. Or at the sight of a Westerner in his yard. He jerks his arm from his wife's hand and stomps off in the direction of the table.

The grandmother follows behind him, wiping her forehead and waving at us to join them.

Once we're settled around the wobbly table, Julia and the grandmother pick up where they left off.

Clueless to the words flying between them, I sit back in my chair and observe the grandfather marching around the table like Joshua circling Jericho. He walks briskly with his hands behind his back, causing him to hunch over and look smaller than he is. I can tell from the grim line of his mouth and occasional snorts he's not happy with the situation unfolding here.

"Their daughter-in-law had twin boys and then became pregnant with another child unexpectedly two years later," Julia informs me when the two women pause to catch their breath. "When the baby was born—a girl—they hid her. They were worried what the local family planning officials might do if they discovered her since they hadn't obtained a birthing permit and already had the maximum number of children allowed under the law."

"That must have been hard. Did the officials find her?"

Julia frowns. "Someone ratted them out when she was a year old. They were fined heavily, and the Family Planning officials ordered the daughter-in-law to be sterilized."

"Sterilized?" I choke back a sob. "Can they really require that?"

"They can, and they do."

I shake my head in disbelief. "I'd heard stories about that, but you never want to believe it could be true."

"Not the best decision my country has ever made." Julia's voice is laced with sadness. "They managed to pay the fine, which was quite steep, but the daughter refused to be sterilized."

My mouth falls open. If I were in the same situation, would I be as willing to stand up for my beliefs and convictions as well? "She must be a very courageous woman."

"Indeed. And because she was determined not to give in, their son and daughter-in-law left for Shanghai, in part to avoid any consequences of her decision and to earn money to pay off any fines that might be levied on them for their defiance," Julia continues, "The children stayed here with the grandparents, which is not uncommon. Most Chinese children are raised by their elders."

The grandmother pours two cups of tea and hands them to us.

"*Xièxie*," I tell her before taking a sip. "What happened after the parents left?"

Julia brings the cup to her lips and drinks the warm green liquid before continuing to fill me in. "Sometime later, the children were playing outside, and someone came by on a motorcycle and took the little girl. They reported it to the local police, but they knew it was the Family Planning officials punishing them for breaking the law by refusing sterilization."

My chest tightens as an unexpected surge of grief rises up within me. I can only imagine the pain that would have caused the family. When I look at the grandmother, tears weave through the wrinkles on her face.

"*Duìbùqǐ*," I whisper my apologies for her suffering.

I shift my attention back to Julia. "What did the police do?"

"Nothing, which, after our visit there yesterday, doesn't surprise me." She frowns. "When the parents returned home and questioned the Family Planning officials, they were told that the baby had already been adopted out and there was nothing they could do to get her back."

"So quickly? Is that even possible?"

"Probably not. It's likely what the officials said to keep the parents from bothering them. That's why the parents started putting up fliers and placing ads on the Internet, hoping to find her. The parents refuse to believe she's been given to another family. They've had a few leads, but nothing has panned out so far."

"Oh." I try to hide my disappointment. "But why did they leave again? Wouldn't they want to stay here in case she was brought back?"

"I'm sure they couldn't afford to stay. There aren't many employment opportunities here for them." She looks around the courtyard. "Parents do what they have to do for their kids, even if it means going away for a while."

Once more, my chest constricts. Although I'm not a parent yet, I understand their reasoning. I imagine there'll be a time when I'll have to do the unthinkable for Lei Ming too. I pray that if and when that time comes, I have the courage I need to do it.

I push down my emotions and refocus on our purpose for being here. "Would they be willing to do a DNA test since the parents aren't here?"

"I can ask." Julia jumps back into her translator position.

As the three of them discuss my request, I survey the courtyard again and spot a familiar pair of eyes peering over the doorframe. I freeze and lock gazes with the youngster staring back at me. It's as if I'm looking directly into Lei Ming's large eyes. I force myself to move and wave as the stare remains fixed on me.

I leap from my chair and toward the child. What does the rest of him look like? Does he have the same round face and chubby cheeks as Lei Ming? In looking upon him, would I know for certain that Lei Ming belongs to this family? And not mine?

My steps quicken to close the gap between us.

Just as I'm about to make contact, a loud racket from behind stops me in my tracks.

I turn to see the grandfather waving his arms and barreling toward me.

"*Li ta yuan dian! Tao li,*" he says repeatedly.

As his frame closes in on me, my gaze shifts toward Julia. I'm hoping she can quickly explain the situation to me before the elderly man overtakes me.

"Nicki!" She races over to my side. "What are you doing?"

"Nothing." I hold out my hands as proof of my innocence. "I just saw someone in the doorway and wanted to see who it was. That's all. What's he saying?"

"He wants you to get away from the door ... and the boy."

"But I was just looking. I wouldn't hurt anyone or anything."

Julia conveys my message, but from the fervent back and forth of his head, I can tell he doesn't trust my intentions.

It takes several minutes for Julia to calm him down and, hopefully, reassure him I don't want to harm anyone. But from his flaring nostrils and menacing growl, I take it her efforts aren't going well.

Waiting for their conversation to end, I peek over my shoulder.

The entryway stands empty.

Heavy-hearted, I return to the heated exchange. "Julia, please tell them I'm sorry. I didn't mean to upset anyone."

She holds up a finger to them and looks at me. "He wants us to leave."

"Leave?" I thrust my head back. "But what about the DNA tests? Will they do it so we can know the truth about Lei Ming?"

"I'm afraid not." She pulls me aside. "Mr. Zhong doesn't trust Westerners and is worried about what you might do with their samples."

"What I would do? You told them why we want to run the test, didn't you?"

"Of course."

Sucker-punched, I step back. "But we need them to help us. It's the only way we can know for sure."

"I can ask—"

I run back to the table where I left my bag.

"Nicki." Julia traipses after me. "They won't take your money."

"I'm not offering them money!" Between my shaking hands and teary eyes, I struggle to open the zipper. When I do, the fuzzy pink blanket escapes from its hiding place.

"*Ta de tanzi!*"

I pop my head up at the grandmother's shrill voice and watch her fall into her husband's arms.

"The blanket," Julia yells before dashing over to help the elderly woman.

I remove the coverlet from my bag and quickly join them, then drop down on the ground where they've moved.

"*Ta de tanzi!*" The grandmother points at my hands. "*Ta de tanzi!*"

"What is she saying?"

"Her blanket." Julia takes it from my hands and holds it out to the couple. "She says the blanket belongs to her granddaughter."

When both grandparents start crying, my heart drops to my stomach. Between the familiar eyes hiding in the doorway and the grandparent's response to the blanket, I'm afraid I might have my answer.

But I have to know for certain.

As they clutch it to their chest and sniff for any evidence of their granddaughter, I stand and gather my strength. "Will you ask if they'll take the test now? Maybe having seen the blanket will change their minds."

Julia nods.

It takes several more rounds of fast-paced back and forth before Julia translates for me. "The grandmother seems willing, but the grandfather said no. He doesn't trust you."

"But I'm only trying to help and get the truth."

"I know, and I tried to explain that to him, but he refuses to change his mind." She rises and wipes the dust from her pants. "We should respect that."

The grandfather pulls his wife back on her feet before

blurting out a few more words. Without giving Julia a chance to reply, he ushers Mrs. Zhong inside.

Watching them leave, I tug on Julia's arm. "Don't let them go."

She places her hand over mine. "I'm sorry, Nicki, but we have to respect their decision. If we don't, we'd be causing them to lose face."

"But the blanket." I stay glued in my spot while she retrieves our belongings.

"Come on." She nudges me toward the courtyard exit. "I can come back later and talk to them again when they've calmed down."

"I can't leave without the blanket."

"I'll ask for it when I return, I promise." She hands me my bag. "But for now, we need to go. I don't want them to make a scene and call the police."

Aware of how that might play out, I quickly follow her lead.

It's not until we're safely back on the sidewalk, a few doors down from their house, that I'm able to talk again. "Now what?"

Julia glances back in the direction of the Zhongs' house. "Let's hope they'll be more open once they've had time to think about it. If not, then I'm afraid ..." She looks at me with sorrow-filled eyes. "I'm sorry, but I'm afraid we may be at a dead end."

I clench my jaw. "No, just an end."

"What do you mean?"

I take a deep breath. "If you come back later and they still aren't willing to give us solid proof that Lei Ming and their granddaughter aren't one and the same, then I'm not going to put my life on hold any longer."

"I don't understand." She rubs her temple. "Are you saying you're not going to keep looking for the parents?"

"Yes." I lower my head and pound the dirt with my shoe. "I'm sorry for what happened to them, and I'm trying to do the right thing here, but if they won't cooperate, what other choice do I have?"

"You're right. You've done more than most people would, but I know you, Nicki, and I think not having the truth will bother you in time."

"You're right." I press my lips together and grimace. "Without solid evidence, there will always be a part of me that will wonder what if, especially since we didn't get the chance to ask if their granddaughter had a heart condition. But I can't force them to do anything, and clearly, they don't want to, so I'll do the only thing I can do."

"Which is?"

I square my shoulders and hoist up my backpack. "If they won't help us get the proof we want, then I'm heading home and starting my family."

12

Sweeping off the dust and trying again.
~ Chinese Proverb

S HE'S OURS!!
Waiting in the New Hope lobby, I reread the text I sent
Ben last night.

I wasn't sure I would ever be able to type those words, but
when Julia returned from the Zhongs' yesterday afternoon
without the blanket or the requested DNA samples, I had to
stay true to my decision.

There is no point in putting our lives on hold any longer. I'm
ready to do whatever it takes to make this unconventional family
of ours a reality as soon as possible. And that starts with
discussing the next steps with Ben this morning—while spending
some quality time with our soon-to-be-daughter.

"Hey there, global traveler," Ben whispers in my ear.

I spin around in my chair at the familiar voice and hint of
woodsy cologne. "Ben!" Without thinking, I jump into his arms.

"If this is the kind of reception I get when you leave and
come back, maybe you should travel more often."

I ignore his quip and squeeze him tight.

"Is something wrong?" He leans back and scrutinizes me. "Is Lei Ming okay?"

"She's better than okay." I smile so big it hurts my cheeks. "She's ours!"

"I read that last night, but you didn't explain much, so I wasn't sure exactly how to interpret it."

My joy overflows. "It means we've done our due diligence and did everything we could to make sure we weren't adopting a baby that someone was looking for. Now there are no more obstacles standing in our way, and we can do what we wanted to do since we came up with this crazy idea." I bounce on my toes. "We can start our family!"

"I'm glad to hear it. Fill in the blanks for me?"

I bend down and grab his lanyard from the chair and wrap it around his neck. "I'll tell you everything on our way to the Recovery Unit."

Arm in arm, we stroll down the maze of hallways to the medical area where Lei Ming is still receiving care. As we do, I tell Ben everything that happened in Fujian province during our whirlwind trip. I don't leave out any details, including the Chinese propaganda spray painted on the side of the building and Julia's last-ditch effort to get the elderly Zhongs to supply us with more information. Either their DNA or the contact info for their children.

"And they wouldn't give it to her?" Ben rakes his hand through his hair.

"No. Julia could tell that the grandmother wanted to help us, but the grandfather was convinced I was a Westerner up to no good. Despite me offering up what could very well be their granddaughter's blanket, they refused to cooperate."

"You let them keep her blanket?"

"I didn't intend to." I wince, thinking about losing what might be Lei Ming's only connection to her past. "But they took it inside and demanded I leave. When Julia went back later to ask them one more time to help us, they refused to return the blanket and threatened to call the police on her."

He stops in the middle of the hallway. "So, you feel as if we've explored every option out there and feel good about moving forward with our plans?"

"Yes. I mean, what more can we do? We did everything we could, and it led to a dead end. I feel bad for that family and what they've had to go through, but if they aren't willing to provide what we need to verify that Lei Ming is or is not their child, then we are free to move on with our lives." My breath hitches. "You still want that, don't you?"

"Of course, more than anything." Ben inches closer to me and takes my hands in his. "I just want to be one hundred percent certain you're going to be okay without any concrete evidence. That you won't always be looking over your shoulder or questioning if we didn't do enough."

While I knew there might be moments when fear might rear its ugly head and tempt me to travel down that road, there really wasn't any way the Zhongs could change their minds and track us down. I hadn't given them any information that would lead them here to us. We were safe. And so was our future. I was certain of it.

I stand on my tiptoes and kiss him on the cheek. "You don't need to worry about me. I'll be fine. All that matters is that the three of us are together now. We've overcome the worse, and now it's time for the better, wouldn't you agree?"

"I do." He chuckles. "And I mean that in more ways than one."

When we enter the Recovery Unit, I spot Lei Ming sitting up in her crib, playing with the bear I'd bought for her at the hospital gift store. I rush to pick her up. Unlike last time, however, she doesn't cry at my embrace. Instead, she smiles at our presence and runs her stubby fingers through my curls.

"I think she knows everything's okay now too."

Ben rubs her back. "Maybe she does."

A nurse sidles up to us and begins talking in rapid Mandarin. My eyes flit to Ben for translation.

"She says now that Lei Ming's no longer connected to all the wires and cords, we can take her outside for some fresh air. But just for a little while. They don't want her to get too worn out."

"Really?" My heart thumps wildly. Finally, things are going our way. "What are we waiting for?"

The morning sun breaks through the thick haze that constantly shrouds the city and bathes us in warmth and light. We alternate between carrying Lei Ming and letting her walk, each of us holding onto one of her hands as she tries to regain her muscle strength and coordination.

"I guess we'll have to wait until later this evening to call our moms and reassure them we're still good to go." Ben looks down at Lei Ming, who stops to study a rock on the sidewalk.

"Yes, I've been so vague with all their questions lately. I'm afraid they may have had some doubts about whether we'd go through with this. But now I don't have to be." I wink. "In fact, I'm going to ask them to move things up a few weeks. That should calm any fears they might have been having."

Ben's head pops up. "Move things up? Why would we do that?"

"Because we don't need to wait the whole month now." I bend down and remove the rock from Lei Ming's hand before she swallows it. "As soon as I get things wrapped up at New Hope with the director's position—and I think I've found the person the Board will approve—we can head home and get married right away."

"Except we can't."

"What do you mean?" I stand up and lock eyes with him. "You said you still wanted to move ahead with our plans, so what's stopping us?"

"My new job." He blinks.

"A job?"

"Yes, here. In Beijing."

"When? Where? How?" I shuffle backward. "And why didn't you say something earlier?"

"It all happened so fast I've barely had time to make sense of it all myself, and, of course, the news about our daughter took precedence."

Lei Ming takes a few more steps ahead of us and sits down on the grass, momentarily bringing our conversation to a halt. We amble over to her and crouch down beside her. She giggles as she pulls clumps of greenery from the dirt and lets the wind carry it from her hands.

"In fact, I just found out last night at church." He manages a half-smile. "You're looking at the new interim pastor of the International Christian Fellowship."

"P-pastor?" I gulp. "I don't understand. A few weeks ago, you told me that wasn't your calling."

"It's not, but it was the only option available for me to remain in the country before my 144-hour visa expires." The muscles in his jaw tighten. "If things had worked out differently with the Zhongs, I would have needed to stay. So, I jumped at the first opportunity I had."

While I appreciate all his efforts to find employment that would allow him to be here with me, I can't deny I'm disappointed. Now that we can finally become a family, it seems like it's going to take forever to actually bring it to pass. But I guess I just have to remind myself that at least there will be a wedding, even if it isn't as soon as I'd like.

"No, you're right, it was the only option, and I'm grateful you can stay here with me—I mean, us." I brush my hand over the crown of Lei Ming's head. "I still need to finish up here at New Hope anyway, so now there's not so much pressure." I bite my lip. "But how long do you think it will be until they find a full-time pastor?"

"I'm not sure." He shrugs his shoulders. "But I told them I'd be willing to stay at least three or four weeks."

"That long?" I arch my eyebrows.

"I know you're anxious to put all this behind us and move on with our family. I want that too. But I'm a man of my word, and when I make a commitment, I follow through."

I did know that about Ben. And I was certainly the beneficiary of that character trait. It was only right that the church was too. "That's one of the things I lo—" I catch myself before saying more and cough. "One of the things I admire most about you."

"Then you know I have to stay the for the time they've asked me to fill in unless, of course, they find someone sooner."

"I do." I lift Lei Ming into my arms. Even though I would have liked to head back right away, it wouldn't be fair of me to ask Ben to get a job to stay in the country, have him do it, then tell him to ditch it because of my personal desires. "I can use the extra time to make sure New Hope is on solid footing, we can spend more time with this little girl, and maybe I can try and convince our mothers to lose the fancy wedding hats."

"Thank you." He inches closer and wraps both Lei Ming and me in his large arms.

Standing there together, everything feels right. The way it's supposed to.

"Nicki." Ben's fatherly voice brings me back to reality. "We should get Lei Ming inside. I think she might be getting cold."

"Really?" I look down at Lei Ming's face and see that there's a slightly blue hue to her lips. "We should get her back inside so the doctor can take a look at her. That's what happened right before she needed surgery last time." My heart beats faster.

"Don't let your motherly instincts go into overdrive, Nicki." He reaches for Lei Ming, who happily falls into his arms. "She's just cold, that's all. I'll keep her wrapped up tight, and you'll see she'll be fine."

Empty-handed, a shiver courses through me, and I realize he might be right. It is cool out today.

"After we get her inside and warmed up, we can look for a

quiet place to talk and plan out our next steps," I say as we stroll back toward the building.

"There's nothing more I'd love to do than spend more time with you right now." He glances at his watch. "But I need to head back into the city before church starts. You know, my job and all."

"Yeah, right, your job." I lilt my voice higher to mask any disappointment that might betray me. "Of course, we can catch up later."

He snaps his fingers. "I've got an idea."

"I'm listening."

"How about we head over to Gubei for an evening canal ride? We can talk all night if you want. I'm all yours."

A flash of adrenaline rushes through me. "You mean ... like a date?"

"Yes, it could be our first official one."

Funny. I'm ready to marry this man, but the idea of a date throws me for a loop. What if spending one-on-one time together highlights the fact that we may *not* be a perfect match? Then what?

The only way to know for sure is to take him up on his offer.

"Okay, what time should I be expecting you?"

LIKE ONLY PRINCE CHARMING COULD, Ben arrives at my hotel room exactly on time to whisk me away for a magical evening.

"Where are we going?" I ask as our driver speeds out of the city.

"Gubei Water Town." Ben flashes a bright smile at me. "Also known as the Asian Venice. It's a nearby canal town that's supposed to be very quaint, cozy, and romantic, so I thought it would be an ideal spot for our first date."

Once again, my insides quiver at the monumental occasion

this is. "Don't you think it's a little strange to be going on a date? I mean, we are going to be married soon."

He shakes his head. "I don't think so. We've been on the fast track of life lately, and now that things are settled, we can slow down and enjoy each other's company without all the stress."

A comforting thought and one I hope will come to fruition. But if that's the case, why am I a basket of nerves?

Ben taps my shoulder. "Hey, what's going on in that pretty head of yours?"

Heat rushes to my face at his compliment. "Don't get me wrong. I'm really looking forward to everything you have planned, but what if, after spending time together, we discover we don't have that much in common? That the other isn't what we thought they would be? What would that mean for our future?"

"Nicki, calm down." His eyes hold my gaze. "It will be fine. This isn't some TV reality show where we get voted off if things don't work out at the end of the evening. It's simply two people who've spent the last few weeks going from one crisis to another, who already like each other, spending quality time together. There's absolutely no pressure." He grins. "No matter what happens tonight, I promise I'll call you tomorrow. And the next day. And the next."

I burst out laughing. "Thank you, that's reassuring."

"Good." He reaches for my hand and intertwines our fingers. "It's going to be a great first date, you'll see."

We spend the hour-long drive playing Never Have I Ever.

I start us out. "Never Have I Ever …"

"Gone snow skiing," Ben replies.

"And I haven't ridden a horse." I wink. "But I have a feeling that's going to change."

"Never Have I Ever …"

I tilt my head and try to think of something that will really shock him. "Never Have I Ever … dated someone for longer than a year."

Ben's eyes grow big. "Really?"

"Yep, which means that you'll be my first long-term relationship."

"I gladly accept the position." He grins.

"Your turn," I quickly say, ready to avoid any more discussion about my lackluster romance life.

"O-kay." He rubs his chin. "Never Have I Ever ... shopped at The Container Store."

I stiffen my spine. "Looks like I'll have to wait for another Prince Charming to reach long-term relationship status with then because that may very well be a deal breaker."

It's a relaxing way for us to pass the time and learn about one another in a fun way. Once the driver brings the car to a halt and opens the door for me, my earlier worries about being compatible have fluttered away like leaves in the wind. If this were all the night entailed, that would have been satisfying enough for me.

As the sun bids farewell to another day, leaving streaks of pink, yellow, and purple in its wake, we trek up a small hill for a panoramic view of the city. From there, we can see the twinkling lights of the houses and waterways, as well as those along the Great Wall just beyond the town.

Goosebumps pebble my flesh as darkness envelops us, and the bridges alight in succession, carving a path through the homes and buildings. In the distance, a large pagoda stands erect as if keeping watch over the city and its inhabitants.

We don't talk much as the night begins its reign, each of us mesmerized by the enchanting transformation unfolding before our eyes. I only wish I had a way to capture the memory, but we'd left our phones in the car to avoid any distractions.

"Have you been here before?" I ask, shattering the silence that's slipped between us.

"No, I haven't." Ben keeps his gaze fixed on the scenery below. "I'd heard about it, but I never found the time or the right person to visit with." He flicks his eyes in my direction. "I'm glad I finally do, though."

"Me too."

"Good, because in addition to offering you this spectacular view, I have something else for you." He reaches into his jean pocket and pulls out the ring he fashioned out of a twist tie at my mother's house. "I've been waiting to give this to you, and now seems appropriate." He takes my left hand and slides the homemade jewelry onto my shaky finger.

I study the thin wire metal encased in red. It's too big for my finger and, like the journey we've been on lately, slightly frayed from Ben carrying it around all this time. But I don't care. It's beautiful.

"Thank you." I hold up my hand and admire it as if it were a priceless jewel. "I'm not sure we'll ever find something that can compare to this, but I'll wear it and cherish it until we do."

"Actually, it's 'I do,'" he jokes. "You may want to practice that for the next few weeks to make sure you get it right during the ceremony."

"Ha-ha, very funny." I poke his ribs.

We walk hand in hand back down the hill to the main city center. There, the town is alive with street vendors, food stalls, and people of all ages loitering about. We munch on local cuisine —tasty meat, veggies, and rice—before queuing for a boat ride.

"So, how would you rate our date so far?" Ben asks as we wait for our Chinese version of a gondola.

"Hmm ..." I tap my index finger against my lips. "So far, I'd say an eight, but we still have this trip down the canal, and depending on how that goes, it could take you up to a ten or bump you down a notch or two."

He covers his heart with his hands. "I'm hurt you would question my nautical skills."

The line inches forward.

"Do you have any?" I chuckle.

"No, but how hard can it be?"

A young boy waves to us, indicating that our ride is ready.

"We'll see." I step out from behind the rope and walk toward the attendant, who holds out his hand so I can hop on.

After Ben and the kid converse for a few minutes, either Ben asking for help or the boy giving him firm instructions on what not to do, we take off down the slow-moving waterway.

I watch as Ben glides the small boat through the canal. He effortlessly rows it under the perfectly arched bridges and around guided tour vessels fighting for their space on the water. When we come to an open stretch of the canal where not too many people have ventured, Ben locks the oars in place and tilts his head up to the skies.

"Amazing, isn't it?" He points up at the stars that twinkle in the surprisingly haze-free sky.

I lift my eyes to the heavens and take in the view. "It is. Hard to believe you can actually see anything up there. I guess that's what you get when you go away from the city a bit."

"Yeah, it's breathtaking." Ben gentles his voice. "All of God's creation is, but when you stop and take it all in like this, you realize how small you are and how big God truly is."

Lowering my head, I stop and study Ben. I see nothing but admiration and awe on his face as his gaze stays affixed on the vastness of the sky and the Maker behind it. And while our date up to this point has been fun, listening to Ben talk, I worry a small fissure might be forming.

Although I believe in God and have put my trust in Christ, I know my faith is not as strong as Ben's. Could that be an issue for us moving forward? Especially now that he's pastoring a church and might want to continue doing so? "Ben, can I ask you something?"

He ceases his sky-watching and turns his attention to me. "Yes, of course, anything."

I shift my weight on the small bench, causing the boat to rock a little more than I'm comfortable with. "Are you sure you're not called to be a pastor?"

"What?" His head jerks back. "Where is that coming from?"

"I'm just curious, that's all."

"Not exactly the question I was expecting."

"Yeah, a little strange." I lean forward. "But I would need to know if it's something you might want to pursue later on. You know ... after we're married."

"Honestly, I can't say." He rakes his hand through his hair. "Preaching this morning was fulfilling, but I can't confirm one way or the other right now. I haven't had time to give it much thought or prayer. Why are you asking?"

"I'm just not sure ..." I swallow hard. "I'm just not sure that I would be good pastor's wife material. If that's what you were called to do, I don't know where that would leave us."

Ben slowly rises from his seat and shuffles over to me. "Come here." He holds out his hands and invites me to stand with him.

Trembling, I place my hands in his and join him.

The boat shakes from side to side but doesn't threaten to spit us out.

"Nicki Mayfield, I don't think you give yourself enough credit. You would make a great pastor's wife. I mean, you've shown so much persistence and courage these past few weeks. I have no doubt what you've learned about yourself and your faith would be an encouragement to multitudes of women." He tucks a stray hair behind my ear.

"But I don't think pastoring a church is my full-time calling right now, and if that were to ever change, it would be something I pray God would put on your heart as well so we could move forward together. Because, like it or not, we're a team now."

My breath hitches at his words. We are a team. And soon, we'll be a family.

As our lips are about to touch, a tour boat speeds past us, sending our bodies flailing in opposite directions.

Before I go flying into the cold, dark waters, I'm able to balance myself and cling to the edge of the boat.

"Are you okay?" Ben steadies himself with one of the oars.

What's more upsetting? Not getting to kiss him or being rattled by the water's wake?

"I will be." I push my torso up off the side and resume my position on the bench, which is on the opposite end of the boat. A football field away from Ben. And his lips. "You?"

"I'm good."

When his voice doesn't offer me a clue to how he feels about our almost-kiss, I take that as a sign it wasn't meant to be. "Maybe we need to take this ship back to the harbor before the waters overtake us," I say, deflated that our magical moment has passed and unable to be recaptured anytime soon.

"Aye, aye, Captain." Ben salutes me and begins rowing.

Only when we're back on dry land and returning to the car are we finally able to laugh about the entire situation.

"The look on your face." Ben clutches his stomach. "You were as white as a ghost."

"Well, you weren't the picture of cool, calm, and collected either. For just a second, I thought I saw some fear flash in those pretty green eyes of yours."

We're still in giggle mode when we slide into the backseat of the car, and our driver heads back to Beijing.

"Too bad we didn't have our phones with us." I pull mine from my purse and turn it on. "It was a night I never will forget, and I only wish I'd had a way to capture the expression on your face when we were almost catapulted off the boat. That was priceless."

"Well, I guess you'll just have to recall it from memory when you tell our kids about it one day."

Did he say kids? As in more than one?

Before I can ask him to clarify what he meant, my screen lights up, displaying a long list of text messages and missed calls.

"You're quite popular." Ben winks. "Guess I'm glad we left our phones after all. That way, I had you all to myself."

Although it looked like I was in high demand, there were really only two people trying to reach me repeatedly. Darlene and Julia. I quickly scan Darlene's texts, where words like caviar, chocolate fountain, ice sculpture, and reception float past me.

However, there are no messages from Julia—just calls.

"Would you mind if I called Julia really quick?" I ask. "We discussed something rather important yesterday, and I'm hoping she's reaching out to let me know her decision. If it's not the answer I'm looking for, I'll have my work cut out for me tomorrow."

"Sounds serious. Don't let me stand in the way."

I tap on her missed call notification and bring the phone to my ear.

"Nicki." She answers on the first ring. "I've been anxious to talk to you."

"Sorry, Ben and I were out." I smile at Ben. "On a date."

"Oh, my apologies for interrupting."

"It's fine. We're heading back now. What's up?"

She inhales deeply. "I'm afraid I have some bad news."

I lower my head. I guess she's decided not to take over for Director Wu after all. Looks like I'm back to square one. "Julia, I understand your hesitancy about not wanting to take the position, but I do think you are the right person for the—"

"It's not that, Nicki. It's something else." She pauses. "The Zhongs phoned me."

"They called you?" My pulse races. "How did they even have your number?"

"I left it with the grandmother in case she wanted to return the blanket." Her voice is laced with guilt.

"Oh." While I want to believe in my heart of hearts that the grandmother was only reaching out to obtain my address, I have a sinking suspicion it's not. "What did she want?"

"It wasn't the grandmother who called, Nicki. It was her son."

Removing the phone from my ear, I place the call on speaker so Ben can hear. He'll want to be part of this conversation. "You mean the father of the missing child? He's the one who phoned you?" My mouth goes dry.

"Yes."

"What exactly did he want?" Ben asks before I can.

"He and his wife want to provide DNA samples." She hesitates slightly. "After seeing a photo of her blanket, they believe Lei Ming is their daughter."

13

The trees prefer calm, but the wind does not stop.
~ *Chinese Proverb*

Rather than have the Zhongs come to Beijing and within such close proximity to Lei Ming, Ben and I offered to visit them in Shanghai. That way, we can gather their samples at a lab of our choosing and guarantee there won't be any issues receiving the results, finally putting this nightmare to rest once and for all.

Between making late-night arrangements to travel to Shanghai on Thursday—the earliest we could leave because of Ben's preaching and job responsibilities—and worrying about the discussion with Director Wu I can no longer avoid, I can't sleep for more than an hour or two. Add in a workout from tossing and turning while processing it all, and I stumble catatonic into New Hope the next morning, thanks to my brain's refusal to switch off.

While I'm in no condition to be undertaking such an important task, I need to inform the director of the Board's ultimatum, as well as the limited timeline in which to find a suitable replacement. Julia hasn't provided me with an answer one way or the other, leaving me no choice but to break the news to Director Wu today, regardless of how she might take it.

"Good morning," I say with as much enthusiasm as I can muster when I enter her office.

"Nicki, you look terrible." She steps out from behind her desk and greets me.

"Thanks." I pat my hair and try to remember if I actually fixed it or not this morning. From the gentle way Director Wu brushes my curls away from my face, I probably hadn't.

The director scrunches her nose. "And why do I smell coffee on your breath?"

I shake the thermos in my hand. "Because I've been attempting to drink it without the help of milk or sugar for the last hour."

"But you don't like coffee."

"I have to get through the day somehow. I didn't sleep much last night."

"I can tell."

She takes the thermos from me and sets it on the corner of her desk, which is surprisingly clean.

"Have a seat. I know something that will infuse you with the strength you need."

From the tenderness that fills her eyes, I know she's not referring to a strong alcoholic drink or a magic elixir. No, her answer is only found in the heavenly realm.

Prayer.

I drop in the seat and bury my head in my hands, thankful to have her intercede for and with me. Standing over me, she lays her hands on my shoulders and then speaks in her native tongue, the words tumbling beautifully from her mouth.

Although I have no clue as to what she's saying, the soft cadence of her voice soothes my spirit. It also draws me into a sense of worship. Something I've struggled with these past few weeks as my life has been a tilt-o-wheel of sorts.

She squeezes my shoulder and says, "Amen."

"Thank you," I lift my head, a sense of lightness immediately overtaking me.

"You're welcome, dear." She flashes a grandmotherly smile at me. "Never underestimate the power of prayer in any situation."

"You sound like my mother."

"She seems like someone I'd like to meet." She takes a seat next to me. "Maybe one day I'll have the pleasure."

"She'd love that, as would I."

The Director narrows her eyes. "Now, why don't you tell me what has you so bothered?"

I rub my thumb into the palm of my other hand before quickly bringing her up to speed on the roller coaster ride Ben and I have been on these past few days as well as our current situation with the younger Zhongs. When I finally finish retelling that fiasco, I force myself to discuss my reason for being here in the first place. "And then there's New Hope."

"What about it?"

"Well, you're aware that I met with the O'Connor Foundation when I was back in the States, correct?"

"You touched on it lightly when you and Ben came to my house. However, you seemed hesitant to talk about it at the time. I'm assuming you have something you need to share with me?"

I cringe and search for the gentlest words I can find to deliver the blow. "They want ... no, they've requested ... I mean, they would like the orphanage to be run by someone other than you."

"I see." She runs her fingers over her pearl necklace. "I can't say I'm all that surprised, really. I'm not completely innocent in what happened with AD Chang. And I've told you before it might be time for me to step down anyway." She removes her hand from her favorite piece of jewelry. "Plus, the way Victoria has been glued to my side around here lately, well, let's just say I'm not enjoying my work all that much."

"You're not upset then?"

"With you? No." She winks at me. "But as for my position, I have to believe it's for the best. As it says in Ecclesiastes, there is a season for everything, and perhaps my season as New Hope's director has come to an end." She eyes me over the top of her glasses. "I only wish you wouldn't have been afraid to speak with me about this. With everything else you have going on, I'm sure it must have been a heavy burden for you to carry."

"I wanted to tell you." I squirm in my seat. "But honestly, I was scared. I know how much you love this place and these children. It felt like telling you would rob you of something you hold near and dear to your heart. I didn't want to do that."

"I appreciate you thinking of me like that, Nicki, but I'm an old woman who has seen many things, both good and bad, in my life. Trust me when I say this is not the worst." She retreats to the chair behind her desk. "So, what needs to be done now?"

"We need to find your replacement. Fast. The Board wants someone new at the helm in a matter of weeks."

"How many weeks exactly?"

I quickly calculate how much time has passed since my unpleasant meeting with the powers that be until today. "Four weeks."

"That doesn't give us much time, does it? I mean to post the job opening, take applications, hold interviews, and then do the required background checks and training. I'm not sure it's feasible." She sighs. "And I assume that if we don't meet the Board's timeline, our funding is at stake."

I nod.

"Then I don't think the normal way of hiring someone is the route for us."

"Probably not. And with as much trouble as New Hope has faced recently, I doubt many people would apply for the job anyway. Bad luck and all."

A small chuckle escapes from under her breath. "Yes, the Chinese can be quite superstitious."

"In fact, I was thinking ..." I perch on the edge of my seat.

"Perhaps it might be better if we looked for a replacement within the circles we know? People whom we think might be a good fit to replace you?"

"Do you have anyone particular in mind?"

"Actually, I've already asked Julia to consider taking over. With her background and experience working at Mother's Love, I think she'd be perfect for the job."

The director's eyebrows rise to the top of her hairline. "Has she indicated whether or not she's interested?"

"Not yet. She's praying about it."

"She's definitely a possibility, but I think there might be someone even better suited for the position."

"You do? Who?" Beads of sweat prickle the back of my neck. Not just anyone can run New Hope. It would require someone with a special heart and understanding to steer this ship into the future.

"I think *you* would be the perfect person to replace me."

"Me?" I gasp. Now I know how Julia must have felt when I broached the subject with her the other day.

"Yes. I believe you'd do a superb job, and I know Ms. O'Connor would approve."

Tears well up in the corner of my eyes. There isn't anything I wouldn't do for my former boss but running New Hope isn't the call of my heart. My priority is the family Ben and I are creating together. And if this last hurdle proves to be nothing more than a blip on the radar, we'll be well on our way.

"I appreciate the offer, but trust me when I say I'm not the person for the job. As much as I love your country, your people, your food, and this orphanage, I have to return home. With or without a family, staying here just isn't possible for me."

"I understand, but you had to know I would ask."

"That you think that highly of me means a lot, but I can probably do more for New Hope if I'm not here."

Director Wu tilts her head. "How so?"

"Heather has offered me a position at the Foundation, and it might help if I'm part of the system." My confidence rises. "I can be an advocate for the orphanage and ensure it gets the money it needs to keep doing the work Mr. O'Connor, and even Ms. O'Connor, envisioned."

"It would definitely be a detriment to our efforts if we lost the Board's financial support. Without it, New Hope would have no choice but to seek other sources of funding, and they would likely insist on having one of their people in charge." The corner of her mouth dips.

"You mean the government?" My tone comes out a bit too harshly. While I don't mean any disrespect, I know they will choose anyone available and not necessarily the best fit. Certainly not someone whose heart beats for these children like Director Wu's.

Or who would want to see Lei Ming in my arms should I be blessed with that?

"Let's just pray it doesn't get to that point. God is keenly aware of what we need, and I have no doubt He will bring the right person along."

Rapid knocking on the door interrupts our conversation.

"Excuse me, Nicki." The director rises and shuffles to admit whoever is so desperate to enter.

When I see the lobby receptionist at the door and not one of the Recovery Unit nurses, I relax and loosen my coiled muscles.

The two women exchange words for several minutes before Director Wu shuts the door and turns back toward me. When she does, her complexion is pale, and deep worry lines are etched between her eyebrows.

"What's wrong?" My pulse races. "Is it Lei Ming?"

"Yes and no." She returns to the chair behind her desk.

"I don't understand. How is it both? Either it is, or it isn't."

"I'm sorry to be so vague, but I just received some startling news."

I grip the armrests. "Why? Has she had a relapse?" She

seemed to be doing well yesterday when we were with her, but with her condition, there were never any guarantees.

"Nothing's wrong with her per se." She blinks rapidly. "Medically, she's fine."

I release my white-knuckled fingers from the chair and cover my heart with both hands. "Good. As long as she's okay, I can handle anything else." I exhale. "Then what's the matter?'

She locks eyes with me, and the intensity of her gaze causes my stomach to do somersaults.

"Director, what is it?" I ask more sternly, out of both fear and impatience.

"It seems we have some unexpected visitors."

I rack my brain trying to determine who she might be referring to, but I can't come up with anyone. "Who?"

"Well." She clears her throat. "It seems that the parents you arranged to meet in Shanghai didn't want to wait until Thursday to confirm whether or not Lei Ming might be their daughter. They're here to give their DNA samples."

Sucker-punched, I push back in my seat. "The Zhongs? They're here, at New Hope?"

"It seems so."

My mind whirrs at the news. How is this even possible? When Ben spoke to them on the phone last night, they said they would meet us at the airport Thursday morning. Why have they suddenly changed their minds?

"That's not all," she says, interrupting my stream of thought.

I look back up at her. "What?" I grip the armrest once more in an effort to brace myself. I'm not certain my heart can take many more surprises these days.

"They've asked to see Lei Ming."

"They want ... to see her?" I ask, making sure I understood her correctly and praying that I didn't.

"According to the receptionist, that's what they said."

"Can they do that?"

The director clasps her hands together and places them on

top of her desk. "I've never been in this situation before, so I'm not even sure what to make of their request myself. Since they did not respond to the finding ad we placed for Lei Ming within sixty days, they technically have no rights to her at all. It's solely my discretion."

I purse my lips and attempt to digest all the information that's been thrown at me like sharp daggers. Last night we had everything perfectly arranged. And even though I wasn't happy about waiting, I could handle that. But now that everything's been turned upside down once more, I'm not sure I'm up to the challenge.

"Nicki?" Director Wu waves her hand in front of my face.

I flinch. "Yes, I hear you. I'm just trying to wrap my brain around it all."

"It is complicated."

"You can say that again." It seems like ever since Ben and I made the decision to go through all of this, we've faced nothing but obstacles at every turn. Was that a sign we'd made a mistake? Had we misheard or misunderstood God's will for us in this?

I look down at the red thread wrapped around my wrist. I have to believe that if we are truly meant to be with Lei Ming, then even in the face of all these challenges and setbacks, we'll still be together somehow. God would see to it.

"So, what are you going to do?" I ask.

"What do you mean?"

"Are you going to let them see her?"

She wrings her hands together. "As I said, I've never been in this position before. However, I want to do what's best for everyone involved. And that includes you."

My eyes widen. "You're asking me what I want?"

"I am."

"Hmmm, I'm not sure what to say." I bite down on my lip. "I mean, part of me wants to protect Lei Ming until we have solid proof of exactly who she is, but then there's a part of me that feels for this couple and the terrible time they must be going through as they search for their daughter."

"As I said, it's complicated, but I want to make sure, whatever I decide, your feelings and thoughts are considered."

My heart swells for admiration for this woman even more. By all accounts, she doesn't need my input or to even worry about my emotions. If I weren't a factor in any of this, her Christian faith would guide her, and she'd let them see the child. Not only because it would be the right thing to do but because doing so might solidify the truth.

And while I want to do what's right for everyone, I need to discuss it with Ben first. We're a team now, and we need to be in agreement about the decision.

"Before answering their visitation request, can you ask them to go to the lab and give their samples first?"

"Of course, but they're going to want an answer about Lei Ming. What should I tell them?"

I grab my purse and sling it over my shoulder. "I'll let you know as soon as Ben and I are able to decide one way or the other."

14

A sharp stick protrudes.
~ *Chinese Proverb*

U nlike the other times I've been to the International church, the hallway leading to the sanctuary is dark and empty. This time, no baked goods perfume the air, and no raucous laughter fills the space either. Just the sound of my shoes clacking against the tile, resonating in my ears.

"Ben?" I call out, only to have my own answer back.

I glance at my watch and double-check the time. I promised Director Wu we'd let her know our decision within the hour.

"Ben?" I search the foyer one more time for any signs of life.

Finally, I spot one of the heavy double doors leading to the worship center cracked open. Praying that's where I'll find him, I veer in that direction.

The large makeshift auditorium is shrouded in darkness except for one lone spotlight illuminating the stage.

And Ben. Who, I presume, is practicing his sermon for Wednesday night.

Although I'm anxious to speak with him about our unexpected visitors, I'm hesitant to interrupt. From the serious expression on his face, I can tell he is in the zone at the moment, and watching him like this, in his element, is inspiring. Waiting two minutes won't hurt anything, will it?

I wedge through the door's opening and tiptoe inside the auditorium. I watch Ben move in and out of the light as he paces across the stage, my breath hitching every time he teeters too close to the edge. Yet, as if by instinct, he knows just when to pivot back to safety.

Finally, I stop focusing on his movements and listen to his sermon.

"Then the king said, 'Bring me a sword' ... he then gave an order: 'Cut the living child in two and give half to one and half to the other.'" Ben chokes up.

"The woman whose son was alive was filled with compassion for her son and said to the king, 'Please, my lord, give her the living baby! Don't kill him!' But the other said, 'Neither you nor I shall have him. Cut him in two!'"

At his last words, a cry springs from my lips as the passage hits a little too close to home.

Ben spins in my direction. "Is someone there?" He tents his hand over his eyes.

"It's me." I regain my composure and wave at him.

"Nicki, why are you standing in the shadows?" He jumps off the stage and races down the aisle toward me.

"I was waiting for the right time to grab your attention."

He stops inches from me. "You always have my attention."

No one has ever said that to me before, and my heart melts at the tenderness and sincerity in his voice. It's nice to know that I matter to someone.

He leans toward me, and for a moment, I think he may kiss me. My pulse skyrockets. But when he reaches behind me and flicks on the lights, I'm not sure whether to be relieved or disappointed.

I blink rapidly. "Interesting sermon topic."

"Yeah." He rubs the back of my neck. "Under the

circumstances, I wasn't sure it was a passage I wanted to use, but it felt right somehow."

"What do you mean?"

He stuffs his sermon notes in his back pocket. "Let's have a seat."

I traipse behind him to one of the few chairs left unstacked in the large space.

Once we're settled in our seats, he continues, "I've spent my entire life in church listening to men preach the Bible from the pulpit. And don't get me wrong, I'm not bashing pastors, but it always seemed that whenever they shared, they were disconnected from their sermon somehow ..." He knits his eyebrows together as if searching for just the right words.

"... as if they had no real-life connection to the verses or passages they were discussing, which always left me a little confused. I mean, how was I supposed to relate to what they were saying if they couldn't?"

"O-kay," I say, not quite sure that I'm completely following him.

"What I'm trying to tell you is that when I decided to take this job, I didn't want to do that to the people I was preaching to. I wanted to make sure that whatever Scripture I shared, I could help them see it lived out in the real world, to understand that the Bible is still relevant today even though it was written thousands of years ago."

His face is damp, and sweat lines his upper lip. "If I'm preaching it, I'm living it."

"So you chose the story of two women fighting over a baby because of what we're dealing with now?"

"Yeah." He wipes his mouth with the back of his hand. "I want to be authentic, and now that our situation is finally in the clear, I thought it would be a good time to talk about our struggles in hopes that it might encourage others with theirs."

Seeing my opening to tell him about the Zhongs showing up

at New Hope, I clear my throat and say, "Well, things have actually—"

"Oh, hey." A voice booms from behind me. I turn my head to see a middle-aged Westerner with chestnut brown hair and a matching mustache heading toward us.

Ben jumps from his seat. "David, good to see you, man."

They shake hands and embrace in a "bro hug."

"And who do we have here?" David flits his eyes in my direction.

"Hi, I'm Nicki." I stand and hold out my hand. "Ben's ..."

"Fiancée." Ben hovers back towards me like a knight in shining armor.

David's eyes bulge. "Really? I had no idea." He shakes his head. "Well, congratulations."

"Thanks." Ben and I say in unison.

"So, when's the big day?"

"In a few weeks back in Texas." Ben's face lights up. "Our moms are handling all the details for us while we finish up some commitments here."

I'm tempted to scream, 'Maybe not!' but refrain. A guy I just met doesn't need to be caught up in our made-for-television drama. Nor do I want to catch Ben off-guard. That's news he needs to be sitting down for. In private.

"Wonderful." David clasps his hands together. "Well, I didn't mean to interrupt. I was just grabbing the carafes to clean out before Wednesday night's service and saw the lights on and stopped to check in case someone forgot them."

"No, just me, practicing. I hope that's not a problem."

"Not at all. I heard nothing but raving reviews on your sermon yesterday. Maybe after you two tie the knot, you'll consider throwing your name in the hat for the full-time pastor's position. I have no doubt you'd be the lead candidate." David cracks a smile. "Well, I gotta grab those carafes and run. Great meeting you, Nicki. See ya, Ben."

As David slips out the door, I lower back into my seat.

Hearing him encourage Ben to apply for the position full-time causes my legs to wobble and my stomach to somersault.

"Hey, are you okay?" Ben rushes to my side.

"Just a little shell-shocked, that's all." By so many things.

"Let me guess—you're put off by David's comments about me applying for the full-time position. Am I right?"

My heart pounds against my chest. Ben really has no clue how gifted he is at preaching. He was created for just this purpose. And although he may not see it yet, there's no doubt in my mind—and clearly in others as well—that he's meant to be a preacher.

The question is, what will happen when he realizes it too?

"Look, Nicki. I wouldn't worry too much about that right now. We have a wedding to look forward to. Let's not spoil that talking about something that may or may not happen."

"Ben, preaching is your calling."

A flash of doubt weaves across his face. "You think so?"

"I know so." I push down the fear lodged in my throat. "The only problem is, it's not mine." I pause. "I have no desire, much less the skills, to play the piano or head up the preschool ministry on Sunday mornings. Being a pastor's wife is not my calling. At all. But I don't want to stand in your way if it's something you're supposed to do."

Ben lays his hands on top of mine. "Like I said last night, Nicki, if it were something I was going to do, we'd figure it out together as husband and wife."

I gulp hard. "Yeah, about that."

Forcing back the tears, I tell Ben about the Zhongs' arrival at New Hope and their request to see Lei Ming.

"Wow." He leans back in the chair. "That's a lot of information to unpack and ask about, but the one that's most pressing is whether or not the director is going to accommodate their request to see Lei Ming."

"She asked what I thought about allowing them access, which I thought was sweet of her."

"It was." Ben rubs his hand over his face. "What did you say?"

"I told her to instruct them to deal with the DNA samples first. I wanted to talk to you about the rest. I thought allowing them to see Lei Ming is a decision we should make together." I swallow. "But I told Director Wu we'd let her know as soon as possible. If the Zhongs are in a hurry to get tested, it's likely they won't want to wait too long to see Lei Ming."

"That's true." He rakes his hand through his hair. "What do you think?"

About what? I want to ask him. Conflicting thoughts speed through my head like a car race on steroids. Honestly, I'm not sure what to think about anything anymore. "I'm not a hundred percent certain we're still supposed to be doing this."

"Doing what?" He furrows his brows.

"All of it." My voice raises a notch. "Marriage. Parenthood. What if we just got caught up in the moment and thought we were following God's lead, but it wasn't Him leading us? What if everything that's gone wrong since day one is proof that we're not meant to be?"

"Yes, it's been hard, Nicki." Ben exhales. "And yes, we've faced lots of obstacles, but just because things are difficult doesn't mean they're not supposed to be. We're never promised smooth sailing on any road we walk with God. If the path was always easy, then why would we need Him?"

He grins before continuing. "Look at all the people in the Bible who followed God's call. At some point, they faced adversity, but it doesn't mean they were wrong."

Heat rises up my neck. "I don't think we were wrong. Loving that little girl and wanting to give her a home and a family is the right thing to do. I'm just not sure we're the ones supposed to do it. Don't tell me you don't have doubts too."

"I've had doubts." He lowers his head.

"Then why didn't you say anything?"

"Because ..." His chin trembles. "I've lost so much already, and the thought of losing you and Lei Ming is more than I can bear. So I'm choosing to walk by faith and not by sight. It's all I can do."

My chest tightens at his admission. And at my failure. I'd been allowing what had been happening to us to overshadow what I knew about who God was and what He was able to do. Regardless of the circumstances. It was time for me to stop focusing on the road bumps and instead, follow Ben's example. I needed to look up and keep my eyes on the One with whom all things are possible.

"Thank you, Ben."

His head pops up. "For what?"

"For being vulnerable and speaking the truth." I clear my throat.

"I will always tell you the truth. Always."

"I know you will, and I appreciate that." I glance at my watch. "It's been longer than the time I promised to reply, so I should call the director as soon as possible." I level my gaze with Ben's. "What do you want to do?"

He lowers his head, seeming to contemplate our next steps.

Not that I need an answer. Even though I've only known this man for a few months, I have no doubt as to what he will say. My only worry is that the results might fracture my heart so much there wouldn't be enough glue in the world to put it back together.

"I think we should let the Zhongs see her." Ben slowly raises his head.

We're taking a huge risk, but I know it's the ethical thing to do. We can't deny them this opportunity. Plus, there's one question still left unanswered I need to know.

"Okay." I take a deep breath. "I'll have Director Wu make the arrangements."

15

Returning the jade bi to Zhao.
~ *Chinese Proverb*

The Zhongs have arrived at New Hope.

While I should be dreading every moment of this meeting and what it might reveal about the relationship between parents and child, I'm actually eager to meet them. There's still one burning question I must ask them. Did their daughter have a heart condition?

Their answer could determine my future even before we receive the official test results.

It's the hope I've been clinging to since Ben and I agreed to have Director Wu call and arrange for the Zhongs to visit with Lei Ming in our presence. With a child as sick as she is, I don't think it's possible she could be their daughter if theirs didn't have a medical condition.

We step inside the room the director had set up for our gathering. Toys lay hodge-podge on thick blankets, and chairs form a circle.

"Is all this for us?" Ben whistles when we step inside the room.

"The director thought it would be better if we visited in here away from the other kids and workers." I'm touched by the elderly woman's efforts to make us comfortable in the midst of an awkward situation.

"Would it be okay if we prayed together before they arrive?" Ben drops the toy he was fiddling with and walks toward me.

"Of course, but God may be tired of hearing my prayers. It's all I've been doing for the last twenty-four hours."

He winks. "Me too, but one more won't hurt."

We hold hands and bow our heads.

Before closing my eyes, I notice a red string wrapped around Ben's left wrist—just like the one I wear to remind me of my connection to Lei Ming. Joy swells within my heart. This one small act lets me know he wants us to be a family as much as I do.

"Lord," Ben says. "We don't understand everything that's going on with this situation, but we know You. We trust that You only want what is best for everyone here today. Help us to walk by faith and not by sight and to accept Your plans and purposes, whatever the outcome may be."

As I listen to the words roll smoothly off Ben's tongue, my swirling emotions settle down. His prayers for us, for the Zhongs, for Lei Ming, and above all else, for God's will to be done causes peace to flood my soul.

Once our "amens" float between us, I open my eyes to find Director Wu standing at the doorway with a petite young couple.

"Nicki, Ben, this is Mr. and Mrs. Zhong."

I reluctantly let go of Ben's hand and wave them inside. "Please join us."

"I'm Zhong Bao," the husband says. Dressed in a faded brown suit, he holds out his hand to Ben. "And this is my wife, Shihong. Thank you for seeing us."

"It's nice to meet you. I'm Ben Carrington, and this is my fiancée, Nicki Mayfield."

While the two men shake hands, I attempt to make eye contact with his wife, but her gaze is glued to the toys spread around the room. A tiny smile breaks out across her face, temporarily erasing the worry lines from her forehead.

Director Wu clears her throat. "Well, I'll give you some time to visit." She reaches for the door handle. "Let me know when you're ready for me to bring in Lei Ming."

Mrs. Zhong's head snaps around, her features drawing tight once more. "Lei Ming?"

"Yes, that's the name we gave her when she arrived at New Hope."

"Thunder rolls?" Mrs. Zhong grimaces, seemingly offended by the description.

The director chuckles. "We thought it was appropriate for her personality." Without offering any further explanations, she shuts the door behind her, leaving the four of us alone.

"Would you like to sit down?" I point to the chairs placed around the makeshift play area in hopes that it might make it easier for us to talk.

"Thank you." Mr. Zhong guides his wife away from the door and toward the middle of the room.

"You speak excellent English," I say, grateful there's no language barrier between us.

"Working in Shanghai, it is necessary for us to make money." He removes his blazer and drapes it over the chair. "We sell more to tourists that way."

We engage in small talk for a few minutes before Ben steers the conversation to our real reason for being here. "Nicki spoke with your parents, and they told her what happened with your daughter, but we'd like to hear your version of the story if you don't mind."

I assume Mr. Zhong will continue being the one to communicate with us, so I turn my attention to him. Yet, much to my surprise, his wife speaks first.

"It's my fault, really." Her voice is barely louder than a stage whisper. "I refused to do as the government instructed, and they took away my sweet baby as punishment."

She removes a tissue from her purse. "As you may know, China has had very strict policies regarding the number of children a family was allowed."

"Sadly, we do," I confirm.

"After our twin boys were born, I was told I could not have any more children. They even suggested I become sterilized. But I would not. I'd hoped that one day the child policy would change, and if it did, I would want to try for more children. I dreamt of a house full of them." Tears spill down her cheeks.

Mr. Zhong caresses her back.

"Then one day, only two years after first giving birth, I discovered I was pregnant again. My boss informed the Family Planning Officials in our village, and they said I had to have an …"

Her words trail off, but I don't need her to finish her sentence. I know exactly what was required of her. And because of it, my heart twists in a knot of frustration and sadness for this poor woman.

"But you didn't go through with it, did you?" I soften my voice.

"I had no choice." She wipes her nose with her tissue. "I lost that baby at the hands of the village doctor."

A lump forms in my throat. I can't imagine how extremely difficult that must have been, and probably still is, to live with.

"So, you became pregnant a third time?" I do my best to tamp down my surprise.

"Yes, I wasn't trying … it just happened."

"What did you do?"

"I refused to endure what happened before, so I hid my pregnancy." She squares her shoulders. "I wore baggy clothes to work, and I stayed in as much as possible. When the time came to give birth, I had Xiuying—that was … is her name—in our home. My husband's mother watched her during the day while I was at work, and at night, I did my best to keep her quiet so no one would know she was alive."

"But then someone in our village informed the Family Planning Officials that we had been hiding our baby." Mr. Zhong's face grows flaming red. "They barged into our home one night and demanded that my wife be sterilized. We begged them to let her have a few months to finish nursing the baby before doing the procedure, and they agreed. But months later, when Shihong never complied, they found other ways to punish us."

His right leg starts to jiggle, and his wife places her hand on his thigh to stop the rapid movement.

"At first, it was small things," he continues, "but then it became more intense. Fines, destroying our property, troubles at work. Finally, we had no choice but to leave for a larger city to work so we could support my parents and our children."

"And while you were away, that's when they came and took the baby," Ben says solemnly.

"Yes," Mrs. Zhong whispers. "It was a parent's worst nightmare. However, we refused to believe that she was no longer ours and committed to looking for her. We've placed ads as our finances would allow, but those do not come very cheaply."

Mr. Zhong clasps his hands together as if praying. "When my parents called and told us about your visit, I knew it was an answer to our prayers after all these long months of wondering and waiting. We've had many false leads, but I'm hoping that we will finally be reunited with our beautiful baby today."

"I'm so sorry for your loss." I wipe my cheeks. "I can't imagine how difficult these past few months have been and how anxious you must be to see if Lei Ming resembles your daughter. But there's one more question I must ask you before we go any further."

Both parents scoot to the edge of their seats.

Taking that as permission to inquire more, I continue. "Did your daughter have a heart condition?"

The couple exchanges bewildered glances before looking back at me. My heart races, waiting for one of them to respond.

"Not that we are aware of," Mr. Zhong says. "Why do you ask?"

I expel a huge sigh of relief. Then I dredge up the courage I need to break the bad news to them.

"Lei Ming suffers from a serious heart condition, which likely would not have gone unnoticed by her birth parents and is probably why she was left at New Hope. Thanks to the support the orphanage receives for children with health issues like hers, she's already had two surgeries. But she will need a lifetime of medical care."

Mrs. Zhong's hand flies to her mouth as fresh tears pool in the corners of her eyes.

Watching her, I'm unsure if she's upset by my statement, the fact that this may be another dead-end, or both. Either way, my heart breaks even more for her.

"What are you trying to tell us, Miss?" Mr. Zhong crosses his arms over his chest.

I sit up straighter. "I'm sorry, but if your daughter didn't have a heart condition, then I'm not sure Lei Ming is the child you're looking for."

The couple draws their heads together and reverts to their native tongue. After several minutes of rapid back and forth, the couple finally addresses us.

"Even if what you say is true ..." Mr. Zhong's face turns a deeper shade of red than before. "That does not mean she is not our daughter. We know our child, and once we see her, we will be able to tell."

Before I can say anything else, Ben rests his hand on mine. A signal, I presume, to let him handle things from here. Everything in me wants to speak up and convince them that Lei Ming can't be their daughter, but I acquiesce and stay silent.

"We're not trying to upset either of you." Ben's voice is gentle. "But you have to understand, Lei Ming's health is critical.

I think what Nicki is trying to get across is that if she were your daughter, you probably would have known about her condition, making it less likely you're a match. That's all."

Mrs. Zhong sniffles. "Thank you for this information, but that does not mean anything. Her problems could have developed after she was taken from us." She narrows her eyes in my direction. "Unless you are a doctor, you can't say for sure."

I purse my lips. She's right—I'm not a medical professional. But I've seen everything this child has endured, and I have a hard time believing her condition could have gone unnoticed as a baby or that it developed suddenly after she was abducted.

"I know this is not the news you were expecting, and of course, the results will confirm one way or another," I say. "But we thought you should be aware of the possibility of this complication."

"We understand. However, we would like to wait for the tests to tell us who this child really is." Mrs. Zhong brushes a strand of hair from her face. "Would it be possible to see her now?"

"I'll let the director know to bring her in." Ben slips his hand out of mine and leaves the room.

An awkward silence hangs over us as we wait for his return. I use the opportunity to search for any physical similarities the Zhongs may have to Lei Ming. As I do, the blinders I've been wearing since first being introduced to them slowly come off, revealing the facial features they have in common. In them, I see the same cheekbones, forehead, and nose shape as Lei Ming.

A tremor of fear and dread shoots through me.

Although I was confident Lei Ming couldn't be their daughter earlier, now I'm not so sure. The resemblances are too strong to deny the possibility.

I pull my eyes away from the adult versions of Lei Ming when the door creaks open a few moments later. Fully expecting to see Director Wu walk into the room, cradling Lei Ming in her arms, I'm shocked when I see my sweet girl and her beloved bear nestled against Ben's chest instead.

The two of them together are more than I can handle. My heart swells with so much love at the sight of them, I'm afraid it might explode out of my chest. I let out a whimper but quickly realize I'm not alone in my crying.

Mrs. Zhong leaps from her chair, weeping. "Xiuying, Xiuying." She opens her arms and reaches for Lei Ming.

Possibly out of protectiveness, Ben instinctively draws back.

"It's okay, Ben." The words tumble out of my mouth though I can hardly believe I'm saying them.

Slowly he hands Lei Ming over to the Zhongs and then joins me across the room.

The couple plops down on the floor with Lei Ming and carefully checks her over.

Despite being studied like a lab specimen, Lei Ming is unfazed by all the commotion. She entertains herself with an old-fashioned Jack-in-the-Box, giggling each time the box pops open.

Her laughter takes my breath away. All I want to do is pick her up and wrap her in my arms. Yet, Ben and I can only stand to the side and watch.

And pray for a miracle.

"So." Ben clears his throat. "Do you think she's your daughter, Xiuying?"

Mr. Zhong lifts his head, joy radiating across his face. "I do."

"How can you tell?" I drop to my knees next to the three of them.

"A mother knows," Mrs. Zhong says without taking her eyes off Lei Ming.

Ben squats down next to me, and for the next twenty minutes, the four of us take turns showering love on this child.

Eventually, Lei Ming stands up and studies each of our faces one at a time, her own scrunched up in confusion. When her eyes land on Ben, she waddles over to him and falls into his lap.

He quickly wraps her up in his embrace, planting raspberry kisses on her chubby cheeks.

I turn my head and hide the tears streaming down my face.

"You've grown quite fond of her," Mrs. Zhong says.

I rub my checks clean before swiveling back in her direction. "Yes, we were about to start the process of adoption, but then we discovered the ad you placed. We returned to China to make sure that we weren't giving a loving home to a child who already had one."

"That is very kind of you." Mrs. Zhong bows.

"We just want what's right for everyone and what's best for this little girl."

"As do we," Mr. Zhong says, his eyes transfixed on Ben and Lei Ming.

"I don't doubt that for a second, but ..." I swallow. "If you gave birth to her without permission, without *hukou*, she will have a difficult life if she doesn't have access to an education or healthcare. What will that mean for her future, then?"

Mr. Zhong puffs out his chest. "We can provide for our children."

"I understand, but what if she dreams of a future where she's a doctor or a teacher? How will she ever be able to accomplish those things in life if your country doesn't even acknowledge she exists?"

"You are correct." Mrs. Zhong pats her husband's shoulder. "But you must understand that people from the countryside don't have dreams. Our only hope is to be happy and—"

"I'm sorry to interrupt." Director Wu's voice slices through the tension-filled room.

I turn my head in her direction. When she refuses to make eye contact with me, pricks of unease nip at the back of my neck.

"The lab we submitted the DNA samples to was able to expedite the tests as we requested." She purses her lips. "They just called with the results."

I scoot closer to Ben.

"And?" Ben sucks in his breath.

"The results prove that Lei Ming is the Zhongs' daughter."

A loud sob escapes from my lips as my eyes flick from the director to the Zhongs. And to the little girl who wouldn't be mine.

The Zhongs leap from the blanket toward Lei Ming.

"Are—are they sure?" Ben reluctantly hands her over to them, despite her wails at being removed from his arms.

"Yes." Director Wu says over her cries.

I squeeze my eyes shut and drown out the world. Why would God bring us this far only to take everything we'd hoped for away from us? I rack my brain, trying to make sense of it all, but I can't.

Yet deep in my gut, I know it's true. I've known it since the elder Mrs. Zhong recognized Lei Ming's blanket. I just didn't want to believe it and foolishly allowed myself to cling to the hope Lei Ming's health issues might be the one thing that made the difference.

But now, it seemed, I had no choice but to believe.

"Thank you for the good news, director." Mr. Zhong springs up from the floor. "What needs to be done so we can take our daughter home?"

A muscle in the director's jaw twitches. "I'm sure you can agree that this is an unusual circumstance, so I'll need to make some calls to determine how we can legally return Lei Ming—"

"Xiuying," Mrs. Zhong corrects her.

"My apologies." The director bows. "I'll need to make some calls and determine how we can legally return Xiuying to you."

"May we stay with her?" Her father asks.

"For the moment. She'll need to return to the recovery unit soon for a nap. Her health is still very fragile."

"Of course. We will remain here until you direct us to leave." He returns to his family on the floor.

"Nicki, Ben." Director Wu turns to us. "May I speak with you out in the hallway?"

Ben and I look at each other and pull our weary bodies up off the floor and out into the hall.

"I'm so very sorry." Director Wu holds out her arms to me.

I fall into them and let the sadness spill out. While I know it's impossible to hear a heart breaking, I'm sure I can hear mine shattering into a million tiny pieces.

"So now what?" Ben whispers.

The director pats my back. "It's hard to say. It's likely they will have to go to court to have her legally returned. But the government will not be happy about that and may rush to have her adopted to avoid admitting a mistake on their part."

"What are you saying?" I pull away from her and wipe my face.

"I'm just listing out the possible outcomes, that's all." She tugs on her shirt, which is damp from my tears.

"Director, can Nicki and I speak privately?" Ben places his hand on my back.

"Of course, I'll be in my office if you need me." She shuffles back down the hall.

Once she's out of hearing range, Ben looks down at me. "Do you think she's implying there's still a chance for us?"

"I do."

"If that were the case, would you still want to go through with the adoption?" His lips press together in a slight grimace.

The knots in my stomach tighten even more. Only moments ago, all hope was lost. Now it seemed there was still a chance— even if it was a small one.

"I just don't know if I can let Lei Ming go, Ben." I wring my hands. "And if Director Wu is hinting we may still have an opportunity to be a family, wouldn't you want to take it?"

He rubs his hand over his forehead. "You know I would do anything to make that happen, but could we live with ourselves knowing that we'd taken a child from a family who truly wanted her and who lost her by no fault of their own? And what would we say to Lei Ming when she got older and started asking questions about her birth parents?"

"We'd cross that bridge when we came to it, but in the meantime, I'm thinking about Lei Ming right now. Considering her medical issues, we could provide everything she needs to stay healthy. We both know how expensive it's going to be, and I'm not sure they'll have the means to take care of her. And knowing what challenges await her in the future, it would be better for her if we adopted her."

"Nicki ..."

Fresh tears sting my eyes. We're so close. But Ben's point is valid. We wouldn't be able to live with ourselves if we did go through with it. And if Lei Ming ever did discover the truth, she probably wouldn't forgive us either. Then I'd really lose her.

No matter how much it hurt, we had to do what was best for this little girl.

"You're right." I push down the lump in my throat. "We should do everything we can to help the Zhongs fight to get their daughter back. I have a feeling it will be a rocky road."

"I knew you'd want what's best for Lei Ming, even if it hurts right now." Ben tucks a strand of hair behind my ear. "And yes, we'll do whatever we can to reunite their family."

Family. I gaze down at the floor and ponder what the days ahead hold for us now that we don't need to jump through hoops to make our own.

"Nicki?" Ben gently lifts my head with his fingers. "What is it?"

My breath hitches. "If we aren't going to adopt Lei Ming, what does that mean for us?"

16

Love won't let go of hand.

~ *Chinese Proverb*

Numb.

It's the only way to describe how I've felt these past few days since learning the truth about Lei Ming's identity. I'm doing my best to go through the motions of living, but my heart and mind are desensitized to everything around me. If only the world could stop until I had a handle on my grief and heartache.

But it hasn't.

New Hope has been a flurry of activity with attorney visits, calls from various officials demanding explanations, and reporters lurking around looking for a juicy scoop.

We finally broke down and shared the entire story with our families, who have been bombarding us with non-stop phone calls, emails, and text messages. They want to know how we're doing—and what we want to do about the wedding.

Add to that our own work responsibilities, and it's been impossible for Ben and me to have the time we need to determine our next steps. But we can't put it off any longer. We have to move on with our lives and figure out where we go from here.

Either together or apart.

At the orphanage that day, we agreed we wouldn't make any decisions about our future together right away. We both agreed that it would be best if we gave ourselves space and time to think. Our hope was that in doing so, we wouldn't let our sensitive emotions, which can never be trusted, override logic. Now that the time had finally arrived to have the discussion, I'm a jumbled mess and not sure I'm capable of thinking clearly.

I do my best to put on a happy face when I enter the restaurant where Ben asked me to meet him after church on Sunday. "Hi." I linger next to the table where he's seated.

"Hi." He jumps up from his chair and gives me a hug. "It's good to see you."

I inhale the familiar scent of his cologne before pulling out of his embrace. "You too." I sit down opposite him. "Thanks for inviting me."

"A girl has to eat, right?"

"I haven't had much of an appetite lately." Or at all, really. A side effect of a broken heart.

"We don't have to eat if you don't want to. We can just talk."

"Thanks." I push my menu to the side. "I'd like that."

He reaches down underneath the table and then lifts out a large bouquet of white flowers. "These are for you."

"They're beautiful." I bury my nose in the arrangement. "What are they?"

"Orchids."

"Did you know that, or did the gardener who sold them to you tell you that?" I poke fun at him, a reminder of our garden trip a few weeks ago when we came up with the crazy idea we could be a family.

"Good one, but no, I'm familiar with these flowers. I chose them on purpose."

I take one last sniff of their sweet fragrance and set them on the table. "What do they symbolize?" Almost all flowers in China stand for something.

"Love."

I freeze. Is he talking about the romantic kind or the one he and I share for Lei Ming?

"Sorry." His cheeks turn a deep red. "I didn't mean to make you uncomfortable." He clears his throat. "I just wanted to give you something I hoped might make you feel a bit better. I know I feel terrible, so I can only imagine what you must be going through."

"I'm doing my best." I move my pre-packaged chopsticks from one side of the salad plate to the other.

"I'm sure it hasn't been easy, and I wish I could have been there for you more, but things have been crazy at church, and I can only guess it's been even more so at New Hope."

"It has." I fill him in on the latest news concerning the Zhongs and their efforts to take Lei Ming, or should I say, Xiuying, home. "Then there's also the ticking clock for Director Wu's replacement. When I asked Julia this morning for an answer, she regretfully declined, saying God had placed something else on her heart to do."

I shake my head. "I can't blame her. It won't be an easy role for anyone to take over. But I need to find a replacement immediately, and considering the director's present condition, I'm not sure she'll be able to assist me."

"Why? Is Director Wu feeling bad?"

"No, I'm just worried about the toll all of this is taking on her. She's still weak from her fall, and none of this is helping matters. It's been difficult for her to juggle her responsibilities and deal with government officials and lawyers."

"I hate to hear that. Director Wu is a lovely woman."

"She is, but she's fully aware that her tenure at New Hope is coming to an end." I take a sip of water. "Now that Julia has declined the position to replace her, I don't know who will be in charge at New Hope."

An icy chill crawls down my spine. What will happen to the orphanage if I don't find a replacement? More importantly, what will happen to the children?

"Well, this may be a stretch," Ben continues. "But have you considered taking the job?"

I sigh. "Heather asked me the same thing when I met with the Board, as did Director Wu."

"What did you tell them?"

"I graciously declined."

"Why?" He props his elbows on the table. "I was kidding at first, but I think you'd be ideal."

I glance out the window. My answer will usher us into our true reason for being here, and I need a moment to prepare myself for what is to come. Good or bad.

"It's not my calling," I admit when I'm finally able to look back at Ben. "But then again, I thought I was called to be a wife and mother too."

"Maybe you're still called to do all those things, just differently than the way you imagined."

"I'm not sure of anything anymore." I lower my eyes so he doesn't see the pain hiding behind them.

"I keep saying I'm sorry, and I truly am. I thought we were going to be a family too."

I blow out a big puff of air before looking at him once more. "When they said their daughter didn't have a heart condition, I honestly believed—hoped—we were in the clear, but there's no debating science, so ..."

Ben pushes his chair away from the table. The legs screech against the floor under his weight, only stopping when he stands. He quickly drops down in the seat next to me.

"Nicki, I know things didn't turn out as you or I had thought, but that doesn't mean it has to be the end of the road for us. We can still have a relationship even if Lei Ming isn't the center of it any longer."

"What are you saying?" I shift in my seat and face him directly. "You still want us to get married?"

"Yes and no?" He lilts his voice higher.

I narrow my eyes. "I'm not following you, Ben."

"I'd like to think marriage is still in the cards for us, but I thought we could start from the beginning and work our way up to it like normal couples do. We sort of rushed into this arrangement, and now we've been given the time to slow down to really get to know one another."

"You mean date?"

"The first one didn't go that bad, did it?"

I tilt my head slightly. "Umm, if you don't consider almost falling into a canal too bad."

"Come on, you know that wasn't my fault, and you were laughing about it afterward."

For the first time in days, I manage a smile. "Fine, I admit it wasn't terrible. In fact, it was a night I'll never forget."

"Me neither. Sitting there with you under the stars, I knew we were meant to be together. Forever. And that what we shared was more than just friendship and the well-being of a little girl."

My heart thumps hard against my chest. I knew how I felt about Ben but wasn't sure if he had the same feelings for me. There was no doubt in my mind that he cared for Lei Ming, and that's why he agreed to our marriage of convenience. But from the way he's talking, maybe it wasn't just about giving a little girl a forever home. Perhaps there was more.

"Are you saying you like me?" My stomach flips at my middle school response.

"Yes, Nicki Mayfield, I like you. A lot." Ben places his hand on my face and rubs my cheek. "And I'm hoping you feel the same way about me too."

I rest my hand on top of his as the barren parts of my

wounded heart slowly fill with joy. "I do." I throw back my head. "Okay, maybe that wasn't the best phrase to use under the circumstances, but yes, I have feelings for you and would love for us to build a relationship like normal people. I think it would be nice."

"Thank heavens." He grins. "Not only was I worried you might not reciprocate my feelings but having to tell my mother to cancel everything would have been terrible. Now I just have to ask her to postpone things for a while, but hopefully not too long."

"Will she be okay putting things off after she worked so hard to make it all happen so fast?"

"When the time is right, and we let her have the big Texas wedding she's been wanting all along, I think she'll be fine." He winks.

"I don't even want to think what all that will entail and the can of worms it will open for my mother."

"We'll let them worry about that, but in the meantime, maybe we should seal the deal?"

"Of course." I lift my hand from his and offer to shake on our commitment to one another.

"I was thinking something a little more personal." He leans forward.

Picking up on his cue, I inch closer to him. I lick my lips and slowly jut my head out. Our lips are just about to meet when a shrill ringtone causes both of us to jump, nearly bumping heads.

Really, another interruption?

"It's me." He grabs his phone from the other side of the table. Looking at the screen, he frowns. "I'm sorry, but I have to take this. It's the church."

"Sure." I lean back in my seat and try to hide my disappointment. "Go ahead."

His fingers graze my shoulder as he stands and takes the call.

Sitting here by myself, it dawns on me that for the first time in almost a week, my heartache isn't front and center anymore.

For the past few days, I was certain there was nothing but a bleak future awaiting me. Maybe that's not the case anymore. Although losing Lei Ming is a wound that will take a long time to heal, at least something good did come out of all of this.

Ben and I found each other.

And now we have the opportunity to give our relationship a solid foundation to discover all the things you should know about the person you're marrying *before* the actual ceremony—like whether or not they eat asparagus or if they keep their house messy or neat.

Thinking about Ben's house, I grip the edge of the table. Not because I deemed him a slob, but because his house was in Texas. Mine was in Connecticut. Which meant we were looking at a long-distance relationship. Could we make that work? Would we even want to?

It was definitely something we'd have to discuss before sealing the deal, that was for sure. My heart was in a fragile state as it was. Any more pain and disappointment might cut it off from the world. For good. Better to figure that out now rather than later.

"Sorry about that." Ben slips back into his original seat. "I had to take that call."

"No problem." I momentarily bury my concerns. We can list out the pros and cons of a long-distance relationship later and discuss it over a romantic dinner somewhere. "Everything okay?"

"It depends." His expression remains neutral.

"On what?" The hairs on my arm stand up. "Did something happen at the church?"

"They wanted to let me know that they made a decision about a new pastor."

"That's great!" Relief washes over me. I thought Ben was going to share bad news. "That means we can head back home earlier—and leave this heartache behind."

The color drains from Ben's face until it almost matches the tablecloth. "I thought we were staying here for a while."

I sit ramrod straight. "What do you mean?"

"Well, you still have work to do at New Hope and—"

"After everything that's happened, Ben, I can't stay here longer than necessary. It hurts too much. And now that they've decided on a new pastor, you don't have to stay here either."

His Adam's apple bobs. "They want me to be the new pastor, Nicki."

"You? They want you to fill the position?" I blink rapidly. "But you didn't even apply for the job." My breath hitches. "Or did you?"

"No, I didn't." He shakes his head vehemently. "I wouldn't have done that without talking to you first."

"Then how did they come to their decision?"

His shoulders lift to his ears. "They said that after listening to me preach a few times and with the feedback they've been getting from the congregation, they aren't really interested in interviewing anyone else." His eyes light up. "They feel I'm the perfect person for the job."

They're not wrong. Ben is the perfect guy.

After seeing him on stage and listening to him preach, I know he's called to full-time ministry. It's what he was created to do. I understand why the church board would want him for the position. He'd do wonders for the church and impact lives.

"Nicki?"

I lift my head at the mention of my name. "Yes?"

"I'm taking your silence as a sign you're not as excited by the news as I'd hoped you'd be." His mouth curves downward.

"No, I'm thrilled that they offered you the job. Like I said the other day, you're meant to be a pastor, but ..."

"But?"

"But once I finish up at New Hope, I'm planning to go back home, Ben." I slump back in my chair. "And if you stay and I leave, then what does that mean for us?"

"I don't understand." He scratches his head. "I know you said it was hard for you to be in China, but it won't be that way forever."

"You're right. In time I will heal ... but in the meantime, I have to help my mom put her life back together. She can't stay with your parents for the rest of her life. And Heather is waiting on me too. I want to continue Ms. O'Connor's legacy and work for the Foundation."

"I hear what you're saying, but even you said I was meant to preach."

"I have no doubt you were created for just that, but are you sure you're supposed to be a preacher *here*? What if this was just God's way of getting your attention? Your ministry could be anywhere."

"It's true, I don't necessarily feel called to preach in China, but I really love it here and would like to stay. It would be like having the best of both worlds."

"I know how much you love this place and the people, and it would only make sense that you'd take a job preaching here." My lip quivers. "But if I ever hope to put this behind me and let my heart be open to the thoughts of kids one day, I can't do that in China."

"Where would you want to go then? Back to Connecticut?"

"That would be ideal, but I could ask Heather if I could work remotely for the O'Connor Foundation." I wring my hands. "And although the thought of being a pastor's wife gives me the hives, I'd go live in Texas so you could pastor a church there. Heaven knows there's probably plenty to choose from in the Lone Star State."

"One on every corner in town." He chuckles.

"And my mother would probably be happy living close to your mom. They're like best friends now."

"It seems that way." The light in his eyes slowly dims.

"But that's not where you want to be, is it?"

"Not really." He frowns. "But I don't want to lose you either."

"I don't want to lose you, but I can't stay, Ben. I just can't. I have a job back home, a family who needs me, and a life I have to start rebuilding somehow."

"Yes, but here you'd have me," he says, barely above a whisper. "Plus, if you could work remotely for the Foundation in Texas, couldn't you do that here as well? That would help keep you occupied, and together we could find a way to heal."

I pick at my cuticles. I know what I have to do. For him. And for me. If he's meant to be a pastor and wants to remain in the place that is near and dear to his heart, who am I to stand in his way?

The truth is I can't.

I open my purse and remove the twist tie ring he slipped on my finger only a few days ago. I'd kept it tucked away for safekeeping, but if this was where we said our goodbyes, then I needed to return it to him. It may have just been a joke between us, but seeing it again someday would only remind me of everything I'd lost here in China.

I'd never be able to move forward if I kept looking back.

Just like the red string I no longer wear on my wrist, I have to let go of anything that evokes a memory of what might have been.

"I love you, Ben, and because I do, I refuse to stand in your way. I know how much you love being in China, and if it's your heart's desire, then you should stay true to that." I slide the ring across the table to him.

He holds it up like the jeweler had that morning when we were ring shopping, then drops it back on the table and slides it back in my direction. "I'm only going to be happy if you and I are together, so if you need to leave to heal, then that's what we'll do. Once we've fulfilled our commitments, we'll go home to Texas. And if preaching is what I'm supposed to do, then I have no doubt God will open a door of opportunity for me there."

"What are you saying?"

He stands up and walks over to my side of the table. But instead of sitting down next to me as he had earlier, he pulls me up to him. When he bends down and our lips meet, fireworks explode.

"That was nice," I say breathlessly once we finally stop kissing. "But you never answered my question."

He grins and butts his forehead against mine. "I'm saying I love you, Nicki Mayfield. I love you and can't live without you."

17

Wishes of mind and heart are as hard to control as a horse and an ape.

~ Chinese Proverb

For the first time since officially losing Lei Ming, I return to New Hope.

While I'd prefer to wait until my heart isn't so tender, I have to finish what I started. Or somewhat started.

There are only a few more weeks until I have to report back to the Board, and since neither Julia nor I want to take over the position, I must come up with another solution. Fast.

I refuse to disappoint Ms. O'Connor and destroy her legacy, nor will I allow Director Wu's efforts for the last thirty years to go to waste at the hands of someone only interested in keeping her seat warm. Whoever leads New Hope into the future needs to have the same love and compassion as the director, if not more.

And I intend to find that person, regardless of the work it will require of me for the remainder of my time in China.

As I've done for the past six months, I head straight to the registration desk upon my arrival at the orphanage and retrieve my permission slip to enter.

"Good morning, Miss Mayfield." The young receptionist hands me my lanyard. "Should I notify the Recovery Unit you're on your way back?"

I flinch at her remark. Clearly, she didn't get the memo that Lei Ming, I mean, Xiuying's birth parents are supervising her care now. Otherwise, I doubt this sweet woman would have purposely sucker-punched me.

"No, thank you." I sling the badge over my neck. "I'm here to see Director Wu, actually. She's expecting me."

She smiles and nods, completely unaware of her mistake. "Director Wu is popular today."

"Oh, is she in a meeting with someone? If so, I can wait."

"She does have visitors and instructed me to have you join them, but I assumed you'd want to quickly check on Lei Ming first."

"Not today." Or any day, for that matter.

As I race toward the director's office, my mind whirls at who might await me in there. I pray it's anyone but the Zhongs. I'm not ready to face them yet. If at all. It would be another reminder of what I've lost. Certainly, the director would not want to inflict any more pain on me in my current state.

I reach the door to Director Wu's office and lean against the wood to see if I might be able to identify the muffled voices on the other side. I can't.

However, when a shriek of women's laughter escapes underneath the door, I relax, knowing this meeting includes light-hearted conversation rather than a serious one. That I can handle.

Breathing a sigh of relief, I knock on the door.

"Come in," the director says.

I crack open the door and poke my head inside. "Is it okay if I join you?" My eyes dart around the room and land on familiar faces. "Julia? Victoria? What are you doing here?"

All three women smile in my direction. I step inside the door and gently close it behind me.

Julia jumps from her chair. "I'm worried about you." She hugs me tightly.

"I'm fine," I gasp. She's surprisingly strong for someone so petite.

She pulls back and studies me. "That's what you said on our call the other day when we spoke, but I had a feeling you were just saying that for my sake, so I showed up here today to see for myself."

"How did you know I'd be here?"

"I like to think I have a discerning spirit."

"Or ..." I set down my bag on the director's clutter-free desk. "You did some detective work."

"Fine." She holds her hands up. "I checked with Director Wu last night, and she said you would be stopping by here this morning."

I twirl around like a ballerina. "Well, as you can all see, I'm still in one piece."

"You look beautiful as always on the outside, dear, but it's the inside we're most worried about." The director places her hand on my shoulder. "It's been a week since the truth about Lei Ming—"

"Xiuying, Mother," Victoria reminds her.

"I mean, Xiuying was revealed, and you haven't said much."

"What is there to say?" I shrug. "I thought I was supposed to adopt this little girl with Ben, but that's not going to happen now. I guess I misunderstood. I mean, why else would God bring her parents back?"

"Have you asked Him?" Director Wu tilts her head. "He's big enough to handle your questions, you know."

I blow out my lips. "Trust me, that's all I've been doing."

"And?" Julia's voice is gentle.

"Nothing." I frown. "Either He's not speaking, or I'm unwilling to listen to what He has to say. I just feel like I'm trapped in a dark cave with no guidance whatsoever. I've never been in this position before, and honestly, I'm not even sure what to do, so I keep going through the motions, hoping one day I'll get a clear picture."

The director rubs my back. "God's light shines brightest in our darkest moments. He won't leave you there forever. You'll find your way out when the time is right. You just have to be patient."

"I'm trying my best, but I'm not going to lie ... it isn't easy."

"No, it's not." The director grins. "But fortunately, you don't have to go through it alone. You have us." She waves her hand around the room. "And, of course, you have Ben."

"I do." My insides tingle thinking about the plans we've made over the past few days. They aren't quite what we imagined they would be, but at least we're together and moving in the right direction.

"So, if you aren't going to lead New Hope into the future, what are you going to do?" Director Wu arches her eyebrow.

From the sly smile on her face, I know where she's going with her loaded question. And as much as I want to save New Hope, I'm not the person for the job. Despite what she may believe.

"Nice try, Director." I wag my finger at her. "I'm not completely sure of what my next steps are, but I do know it's not this."

"You can't blame an old woman for trying." She winks at me.

"I don't. In fact, I know exactly how you feel." I cock my head in Julia's direction. "I did my best to recruit my friend here, but she said no too."

"I appreciate your vote of confidence and belief that I could carry on such important work, Nicki." She places her hand over her heart. "But after spending some time praying about it, God is leading me to do something else."

"Like what?"

"Well, that's what we were discussing before you arrived." Julia lets go of my hands. "After listening to Nian Zhen talk about how many children had been taken as punishment for violating the country's policies, I was devastated. Not only by what people would do, but that there were families torn apart by no fault of their own. I want to right that wrong."

I take a cursory glance around the room before letting my gaze fall back on my friend. "What—what exactly are you thinking?" While I have an inkling, I don't want to make any assumptions until I hear her confirm it out loud.

"Somehow, I want to find a way to reunite children who were abducted and adopted out with their birth parents. The Zhongs were fortunate to have people like you and Ben who chose to check first, but not all parents are. And I can only imagine them pining for children they loved with no one to help them."

"Julia." I rub my forehead. "That sounds amazing, but you'll be looking for a needle in a haystack."

Her forehead wrinkles in confusion.

"What I mean is there are so many parents in China, and these children could be anywhere in the world. How would you even start such a task?"

"I don't know—yet." Her long ponytail sways back and forth. "I only know that as an orphan myself, it took me a long time to stop questioning the circumstances around my birth and abandonment and have peace about my situation."

"But Julia, you had special circumstances," I remind her.

"Yes, and even though I've come to terms with why my parents did what they did, I know there are many children, both adopted and unadopted, who probably feel the same as me." Her voice grows stronger. "I want to help them put the pieces back together if I can because when you know where you've come from, you can have peace in your heart. If there are children out there who were really wanted and didn't know it, that might change their lives. Drastically."

"I applaud your efforts, Julia." Director Wu shifts her weight from one foot to the other. "However, what you are proposing would be quite an undertaking. One that would require lots of money and research. DNA testing, data analysis, and immaculate record-keeping. Where would you get the funds?"

"Well, I wasn't planning on asking our government for help because that would require them to admit wrongdoing on their part, and we all know that would never happen." She levels her gaze at the director. "Unfortunately, I haven't gotten that far in my thinking just yet. I only know this is what God has called me to, and I must follow His lead, and rest in the knowledge that He will supply my every need."

My chest aches to listen to her. I believed the same about the situation with Lei Ming, and look how that turned out. It's been a stumbling block to my faith lately, and I don't want that for my dear friend.

Yet I can't be cynical, either. If this is the path she wants to go down, then I must do everything I can to support her. "I can help," I blurt.

All eyes fall on me.

"I mean, I know who I could ask for help." My pulse races thinking of the possibilities. "Heather asked me to come to work for her at The O'Connor Foundation to continue Ms. O'Connor's legacy and help the less fortunate. Your vision falls under that category, and I'm sure I could request some of the Foundation's resources to provide help for you to organize a nonprofit and get started."

"You would do that for me?" Julia's eyes bulge.

"Of course." I wrap my arms around Julia's shoulder. "Look at all that you've done for me in the short time we've known each other. I'd be happy to ask."

Julia rests her head on my arm. "Thank you, that would be great."

Finally, a way to pay her back with something much more meaningful than magazines.

"My pleasure. We can talk about all your ideas later, so I can present them to Heather for consideration." I give her a tight squeeze. "In the meantime, since you'll be busy doing good elsewhere, I have no choice but to go back to the drawing board and find someone else to run New Hope."

"Maybe not," Director Wu brushes her hand over her pearl necklace.

At her words, my entire body grows rigid. She isn't planning on staying, is she? I mean, she's fully aware of the Board's demands and would never do anything to jeopardize the children's well-being. But that's exactly what would happen if she doesn't step down.

"I don't have any intention of remaining at the helm."

She must have read my mind as her words are a balm to my soul, and my body relaxes. Momentarily. "Okay, but if Julia isn't going to take over for you, then I have a very short window to find someone who will. And as we've already discussed, that isn't going to be easy."

"You don't need to worry, Nicki, and you don't need to search either." One corner of the director's mouth lifts in a smile. "I've already found someone."

"You have?" I ask with bated breath. "Who?"

"Me."

My head spins from the director to her daughter. "You, Victoria?"

After staying quiet all this time, her face lights up. "Yes."

"But when? How?" I rub my forehand and try to process the news.

"Having spent the last week here at the orphanage, not only have I seen how much this place means to my mother, but I've fallen in love with these kids and understand how meaningful the work is here as well. Like all of you, I don't want to see it fall into the wrong hands, either. However, because of all the problems it's been dealing with lately, no one is interested in taking her spot, and the government has been threatening to fill it with one of their own people."

She reaches for her mother's hands. "I couldn't stand by and let all her hard work be forgotten. So, with personal guidance from someone closely familiar with the job and my legal background, I hope to follow in the footsteps of my mother and continue her legacy."

"That's fantastic!" I throw my arms around Victoria. "I had no idea you were even interested. I thought you were just hanging around so you could keep an eye on your mother."

"It started out as that, but as the days went on and mother's concern over who would take her place mounted, I realized it was something I wanted to do for her and for me. And like you said, having someone in charge who understands what it means to be an orphan and go through the adoption process, I think I'm well suited for the job and in the perfect position to do whatever I can to help these children and honor my mother's legacy."

My mouth drops open. "You're adopted? How did I never know this?"

"You never asked." Director Wu leans against the desk to stabilize herself.

"No, I didn't. I just assumed," I admit.

"It's okay, dear. I don't mention it that often because I never think about my daughter as not being my own. Through and through, she's mine."

Victoria sidles up next to her mother and puts her arm around the elderly woman. "I am, *Māmā*." She gently plants a kiss on the director's cheek.

"Thank you, dear." She pats her daughter's arm. "Nicki, I'm sorry if we caught you off guard with that revelation. That wasn't our intention. With everything that's gone on here since you arrived with Ms. O'Connor last November, it seems we never really had a chance to talk about our personal lives."

She was right. Since discovering the orphanage's existence and doing what I could to convince Ms. O'Connor not to shut it down, followed by the blow of her unexpected death and the craziness that has been my life since returning here in February, we've never really had a chance to sit down and visit like regular people. Now that I didn't have to worry about her replacement, perhaps we could find time over these next few weeks to become better acquainted.

"I would love that."

"When are you heading home, Nicki?" Julia frowns.

"As soon as Ben finishes his commitment as interim pastor at the church. There's not much left for me here now. As much as I'll miss being with you all, I need to move on with my life if I ever hope to heal."

"You will, emotionally and spiritually," Director Wu says, her voice soft with compassion.

I pray she's right. Because right now, neither seems possible.

Before I can expand on that thought, the door to the director's office swings open, and the receptionist from the front desk rushes in.

"I'm sorry to interrupt, Director, but there's an emergency." She wrings her hands together.

Taking that as my cue to leave, I reach for my bag. "I'll come back tomorrow, and we can finish discussing Victoria's new role." I look at my friend. "Want to grab some lunch with me, Julia? You can tell me more about your plans, and we can write up a proposal for Heather."

"I'd love that." She scrambles to gather her things.

"Oh, Miss Mayfield," the receptionist says. "You may not want to leave just yet."

"Me?" I hitch my purse higher on my shoulder. How could this emergency possibly involve me? For all practical purposes, my job here was done. New Hope was in my past.

The receptionist's eyes bore into me. "It's Lei Ming. She fainted and has been taken to the hospital."

My legs turn to Jell-O at her words, and I grow dizzy.

Seeing that I'm about to collapse, Julia grabs my arm and leads me to the closest chair. After a few minutes, I'm able to breathe normally and assess the situation as Director Wu makes several phone calls.

"I was able to talk with her doctor." She sets down her phone and looks directly at me. When she does, her eyes are teary. "He says she's in critical condition and will need surgery by the end of the day."

My stomach lurches. More surgery? "But she seemed to be doing so well. Other than looking pale and her lips occasionally blue, she seemed to be on the road to recovery. What happened?"

"He wouldn't go into any detail with me over the phone. He said he'd discuss everything with me once I was at the hospital." She spins in circles. "Where is my purse?"

"By the door, Mother." Victoria points to a brown leather bag hanging on a hook next to the doorway.

"Thank you, dear." The director wobbles as she makes her way in that direction, her body swaying.

"Director!" I leap from my seat and do my best to catch her before she crashes to the ground. Again.

"Mother," Victoria rushes to her side. "Are you okay?"

Together, we stabilize the director and guide her back to her desk chair.

"I'm fine." She gasps for air and leans her head back.

Noticing that her skin is warm to the touch and sweat beads her upper lip, I say, "I think we should call the doctor."

"Nonsense." The director sits upright. "I must go to the hospital and deal with this situation with Lei Ming."

"Xiuying, Mother, and no." Her daughter crosses her arms over her chest. "Someone else will need to go for you. I'm taking you home so you can rest."

"Someone has to be there." The elderly woman looks at me.

"Me?" I tap my fingers against my chest. "You want me to go?"

"Would you? Please?" Anguish flickers across her face. "Technically, she is still the orphanage's responsibility, and since Victoria hasn't officially been placed in charge, that only leaves you as our representative. I don't know how much this additional surgery is going to cost or whether or not we have the necessary funds. Special arrangements will need to be made, and I can't leave the handling of that to just anyone."

A lump forms in my stomach, weighing me down. How can I possibly be expected to deal with this situation? Going to the hospital would be like pouring salt on a fresh wound. It would stir up so much pain. Pain I don't want to relive again.

Not to mention we'll have to notify the Zhongs. And I can't imagine they'd want me there waiting with them.

Yet not being there would be even worse.

Lord, what am I supposed to do here? I tilt my head up to the ceiling and wait for an answer.

"Nicki?" Julia touches my arm. "I'll go with you if you'd like."

I lower my gaze. "You would?"

"Of course. That's what friends are for, right?"

It is. And I'm so grateful to have Julia as mine.

"Thank you. That will help. A lot." I glance around the room at all the people who think I'm the best person for the job. "Looks like God's not done with this little girl and me yet."

18

Strength + Strength + Strength = Cooperation
~ *Chinese Proverb*

When Julia and I arrive an hour later, the hospital is in complete disarray. Ambulances line the street waiting to drop off the sick while nurses and orderlies scamper through the congested hallways attending to broken bones, vomiting children, and lame geriatric patients.

Where will I find Ben in all this commotion? I retreat to the one place we'd both think to find the other. The waiting room.

Of course, it's as packed as the rest of the hospital. I trudge through the crowded space looking for his sandy blond hair in a sea of black but come up empty. He has to be here somewhere. He promised me he was on his way.

After Lei Ming's last emergency visit, I don't have the stamina to do this without him.

"Nicki," Julia tugs on my arm. "Don't forget to look for the Zhongs. Director Wu said she'd send them here."

I scan the room once more and spot the young couple in line at the information desk. Presumably waiting, like so many others, for answers about their loved ones.

"I'll be right back." I dart off in their direction.

"Mr. and Mrs. Zhong," I shout over the multitude of conversations in Mandarin.

They both pivot at my voice.

I wave them over to a secluded hallway. "I'm glad you're here," I tell them once we're away from the masses.

"The director called to inform us of what happened with Xiuying. Do you know anything about her condition?" Worry clouds Mrs. Zhong's eyes.

"No, not yet, I just arrived, but her doctor is expecting us, so it shouldn't be too much longer before we hear something." I pull my phone from my purse and tap on Ben's name in my contact list.

"Nicki, where are you?" Ben answers, his voice jagged with nerves.

"I'm in the first-floor waiting room by the main entrance. Where are you?" I glance around, searching for his towering frame.

"Our friend Tao, the orderly, helped me locate Lei Ming. We're up on the third floor in the pediatric surgical wing."

My heart melts in relief. Not only because he's here at the hospital, but because he seems to have things under control. "I'll grab the others and be up in a minute."

I gather my sidekick and the Zhongs, and together we race up to the third-floor surgical waiting room.

There, I find Ben pacing.

"Any word?" I ask as soon as we step off the elevator.

"No, but the doctor has been notified that we're here and waiting for an update."

"I guess all we can do is wait, then." The five of us join a few other worn-out parents in a similar waiting room as downstairs, just smaller and much quieter.

Mr. and Mrs. Zhong sit stoically a few seats down from me. Every so often, I lean over to see if I can tell from their faces how they're reacting to the situation, but they remain unchanged.

"Don't stare, Nicki." Ben's voice holds a thread of warning.

"They look blindsided."

"Probably because they are." He stretches out his long legs and crosses his feet.

"I want to make sure they don't mind us being here."

"Why would they?"

"Because we technically don't have any ties to Lei Ming."

"Xiuying."

I slap the palm of my hand against my forehead. "It's going to take some time for me to get used to calling her that. In my mind and in my heart, she'll always be Lei Ming."

"Well, we need to be respectful of their wishes to call her by her birth name if we hope to see her."

He's right. I'm not trying to be difficult, it's just that it's not easy calling her something else. Lei Ming is all I've ever known her as and all I'll remember her by. I stand and peer down at the young couple. "I need to say something."

"I hope you know what you're doing." Ben shakes his head.

My heart rattles inside my chest like a triphammer. "Mrs. Zhong?" I whisper.

The young mother pops her head up and stares at me. "Yes?"

"May I sit down?" I point to the empty chair next to her.

She nods.

"Thank you." I squirm, trying to find a comfortable position. When I don't, I give up and inch closer to the woman. "I hope you don't mind my presence at the hospital."

"You are here on behalf of the orphanage, correct? I mean, Xiuying is technically still their responsibility."

"Yes, the director wasn't feeling well and asked me to come in her place."

"She told me." Mrs. Zhong grips the handles of her purse. "Thank you for coming."

"I wasn't sure you'd want me here," I tell her.

"If things were different and you were standing in my shoes and I in yours, would you want me here?"

"Yes." I gulp.

She arches her eyebrow, doubt filling her eyes.

I steady my voice. "I would want anyone who cared for my daughter, as much as I do, here because we could lift each other up with our common love. I believe that would make a difference. For everyone."

"You truly love Xiuying, don't you?"

Xiuying. Lei Ming. It didn't matter what her name was. Every ounce of me loved that little girl. I always would, even if I was never able to tuck her into bed, braid her hair into ponytails, or dry her tears after a fall.

"I do." I choke back a sob. "Although she will never call me mother, I will love her as if she were my own for as long as I live."

Mrs. Zhong wipes a tear from her eye. "Then you must stay here. Together our love can give her the strength to fight." She holds out her hand to me.

I place my hand in hers. United, we can do more for this child than we can apart.

After an hour of frequent visits to the nurses' station by each member of our party, the doctor steps into the waiting room in his familiar green scrubs.

"Dr. Wong." I leap from my chair and race to his side, ignoring the short, balding doctor next to him. "Is she okay? What's wrong? How did this happen?"

"Miss, please. I can only answer one question at a time."

"Sorry, it's just that we've been here a while and haven't received an update." I glance at all the faces huddled around us, grateful that we have each other during this difficult time.

"I apologize, but I was waiting to confer with my associate, Dr. Han." The doctor's eyes flick toward the man standing on the outskirts of our group, whom I first ignored. "He is also a pediatric cardiologist but much more skilled in these situations than me. I was waiting for him to have a look at Lei Ming."

"Xiuying," Mrs. Zhong corrects him.

The doctor freezes at his reprimand.

Sensing his confusion, I quickly explain, "Doctor, this is Mr. and Mrs. Zhong." I point to the young couple. "They are the birth parents of Lei Ming, whose actual name is Xiuying."

The doctor's eyes bulge. "Oh, I had no idea. Isn't she in the care of New Hope?"

"Technically, yes, but it's a long story and one that doesn't really matter at the moment." I pause to catch my breath. "Please, can you tell us what's wrong and why you wanted to confer with another specialist?"

He nods as if understanding the craziness of the situation, but I'm certain he's just as shocked as we are concerning Lei Ming's true identity.

"Well, unfortunately, it seems that I originally misdiagnosed Lei—I mean, Xiuying's—heart condition."

"Misdiagnosed?" Mrs. Zhong covers her cheeks with her hands.

"Yes." The doctor crosses his arms over his chest. "When she was first admitted a few weeks ago, we thought her condition was nothing more than a ventricular septal defect because of the hole she had in the wall between the two lower chambers of her heart, which, as you remember, we closed up."

"I recall you mentioning something along those lines." My mind flitters back to our conversation only a few weeks earlier. "But you said you fixed the hole, so why is she back here and in such critical condition?"

"When she was readmitted today, we looked at other possibilities since most children treated for a ventricular hole go on to live normal lives, but Xiuying has further complications. Upon another examination, Dr. Han discovered that the ventricular septal defect was just one of her problems. After running several different tests, it's his medical opinion that she suffers from a congenital heart disease known as Tetralogy of Fallot."

Even though I didn't have a medical degree, such a complicated diagnosis couldn't be good news. At all.

"Often these children will have trouble gaining weight, suffer from shortness of breath, or have a bluish discoloration to the skin or lips."

My mouth goes dry. Lei Ming had displayed all those symptoms numerous times. I always thought she was tired, cold, or still recovering from her first operation. Now I see that there was more to it. "Is it normal for these issues to show up so late?" Guilt plagues my question. "Isn't it something that would have been detected at birth?"

Dr. Han clears his throat. "Not necessarily. I've heard of cases where symptoms don't show up until adulthood. Every case is different."

"Can it be fixed?" Mr. Zhong pipes up. "Once you operate, will she be better?"

"It can. However, this is a serious condition. I'm afraid your daughter will need surgery immediately and will likely require a lifetime of highly supervised medical attention and possibly even more operations."

"But she'll live, right?" Mrs. Zhong asks.

"She should." Dr. Han grimaces. "However, there are never any guarantees when we put someone, especially a child her age and in her weakened state, under anesthesia."

"No, we understand," Ben says. "We appreciate your honesty and efforts to help her."

"We will do our best." Dr. Wong bows and then looks at me. "As the representative from New Hope, I assume you will be handling the financial payments? We can't move forward with treatment until we have confirmation and proof of payment."

Panic takes hold of my legs, making them bow and wobble. I can't imagine a surgery of this caliber will be cheap, and I seriously doubt the orphanage's budget can handle such a large expense after AD Chang stole most of its money.

"How—how much will it be?" I mumble.

"The procedure itself will be at least 150,000 yuan." The color drains from Dr. Wong's face. "And that doesn't include any additional care she'll need post-op."

I quickly convert the currency exchange in my head. Twenty thousand dollars. Roughly five times more than the first one she underwent. I blanch. New Hope doesn't have the funds to cover anywhere close to that amount. And from the frantic looks on their faces, I can tell that the Zhongs don't either.

Which can only mean one thing.

I cut a sideways glance at Ben. When our eyes meet, we both nod as if instinctively knowing what the other is thinking.

"Doctor Wong," Ben says. "My fiancée and I will cover the cost of this surgery, and any additional medical expenses Xiuying may incur while in the hospital. Just let me know how I can arrange for the payment to be made so you can do whatever needs to be done right away."

Mr. Zhong's eyes flame, and he lets out a shriek before stomping away to a corner of the waiting room. His wife flees after him.

"Thank you," Dr. Wong says to Ben before turning in my direction. "Since you are New Hope's representative and have given us permission to move forward, we will go ahead and prep for surgery. I'll have one of the nurses bring out all the proper documentation for you to complete. This is a long procedure, so we will keep you updated as often as we can."

Both doctors bow at us, then retreat down the hallway to the hospital's abyss of pediatric operating theatres. Once they've disappeared from our line of sight, we turn and look at the Zhongs, huddled together and exchanging sharp whispers.

"Do you think he's upset about the operation or the money?" I ask Ben timidly.

"Neither." Julia sidles up next to us, having apparently overheard. "When Ben offered to pay, Mr. Zhong lost face."

"But what else were we supposed to do?" Heat scalds my lungs. "It was the only option. I know New Hope doesn't have the money to cover the costs, and I seriously doubt the Zhongs do either."

"You're probably right, Nicki, but we Chinese are a very proud people, and I'm sure he feels terrible knowing that he's incapable of providing for his child."

Her words rattle me to my core. If the Zhongs can't cover this medical expense, how will they possibly pay for the lifetime of care Dr. Han mentioned? Especially if Lei Ming's birth isn't recognized and she has no *hukou*?

A heavy darkness envelopes me as I imagine Lei Ming's future. Although we couldn't raise her ourselves, perhaps Ben and I could fund her medical treatment to ensure she received everything she needed. It's exactly what Mr. O'Connor did all those years ago and what eventually brought me to China in the first place. We could do the same, couldn't we?

I mentally weigh the pros and cons of such a commitment. It was possible on our end, but I have a feeling that if Mr. Zhong reacted as negatively as he did when we said we'd cover this hospital stay, a lifetime donation would be more than his pride could handle. It's an offer I seriously doubt he'd accept.

"Nicki?" Julia shakes my shoulders. "Are you okay?"

I blink back a rush of tears. "I'm fine. I'm just worried about the Zhongs, that's all."

And the very difficult road they face with a seriously ill child.

Just as Dr. Wong had said, the operation takes hours. The five of us remain in the waiting area, but the Zhongs remain on the opposite side of the room, keeping to themselves.

I do my best to keep Director Wu updated on the situation, but after seven hours of back-and-forth texting, I decide to let her rest and promise Victoria that I'll call in the morning. Julia leaves shortly afterward to head back to Mother's Love so she can check on Mingyu.

Nine hours after the doctors first explained the dire situation to us, the Zhongs, Ben, and I are the only ones left in the pediatric waiting room.

"It's late, and you haven't eaten since we arrived here at lunchtime." Ben places his arm around me. "Do you want me to get you something to eat or drink?"

Although my stomach has growled on occasion over the last few hours, I have no desire to eat. I can't stop thinking about Lei Ming on the operating table, her chest splayed open and large instruments poking and prodding at her tiny body.

"I'm not hungry." I rest my head on his shoulder, grateful he is here next to me so I don't have to endure this alone. "But if you want to go get something, go ahead. I'll stay here in case the doctors come out with an update."

"Are you sure? I don't have to eat."

I look up at him with a sheepish smile. "You and I both know how you need food."

"What can I say? I'm still a growing boy, I guess." He shrugs. "I'll just go downstairs to the gift shop really quick, grab something, and be right back." He plants a kiss on the top of my head before scurrying out of the room.

I close my eyes and lean my head back against the wall. At first, to rest. But when I can't sleep, my mind yields to prayer—a task that has been difficult over these past few weeks as my heart and my mind attempt to reconcile all that has happened with what I thought God had planned for Ben and me. And Lei Ming.

While I long to pour out an elegant soliloquy of words that would capture my deepest desires for this little girl, the only words I can manage to utter silently are, *Lord, please heal her.* Over and over again, hoping it's enough.

A kerfuffle in the chair next to me interrupts my pleading.

Expecting Ben's large frame to be seated next to me, I'm startled when I open my eyes and find Mrs. Zhong there instead.

"Is something wrong?" I sit up. "Did you hear something about Xiuying?" I scan the room for any signs of activity but notice that it's empty except for the two of us.

"No. I didn't mean to alarm you." Mrs. Zhong sniffles, her eyes puffy and red. "I just need to speak with you about something."

I rub my hands over my face. "Yes, of course. Anything."

The young mom perches on the edge of the seat. "My husband and I have been talking for the last few hours, and we've realized that as much as we love Xiuying, we cannot give her the care she will need in the future."

I want to reassure her that won't be the case, but I can't. If the doctors are correct with their diagnosis this time, that will be the story of her life from now on. "I'm so sorry. No one could have expected her situation to be so dire. I'm sure you and Mr. Zhong have been taken aback by the news."

"I appreciate your kindness." Mrs. Zhong hunches over and studies the dingy white tile. "We thought the worst thing in the world was never finding her again, but the truth is, having her and not being able to provide what she needs is far worse." She lets out a soft whimper. "That is why we left for Shanghai in the first place, so we could take care of our children and give them the best life possible."

My chest squeezes at her confession. "I can't even begin to understand what a huge sacrifice that must have been and know it could not have been an easy decision for you to make. I'm not even sure I could have made that choice."

"It wasn't easy, but we did what we had to do. And now ..." She takes a deep breath. "And now we must do it again."

"Do what?" I bend down and attempt to make eye contact with her.

She slowly tilts her head in my direction. "We must leave her once more."

"Leave her?" Blood rushes in my ears. Is she saying what I think she's saying? "Mrs. Zhong, what exactly do you mean?"

The lines of her throat tighten. "As much as I want to take my daughter home with me, I can't. Even if we could cover her medical expenses, we wouldn't be able to take off from work to be with her if she needed future operations, and we both know what her life without any *hukou* means. It would be better if you and Ben took her and gave her what we are unable to."

"You want us to take Lei—I mean, Xiuying—and raise her as our own?" My heart pounds faster. Was this really happening? Was what God had planned finally coming to pass, just not the way I imagined?

She straightens back up, fierce determination written across her face. "Yes, that is what I'm asking." She grabs my hands. "Please tell me you will do this for me. For her."

Taken aback but overly thrilled by her request, I say, "I would do anything for her. And for you."

Sobs rack her small body, and she buries her head in my chest. I cling to her heaving frame and do my best to comfort her in her loss. And my gain.

I'm not sure how long we sit there as our hearts join in a common bond of family, love, and motherhood, but when she finally lifts her head and matches my gaze, I see a spirit of peace within her velvety black eyes.

"I have one more request of you, and I promise I won't ask for anything else." She hiccups.

Uncertain as to what else she would need but willing to do whatever I could, I simply nod.

"If at all possible, could you let us be a part of her life? Could you bring her back to China on occasion so we could see her and show her where she really comes from, her true heritage?"

"We—we would be happy to. I mean, I can't promise we would come often, but if it's possible, I would find a way."

"That would mean so much."

"Of course." I reach for my purse, pull out a tissue, then hand it to her.

She takes it from me and daintily wipes her porcelain skin.

Silence descends upon us as we both ponder the ramifications of what just transpired. The promises that were made. The hope that was given.

A few minutes later, Mrs. Zhong shatters the quiet with her soft voice. "Do you remember the other day when I said to you that people from the countryside don't have dreams?"

"I do," I say, recalling the sad observation of her life.

"Well, that wasn't completely true. I do have a dream."

Not wanting to be nosy, I wait for her to continue.

"I dream of my whole family together celebrating the Chinese New Year in the spring, catching fish together in the fall, and having snowball fights together in the winter." She wrings her hands together. "I know that may sound silly to you, but for me, it is all I have ever wanted."

"It sounds like a lovely dream."

"Maybe someday you will bring Xiu—I mean, Lei Ming— back to China during one of those times, and I will be able to see my dream come true."

"If I can, I will."

She slowly rises from the chair. "Thank you, Nicki. I don't know how many more times I will continue to say that, but I hope you know it comes from the depths of my heart." She glances over her shoulder. "I need to find my husband and let him know what we have arranged. He is very shaken by all of this, but in time, he will understand that we did what was best for our daughter."

I press my lips together, unsure of what else to say. What do you tell someone who gave you the greatest gift possible when you have so little to offer in return?

I dig deep and share the words I hope to bring to pass. "Mrs. Zhong, you have my word that we will do whatever is necessary to ensure your daughter—our shared daughter—is cared for. We will treasure her and bring her up to understand her heritage and honor her parents and family, both near and far."

"I have no doubt you will." New tears spill out onto her cheeks. Trembling, she covers her mouth with the tissue, then bolts out of the room.

Left on my own, I sit back in my chair and replay what just happened, pinching myself to make sure it wasn't all just a dream.

But when my nails dig into my flesh, and a tiny red splotch develops on my forearm, I know that our conversation wasn't a figment of my imagination. It was real—all of it. What God said would be, is. Even if it didn't happen the way I expected it to, His purposes for Ben and me and our family were coming to pass.

With this realization, I jump from my seat. I have to find Ben and tell him.

I sprint out of the waiting room and round the corner. As I do, I run smack dab into Ben's arms. And the sound of potato chips breaking into tiny pieces.

"Hey, slow down." Ben grabs my shoulders. "Where are you going? Did the doctors give an update?" His voice cracks. "Is Lei Ming okay? I tried to get back as soon as I could, but I ran into Tao in the gift shop and—"

"Everything's fine." I wrap my arms around him and smile. "No, I take that back. Everything is wonderful."

We return to the waiting room, where I replay my conversation with Mrs. Zhong and her request for us to proceed with the adoption to make Lei Ming our daughter.

"I can't believe it." Ben rakes his hand through his hair. "If we can get the adoption to go through, Lei Ming is ours?"

"Yes!" I say, still in a state of shock. "Never in my wildest dreams did I think that this would happen, but it has, and we're going to be a family, after all."

"God works in mysterious ways."

"He does. I only wish I could have had more faith."

"Don't beat yourself up, Nicki. God uses these experiences to grow our faith so that next time we're faced with a difficult challenge, we can look back at what He's already done and know that He is faithful, and He won't abandon us."

I let his words sink in and soothe my weary spirit. I still had a long way to go with God, but I was grateful that He was faithful, even when I wasn't.

"Oh, there's one more thing."

"What's that?" His forehead wrinkles.

"Mrs. Zhong asked if we could let them see Lei Ming from time to time so she would know her birth family and not forget where she came from."

"Hmmm." Ben props his elbows on his knees. "I mean, sure, we could fly back here every once in a while to visit."

I kick the chair leg with my foot. "What if we didn't come back and visit?"

"You mean like ghost them?" He juts his head back. "I'm not sure I feel comfortable doing that, especially when they've given us such a precious gift."

"No." I dismiss his words with a wave. "That's not what I meant."

"What did you mean, then?"

I shift in my chair and take a deep breath. "What if we don't leave China? What if we stay here and raise our family?"

Ben inhales sharply. "Are you serious?"

"I am." I square my shoulders. "You could take that job at the church, and we could live here full-time. That way, we could easily see the Zhongs. In the end, Lei Ming would have two families that would shower love on her, and she would always know where she came from because she'd still be here."

"You would really be willing to do that? To become a pastor's wife and share our daughter with her birth family?"

Hearing him say it like that sends fear rippling through my body. I'm not sure about the pastor's wife thing, but I know that Ben would love nothing more to develop his preaching ministry here in China. I don't want to deny him that. And as for sharing Lei Ming? I can't think of a better way to show my gratitude to the Zhongs for the gift they've bestowed upon us.

It's a sacrifice I'm willing to make. Because sometimes that's what love requires.

"Yes, that's exactly what I want."

Ben's eyes grow wide. "But what about your mom?"

I pause and entertain his question. After a few minutes, I have the perfect solution. "Maybe I'll ask her to come live with us for a while. If that's okay with you."

"I think we can figure out a way to make it work." He reaches over and kisses me, and once more, fireworks explode.

Officially sealing the deal. And our future.

"Excuse me." Doctor Wong's voice echoes through the empty waiting room.

I quickly pull back from Ben's lips and glance up at the surgeon, who has dark circles under his eyes. "Oh, sorry, Doctor," I say, my cheeks burning.

"Quite all right." He winks. "I apologize for the long delay in providing an update, but things were a bit trickier than we were expecting."

Ben and I leap from our chairs.

My heart beats so loud that I'm sure Dr. Wong can hear it from where he's standing. *Please, Lord, don't let anything be wrong.*

"Is she okay?" Ben and I ask in unison.

The doctor removes the surgical cap from his head. "It was an extensive operation, and it likely won't be her last." He slowly curves his lips upwards into a smile. "But she's going to be just fine."

I jump into Ben's arms. "She's going to be okay!"

He holds me tight. "And she's going to be ours," he whispers in my ear.

"I'll let you two celebrate and return with an update once she's in recovery." He quickly leaves our lovefest.

When we finally let go and put some space between us, I

blow out a huge sigh of relief. I can actually put the last six months behind me and focus on my future. Our family's future.

"So, now what?" Ben asks, his face radiating with joy.

My stomach flip flops thinking about all that must be done in the next few weeks. "I really need to sit down and make a checklist." My brain goes into overdrive. "There's so much to do, but I think with a detailed list, I should be able to manage a wedding, complete the adoption paperwork, set up house, and see if I can convince my mother to move across the world."

Ben throws his head back. "Such the organizer." He steps toward his chair and retrieves his jacket. "Well, while you work on your to-do list, I need to run out on a quick errand."

"What do you need to do at this crazy hour?"

"Sorry, I can't tell you. It's a surprise." He heads for the elevators. "Meet me in the garden downstairs in an hour, okay?"

"Ben!" I follow after him. "You may not know this about me, but I don't like surprises."

"You'll like this one."

I speed around the corner to glean more information from him, but the elevator doors close and whisk him away. Defeated, I march back toward my belongings and do the only thing I can do for the time being. I create the longest wedding, adoption, and moving checklist the world has ever seen.

With my detailed schedule and agenda safely tucked away on my phone, I head down to the garden as instructed. Walking back through the wooden gates, my mind flashes back to only a few weeks ago when Ben and I came here and forged a plan that would change our lives forever. One that seemed so simple at the time. I had no idea it would take me on a journey that would test my faith and my heart more than I could ever imagine.

But, in the end, it was all worth it. That I was sure of.

What I was uncertain of, however, was what exactly Ben was up to. Since he didn't give me any directions other than to meet him here, I park myself on the first bench I see and enjoy the sweet aroma of flowers perfuming the night air and the peaceful sounds of the waterfall behind me.

The serene landscape almost lulls me into slumber when Ben's voice jolts me back awake.

"Not dozing off on me, were you, Sleeping Beauty?" He lowers himself down on the bench.

"No, just closing my eyes and dreaming of our future."

"Good, I hope."

"It depends."

He cocks his head. "On what?"

"On this mysterious surprise of yours."

"Oh, that." He places his arms behind his neck and leans back on the park bench, purposely delaying the reveal.

I nudge him in the ribs. "Ben, the suspense is killing me. Where did you run off to at this late hour? What big surprise do you have for me?"

"Actually, it's not big." He drops his arms and reaches into his jean pocket.

With bated breath, I watch as he pulls out a ring. But not just any ring. *The ring.* The one I fell in love with at the jewelry store right before our lives were turned upside down with Julia's call.

"Is that ..." My voice trails off as my eyes stay glued on the beautiful topaz pear-shaped stone surrounded by tiny diamonds.

"It is ... sort of." Ben holds it up in front of my face.

I wrap my hands around his. "But how? When?" More questions race through my brain, but they're coming so quickly that I can't say them out loud. All I can do is stare at the jewelry encased in our grip.

Ben must sense my oncoming inquisition and clears the air. "Right after you confessed your undying love for me the other night ..." He chuckles before continuing, "I searched all over Beijing looking for a ring that was like the one you'd picked out back in Connecticut. It took a bit of hunting, but I found this one which I think is pretty close."

I take the ring and study it. It's a perfect match. "I wouldn't have known the difference if you hadn't said anything."

"No secrets between us, remember?" He holds out his palm.

I begrudgingly return the topaz beauty. "You did all that for me?"

"I did."

My heart melts at his words. No one had ever done anything so special for me. What did I do to deserve him?

Looking into his emerald green eyes, I see my future, my hopes, and my dreams. I would never have imagined it possible, especially with everything we'd been through lately, but I couldn't wait to become a mother to Lei Ming and a wife to Ben.

Or whatever else God may have in store for me.

"I was planning on presenting it to you in a more romantic setting, but after tonight's turn of events, I don't want to wait one minute longer." Ben slips off the bench and down on one knee. "Nicki Mayfield, will you marry me?"

I can only nod as the tears stream down my face.

Ben slides the ring onto my finger. "Nicki, we've been through better and worse these past few weeks, endured Lei Ming's sickness and her health, and as a pastor's wife, there will likely be days of poorer rather than richer." He grins. "But no matter what we will face, from this point forward, I promise to love and cherish you all the days of my—"

I quickly plant my lips on his and kiss him just as I would if this were our actual wedding ceremony.

When I finally pull back, his smile is as big as Texas. "I thought we kissed *after* we said I do."

I wink at him. "Then I do."

EPILOGUE

The flower of the heart in full bloom.
~ *Chinese Proverb*

Chinese New Year, nine months later

Our tiny apartment in the heart of Beijing bursts with the cacophony of celebration.

Ubiquitous red and gold decorations flank the walls and ceiling, and the aroma of Chinese delicacies permeates the room, causing my stomach to growl. Luckily, we have enough food to feed an army, so I'm confident I won't miss out on any of my favorite holiday dishes.

Every seat in our living room is occupied, and as I scan the twelve-by-twelve space, my heart overflows with love and affection for each person present: Ben, my mom, Darlene and Hank, Julia, Director Wu, Victoria, and, of course, the Zhongs.

Above the din of laughter and conversation, I search for three small bodies which are nowhere in sight. My ears perk up to see if I can hear them in the other room. When nothing pops up on my radar, fear cuts me to the bone as I consider the possible mischief they could be getting into.

Just as I'm about to head off on a search mission, Chao and Bingwen race into the room, their younger sister chasing after them at a snail's pace. I pluck Lei Ming from her pursuit and lift her into my arms.

"Where are you off to, Little One?" I tug on her Chinese New Year outfit and wipe off the sticky peanut butter marring the front of the intricate silk fabric.

"*Xiōngdì*." She points to her older siblings.

"Yes, I know you love your brothers, but it's almost time for your nap." I nuzzle the back of her neck and inhale the fruity smell of her shampoo.

"Here, Nicki," my mom walks over to me. "I can put her down if you'd like." She holds out her arms to Lei Ming, who happily falls into them.

"Are you sure, Mom? I don't want you to miss out on the fun."

"I don't mind at all." She removes the peanut butter rice ball from Lei Ming's fingers and passes it to me. "We have our routine, and it won't take long at all for her to fall asleep. I'll be right back."

The two of them traipse down the hall, and as I watch their figures fade into the recess of our apartment, my heart constricts. What a blessing it is to have my mom here with us. She dotes on her granddaughter every day while Ben and I are at work, and Lei Ming loves being with her. It's as if they're joined at the hip.

Then again, my daughter's attached to anyone who sneaks her an occasional treat and showers her with presents.

Which is pretty much everyone in this room. Especially my mom, who stockpiles her room with more toys than the local department store.

Just not any scary dolls.

A knock at the door grabs my attention, and I drop the half-eaten rice ball in the trash, then rush to admit the last guests missing from our happy fete.

"Longchen!" I open the door to greet our dear friend. *"Zhōngguó xīnnián kuàilè!"*

He grins from ear to ear and steps inside. "Happy Chinese New Year to you as well, Nicki."

"I'm so glad you made it." I take his coat and hang it on a hook next to the door. "Could your wife not come with you?"

"Unfortunately, no. She was playing host at our home while I snuck over here for a few minutes."

"I hope she isn't upset that you left."

He winks at me. "I promised you would let her babysit Lei Ming sometime soon, and she was more than willing to let me go."

"That I can certainly do." I take him by the arm and lead him into the living room.

"Longchen!" Ben jumps up from his spot on the couch and dashes over to us. "So good to see you, my friend. Thanks for coming over."

"I appreciate the invitation. I wouldn't have missed it for anything."

"Let me introduce you to everyone." Ben ushers his friend to the center of the activity.

As the two men skitter off to visit, Julia joins me at the food table.

"What's your Wi-Fi password again?" she asks, her nose buried in her phone.

I cover her screen with my hand. "No working today, remember?"

"I know, and I'm not. Much." She pushes up her glasses and looks at me. "I just want to take a quick look at the lab results that came in from the States and see if anyone was a match."

"Okay, you win." I give her the secret code. "So, did we get any hits this time?"

Julia scrolls through the document. "One." She lifts her head and flashes her pearly whites at me. "That makes thirty-four so far."

Balancing my plate of food, I give her a high-five. "If all goes well, we'll reach our year-end goal of reuniting fifty families who should never have been separated in the first place."

"I can't wait until I get to call this family and let them know we found their child." She lifts a dumpling from a nearby platter and takes a bite.

"Let's wait until tomorrow to contact them. Today is all about our family. Tomorrow can be about theirs."

"Agreed." She looks down at my overflowing plate. "Wow, Nicki. That's a lot of food. If I didn't know better, I'd say you're eating for two."

I purse my lips.

With a squeal, Julia drops her dumpling on a napkin.

"Shh," I hold up a finger to my lips. "Ben and I are planning to tell everyone tonight before the fireworks."

"Okay, I'll do my best to stay mum, but oh my goodness, Nicki, I can't believe you're going to have a baby." She wraps me in a bear hug. "And to think you said you weren't fond of kids. You're going to have a quiver full of them soon!"

After slowly releasing me from her embrace, she picks up her abandoned dumpling and heads back to the living room.

Laughing, I shake my head at her words. She's right. It was only a little over a year ago when I admitted to her that kids and I were not a good combination, and that I would never grow tender toward them. I guess I should never say never ...

I never wanted to live under the same roof as my mother. Now I can't imagine our home without her in it.

I never wanted to marry a Prince, but once I found him, I couldn't let him go.

I never wanted to be a mother, and now I want a house full of children.

Funny how things change in ways you'd never expect.

That God would take a down-and-out organizer and arrange for her to meet a woman whose family secretly funded an Asian orphanage, then place that same organizer back in China to get things in order only to have her fall in love with a little girl and uncover an embezzlement scheme, well—it was all unbelievable.

And finally, when things couldn't get any crazier, He matched her with a Texas preacher to start an unconventional family that brought different generations and cultures together under one roof.

If I didn't know any better, I'd say God had a wild sense of humor.

Or maybe He just knows how to perfectly arrange, place, and match the pieces of our lives to tell a story no one will ever forget.

THE END

AUTHOR'S NOTE

As I've done in the previous two books of this series, I want to offer some insight into how *Perfectly Matched* came to be.

When I first started working on the outline for this novel, I had a story idea, but I wasn't completely sure it would work. In order to make the narrative I was considering believable, I had to do my research. My first source was a book by Karin Evans called *The Lost Daughters of China*. It was a spell-binding memoir of one family's efforts to adopt from China. Then I stumbled upon the documentary, One Child Nation (Amazon), which details the untold history of China's one-child policy. From watching this film, not only did I discover the heart-breaking impact of such a policy, but I also learned about the work that Brian Stuy and his wife were doing to make things right (you can learn more about their efforts at http://research-china. weebly.com/).

I took a bold leap of faith and emailed Brian to see if we could talk. I wanted to share my idea with him and see if it was plausible based on his experience and expertise (even though it was fiction, I wanted to make sure readers could believe it). He happily agreed to chat with me.

After hearing the premise of *Perfectly Matched*, he kindly told me I needed to come up with a new plot. Then he offered some alternative scenarios that I could use. One of those was about a family in Shao, China, whose daughter had been kidnapped as payment for government-imposed fines and turned over to an orphanage, where she was eventually adopted out (you can read the full story in the book, *Orphans of Shao* by Jiaoming Pang). This revelation was eye-opening to me, as I hadn't realized this type of activity was taking place. Like most people, I'd always assumed that orphans were given up because of their gender (girls), the lack of finances to care for them or because of the strict rules in place by the government. Yet, that wasn't the case. At all.

After talking with Brian, I knew the story I needed to tell.

However, I was nervous thinking about the implications of using this information—*would it cause people to think poorly of China, a country dear to my heart? Would it cause parents who had adopted from China to question their child's own reason for being given up? And what consequences might arise from that?*

Even with these worries swirling around in my heart and mind, I knew I couldn't hide the truth. So, I did the best I could to wrap these injustices in a story that was redeeming and hopeful, not only for entertainment value but for educational purposes as well.

While *Perfectly Matched* ends with a happily ever after for Nicki, Ben, and Lei Ming, the reality is that there are still many Chinese parents pining for their lost children. My prayer is that they will be united someday soon.

ABOUT THE AUTHOR

As a multipotentialite, Liana George has many interests and creative pursuits. She claims that's why it took her so long into adulthood to become a fiction author and have her first book, *Perfectly Arranged*, published. Yet if it weren't for the diverse adventures she's experienced on the journey – from being an expat in China and Germany to restoring order in people's homes and lives—she claims she wouldn't have any stories to tell.

Married to her college sweetheart, Clint, with whom she has two adult daughters, Liana lives on a small farm on the outskirts of Houston. When she's not scribbling away, she enjoys watching tennis, reading from her large TBR pile, or planning her next vacation.

ALSO BY LIANA GEORGE

Perfectly Arranged

Book One of the Hopeful Hearts series

Short on clients and money, professional organizer Nicki Mayfield is hanging up her label maker. That is until the eccentric socialite Katherine O'Connor offers Nicki one last job.

Working together, the pair discovers an unusual business card among Ms. O'Connor's family belongings that leads them on a journey to China. There the women embark on an adventure of faith and self-discovery as they uncover secrets, truths, and ultimately, God's perfectly arranged plans.

Perfectly Placed

Book Two of the Hopeful Hearts series

Six weeks after leaving China, Nicki Mayfield returns to complete two critical tasks: restore order at New Hope Orphanage and re-connect with the little girl who stole her heart. However, between a stubbornly stone walling supervisor, missing documents, and personal tragedy, Nicki faces challenges at every turn. Is she the best person to bring order – and longevity – to the place these children call home?

Then, with the help of an unexpected ally, Nicki makes a life-altering decision that upends her well-planned life and the lives of those around her. Will she lose it all, or has she found the way to save what matters most?

YOU MAY ALSO LIKE:

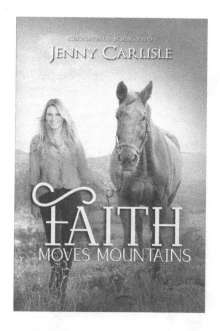

Faith Moves Mountains by Jenny Carlisle

Book Two in the Crossroads Series

John Kennedy (John K.) Billings has spent his whole life living up to his hero inspired name. Now, back from a traumatic incident in the military, he finds himself running from the fact that he is only human, with real-life struggles to overcome.

Faith Caldwell feels free to pursue her own dreams now that her family's regularly scheduled rodeo has ended. After helping care for her cancer-stricken mother she is determined to bring big city medical expertise to small-town Arkansas. While trying to prove she can fulfill her dream on her own, a new admirer seems determined to pull her down.

Both enjoy the idea of seeing more of the world, but find their hearts are still tied to the mountains of Arkansas, and the people who live there.

Can these lifelong neighbors help each other face their weaknesses while following God's plan for their lives?

Get your copy here:

https://scrivenings.link/faithmovesmountains

Forever Home by Hope Toler Dougherty

Book Three in the Forever Series

With a fulfilling job and a home of her own, former foster child, Merritt Hastings, relishes her stable, respectable life. Dreaming for more is a sure way for heartache. When a contested will turns her world upside down, she must reevaluate what's important to her, what's worth fighting for, and what's worth sacrificing.

Patience has never been Sam Daniels' strong suit with his history of acting quickly and asking questions later, and he's ready for changes in his life...now. Too bad the plans for acquiring a radio station didn't include a contract. Now he's out of a job, out of a radio station, and out of prospects.

While his life is in flux, at least he can help Merritt steady hers, or will he rush in and overstep ...again?

Will the sparks flying between these two opposites lead to a happily-ever-after or heartbreak for both?

Get your copy here:

https://scrivenings.link/foreverhome

Scrivenings
PRESS
Quench your thirst for story.
www.ScriveningsPress.com

Stay up-to-date on your favorite books and authors with our free e-newsletters.

ScriveningsPress.com